idioms

John Doriot

idioms

This is a work of fiction. All of the characters, organizations, and events portrayed are either products of the author's imagination or are used fictitiously.

Copyright © 2023 John Doriot

ISBN 979-8-9865958-3-2

Books by John Doriot

Novels:
Litter
The Cures

Short Story Collections:
Intersections
Crossroads
Grimmer Folk Stories

Poetry:
Irritable Vowels
From Sorrow to Tomorrow

Children's Books:
Doozy
Oh, Where'd You Go, Oreo?
A Dog I Know Called Oreo
What Would Oreo Say, If She Could Talk Today?

Table of Contents

Foreword

Curiosity killed the cat. That's how this book got started. Only when I heard the phrase, I didn't think that someone had gotten into trouble for asking the wrong question, or found out something that they shouldn't have by asking too many questions. I wondered who Curiosity was and why did they kill the cat? Did they not like cats? Was it an accident? Were they bad pet owners, just bad people, or even worse, murderers of some kind?

As you can see, the questions were many, and I immediately thought there would be hundreds of similar questions that "popped" into my head with other idioms, so I began making a list of them. And as I wrote, some of them "jumped off the page" and I made notes underneath them as I saw stories that could be told from phrases that had been uttered thousands of times, but not exactly with the same intent as I envisioned.

I think you will find these stories a lot of fun to read and very entertaining. They are meant to elicit laughs, a smile or two, perhaps a tear, maybe a grimace, an "I didn't see that coming" once or twice (maybe even after every story), and several, "What the hell were you thinking?" questions.

At least I hope those are the reactions. And regarding that last question. Don't worry. I ask the same question of myself all the time. The answer is always another story.

Familiarity

Her full name was Clementine Lace Grassley. She was named after a beloved great-grandmother, Clementine, and a favorite "Aunt Lacey" - names that reflected a different era of tolerance. No one ever called her Clementine, not even her parents or teachers. Her teachers called her Miss Grassley because they identified all the young students by the proper prefix reflective of their gender and their last name.

Clementine was extremely shy and had difficulty making friends in elementary school. Her shyness was often characterized as "weird" or "odd" by her classmates and as such, she suffered years of isolation and alienation that unfortunately labeled her as a "strange little girl" and placed her in a world of her own in that environment. By the time she entered the fifth grade, school had become unbearable for her due to the bullying she faced every day. Rather than subject their daughter to any more trauma, she was removed from the public school system and home-schooled by her parents.

She thrived in that home setting and her parents gave her a kitten for her birthday. She fell in love the first moment she stroked the soft fur and heard the kitten purr. She soon realized more happiness than she had ever known in all her years in school when not long after she received her kitten she met her first friend, "Annie," who eventually became her best and only true friend. The two were inseparable as they both loved cats and all the same subjects in school, especially reading. It was her best friend who started calling her Lacy, and as her parents saw the happiness return to their child's face, they followed suit. From that point forward, Clementine Lace Grassley became Lacy to both her parents and Annie.

Lacy and Annie loved playing in the woods behind Lacy's house; depending on the day, they either called the woods "Oz" or "Wonderland." If it was Lacy's turn to name the magic woods, she called it Wonderland because her cat's name was Alice. When it was Annie's turn to pick the name for the woods, she chose Oz, because, as you might guess, her cat's name was Dorothy.

Neither Lacy nor Annie missed any of the elements of school that other children enjoyed as they progressed from elementary to middle and high school because they had each other. When they were together, their shyness and awkward social skills were unimportant because they found all they needed from the love of their parents and their friendship with each other.

Lacy and Annie even enrolled in the same university, Mary Baldwin University in Staunton, Virginia. Unfortunately, Lacy never completed her degree because of an accident her parents had one night coming home from a drive-in movie. Her father, who suffered from sleep apnea, fell asleep at the wheel and ran into a tree while going fifty miles an hour. Both parents suffered severe brain injuries and Lacy spent many months with them in the hospital before she was told they would not get any better. With Annie's support, Lacy told the medical staff she understood, but asked if she could take care of them at home.

The medical staff told Lacy it wouldn't be easy, but she informed them that her friend would help her and they would do whatever was necessary to meet her parent's healthcare needs. She was given the proper instructions on how to care for a person on a ventilator and from that point forward, Lacy, with Annie's periodic help, took care of her parents for the rest of their lives.

Lacy never once thought of this as a burden. As time progressed, she and Annie became even closer and Lacy began to acquire more and more cats. She wasn't sure where they came from, they just started showing up at her door. No matter their condition, she never turned them away and made sure they had a loving home where they could flourish. She and Annie loved having the cats around the house and one day, Annie suggested she start painting pictures of them. She reminded Lacy that she had always been good at art and though Lacy objected at first, she eventually began to paint.

Annie was right. Lacy was very skilled at painting her unique large-eyed cats with vibrant colorful quilt-like fur. Once the local art store owner was shown the pictures and began selling them in her shop, the paintings became very popular. Lacy was embarrassed by the thought of anyone buying her paintings, but she had to admit there were no other pictures like them and she was proud of her work. After the local store placed the paintings on its website, the pictures achieved worldwide acclaim, and became known simply as the "Grassley Cats."

Unfortunately, Lacy's shyness caused her to shun all the publicity and she never left her home. Food was delivered as necessary, and the sales from her art provided her sufficient money to live well and take care of her parents and her ever-growing family of cats. It was at this time, that Clementine Lace Grassley became known as the "cat lady" within the community. Most said that term with respect, but there were a few who used the description to suggest that Lacy was ill-suited to be living in the house by herself or taking care of her parents, and most of all, ill-prepared to care for all the cats that made her house their home.

Some of the eldest folks in her neighborhood said that she had been "tetched in the haid since she was a young'un" but then proceeded to discuss much more important issues like food (past, present, and future), medical visits and ailments (past, present, and future), and their activities within the bathroom and bedroom (past, present, and future). Almost all of her other neighbors described her as eccentric and lonely. Some of the nicer folks would add that they felt sorry for her considering the life she had led and currently endured. But any of those aforementioned neighbors, whether old or young, considered what Lacy had done for her parents as noble, and viewed her as a very talented individual, even if they weren't avid fans of her art.

The man next door, however, also shared those early classmates' perspective of his neighbor with an adult's ability to be even more vindictive and cruel. He referred to her as a menace, often obscenely, when he was certain no one could hear the profanity. But he was only fooling himself. All the other neighbors knew how he felt about the lonely woman in the home next to him and they thought he was a mean and angry man for cursing her or her cats. Some had even seen him try and kick the cats if they strayed onto his property, but the cats were always too quick for him and they often laughed as they watched him make a fool of himself.

His name was Melvin Vance Merkel and he was well known by the Health and Animal Control Departments of the town as he called both quite frequently, complaining of the unsanitary conditions, the loud noises, and the allergies he was subjected to because of the numerous cats that were living in his neighbor's yard and home.

The Health Department and the Animal Control Department, as well as members of the ASPCA, had been to the "cat lady's" home fifteen times over the past ten years as a result of Melvin's complaints. And every time they visited Lacy's home, they were amazed at the cleanliness of the home and yard, and how well the animals looked; though no agent, or concerned citizen, could ever say with certainty just how many cats occupied the "cat lady's" home.

When twenty to thirty cats are lying in the yard or on the porch, health inspectors assume they will be overpowered by the nitrogen smell of cat urine as soon as they step foot on the property. They had been to many homes with half that number of cats and litter boxes and would tell you the stench of urine seemed to seep out of the walls or waft up from the carpet like steam arising from a hot street in summer after a brief rain. But the inspectors and animal lovers who visited the cat lady's home never smelled anything offensive. There were no foul odors in the yard or the home, just the sweet fragrance of tea olives and gardenias that always seemed to be in bloom and made them smile.

They also never found cat droppings littering the yard like land mines or inside the home as if dozens of bags of old and rotten potatoes had spilled out onto the floor. Again, that was something the inspectors expected to see with such a large population of cats, and were pleasantly surprised when they did not, even though they checked in every closet and corner of the home and yard. In addition to the pristine living conditions, the animal control personnel always found the cats to be healthy and were never seen fighting amongst themselves; a rare phenomenon considering both male and female cats are extremely territorial in nature. Regardless if it was their first or fifth or even fifteenth visit, the inspectors were often dumbfounded as they tried to explain what they witnessed.

"How do you do it?" they would ask the homeowner and her reply was always the same. "We are a family here and my cats do their business out in the forest as good cats should."

"Amazing," and a shaking of the head in disbelief was consistently the same response from the inspector who asked the question. And before any inspector left, each of them would then thank the reserved and polite woman for her time and apologize for disrupting her day, to which she always replied, "Come back anytime you want. My cats enjoy seeing friendly people."

As they walked away, the inspectors would comment on that last statement about the cats "enjoying friendly people," which would invariably lead to a discussion of the man who had made the complaint and to whom they now had to provide a report. When they told Melvin they could find no evidence of mistreatment or poor hygiene, they knew that they would be in for a good twenty-minute tirade regarding their inability to do their job. And every inspector, regardless of their department, would say the same thing afterwards, "What an asshole."

Initially, one of the inspectors asked Melvin why he moved next to a home with so many cats if he had such severe allergies, and that led to a ten-minute diatribe on allergies and the fact that there were only a few cats there when he moved into his house.

"Now, tell me, please. How many goddamn cats are living there? Huh? Can you tell me? There must be hundreds! That is against the law and un-hygienic and is creating havoc with my allergies. Why can't you damn people just do your damn job?" he yelled.

Even if they were aware not to ask that particular question, the inspectors would still get an "earful" of words implicating their incompetence until they had heard enough, and then politely tell him they had done their job, and wish him a nice day. Many wanted to ask, "Why the hell don't you move if the cats bother you so much?" but they knew that would only make matters worse, so they never did.

Regardless, the question Melvin raised during one of his rants, regarding the number of cats that lived in the old lady's house, created a lively debate among the inspectors. None of them ever came up with the same number; it varied depending on the inspectors and the time of year they inspected the home. After talking with each other, the inspectors were always befuddled by the number their coworkers said they had documented and how the woman could keep such a clean home with so many pets.

If one inspector said they counted forty or fifty, the other would look at them as if they were crazy and tell him or her there were no more than twenty, at best. Then two or three of them would argue for thirty minutes or more and as they argued, their minds would start to wonder if perhaps the number they had counted was indeed wrong. Usually one of them would say,

"Perhaps they just kept moving around so much that you counted the same cat numerous times." "Maybe," would be the reply. Then the other would say, "It's possible I didn't see all the cats you did in some area of the house or yard," and then they would both nod and realize that either scenario could indeed be true. In the back of their minds, though, all of them were wondering, "Was Melvin right? Were there hundreds?" And they would come to the same conclusion each time – that could not be possible.

Thus, the final reports always said the same thing – "Complaint investigated and no hoarding of cats could be identified that suggested inhumane living conditions for the animals or the human caretaker." And never once did a report denote a definitive number of cats because a definitive number could never be determined.

The "caretaker" described in the report was never labeled as the "cat lady" or as Clementine Grassley, but as Miss Lacy. The initial inspectors had used the term "frail and delicate" to describe the shy and gracious woman so from that point forward, she was known as Miss Lacy to all the inspectors. Since that was a variation of the name her parents and best friend had always called her, she liked hearing them refer to her in that manner.

Occasionally, an inspector might call Miss Lacy "the cat lady," but on the few instances that occurred, it was done to suggest a woman who loved animals, especially cats. When those same words - "the cat lady" - were used by Melvin, it was never just "the cat lady," but always "the damn cat lady with her four-legged abominations." Those words emerged from his mouth as if he was choking on a hairball and were meant to describe a crazy woman who was a threat to society. But the words Melvin used were ignored and his frustration and anger continued to fester and grow which often triggered even more severe allergic reactions.

Her parents lived for twenty years under Lacy's care, but even with the best of care, keeping someone on a ventilator for that long presents problems. Eventually, they both acquired pneumonia and died. The nurses and doctors told Lacy that her parents could not have received better care anywhere in the country and their words gave her a great deal of comfort.

If not for her friend Annie and all of her cats, Lacy would not have made it through the loss. But Annie reassured Lacy, almost daily, that her parents had been truly loved by her for all those years and were looking down on her with pride.

"They knew you were there with them even with their eyes closed," Annie said many times, and those words warmed Lacy's heart and she thanked her for being such a good friend.

For the next twenty years, Lacy continued to paint and acquire cats. She never knew how many cats she had but neither she nor Annie, who never left her alone, cared. Though they both missed Alice and Dorothy, Annie and Lacy had many other cats that they had come to love. Annie said she doubted if Lacy could even say which cat she liked the most and Lacy would just smile because she knew that was true. She loved every one of the cats and felt protected and loved by each of them in return.

Annie told Lacy that her neighbor complained about her cats quite frequently. She could hear him at times when he thought no one was listening, cursing the cats that sometimes came into his yard. She told Lacy that she even saw him try and kick some of the cats and she laughed when they jumped out of the way. They seemed to taunt him by watching him come running toward them before they ran a little farther away and then sat down and waited for him to chase them again.

"They are playing cat and mouse with him," Lacy told Annie as she stood next to the window one day and watched what Annie had described. "But you know, Annie, I'm not sure they should be doing that. I heard one of the inspectors say he has cat allergies. I'm sure it only aggravates him for them to be over there playing with him."

"Well, then he shouldn't have moved next door to you, Lacy," Annie replied. Lacy nodded her head in agreement though, in a way, she felt sorry for the man. He didn't seem to have many friends in the neighborhood and she understood how that felt.

It was on one of the most recent inspections by the health department, brought on by a complaint from Melvin, that one of the inspectors warned Lacy to be careful because there was a very bad man breaking into homes around town and doing bad things to women. He couldn't tell Lacy what it was that the man was doing to the women but advised her to make sure she locked her doors at night and to call the police if she heard anything or saw anyone suspicious lurking around her yard. He even asked her if she had anyone who could stay with her for a while.

Lacy smiled and told him not to worry about her, saying, "My best friend is staying with me and I am under the watchful eye of many other friends."

"Well, I'm glad you have a friend staying with you and you certainly do have a lot of friends watching over you, Miss Lacy," the inspector said as he smiled and tried counting all the cats before he gave up and left.

Lacy watched the inspector as he went to his truck and heard her neighbor complaining again about how he wasn't doing his job if he couldn't do something about all the cats. She heard him mention his cat allergies and even saw him pull up his shirt to show the inspector the hives that covered his chest and back. She turned her head away when she saw how awful that looked. The inspector just shook his head and told him to go to his doctor and heard the neighbor say he was going to several doctors and a lawyer because "you damn idiots can't do your job!"

The inspector looked angry as he slammed the door of his truck and drove away but Lacy heard him say nothing ill toward the man. And though the blisters on her neighbor's back made her shiver, she did not like the fact that he complained about her cats. She agreed with what the inspector had said about going to see a doctor, and the more she thought about his medical problems, the more she remembered her parents and then any animosity that had formed in her mind regarding his dislike of her pets, soon dissolved into concern and sorrow for her neighbor's health.

She wasn't sure what time it was that night when she felt someone on top of her. She opened her eyes and saw a man holding a knife close to her throat. He instructed her not to move as he yanked down the sheets and she felt his hand on her thigh. Just as he started to pull up her nightgown, a cloud of cats leaped out of the darkness and enveloped him, knocking him to the floor. Many of the larger cats covered the man's head and though he cut several of them, they soon tore the skin away from his hand and disarmed him before they began ripping away parts of his face.

When she heard the screaming, Annie ran into the room, sat down next to Lacy, and told her to call 911 immediately. Lacy did as she was told and after hanging up, the two of them sat on the edge of the bed and watched as the cats made the intruder wish he had never come into that home.

"What's wrong, cat got your tongue?" Lacy heard Annie ask the man. When she looked over at the man lying on the floor, she saw that one of her large male cats named Mau did indeed have the man's tongue. She didn't say anything to Annie upon hearing that comment as she didn't want to encourage any additional off-color remarks from her, considering that the cats had now removed both the man's eyes and that his ears were hanging from the side of his head by a thin thread of flesh.

The police found the man in the corner of the bedroom, whimpering, with his arms over his head and a sea of cats surrounding him. As several officers walked toward the man, the multi-colored carpet of cats seemed to anticipate the policemen's steps and moved just enough for them to place their feet onto the hardwood floor. The hisses and moans from the animals that surrounded their feet, suggested that they not step anywhere that was not vacant, and the face of the man that sat in the corner of the room reinforced their cautious movement.

Each of the officers that arrived on the scene winced as they saw the man's face when they placed him into the back of the car. Two officers said they would rush the man to the hospital if the other team would take the report from Miss Lacy. As the first responders were leaving, they suggested to the other officers that they take Miss Lacy's statement outside. When the officers saw all the cats surrounding the bed in Miss Lacy's room, they understood their coworkers' suggestions.

The next day, the police stated that they had captured the serial rapist who had been terrorizing the town but they didn't mention how or where he was caught. They just said that he would "pay dearly" for his crimes. The police department talked for months about the "faceless man" who got what he deserved.

Melvin began to call the health department on an almost daily basis because of his allergies, and with each interaction between him and the members of the health department, the animosity and contempt the officers had for the man grew. They told Melvin numerous times how sweet and nice the woman who lived next door to him was, how she took great care of her animals, and that she was a nationally recognized artist.

He told them he didn't care. Without going into details, they even suggested to Melvin that his neighbor was a "hero," but Melvin didn't want to hear any of what they had to say unless it was that they were getting rid of her "damn" cats.

He became indignant when he heard the officers describe the woman as a hero saying, "Just because she can paint a damn cat doesn't make her a hero," and snorted and spit up a wad of phlegm on the ground. Though the officers wanted to tell Melvin that wasn't why she was a hero, they knew that would be a privacy concern for Miss Lacy as well as give Melvin even more reasons to have the "dangerous" cats removed from the property.

After several more years and hundreds of complaints, Melvin finally obtained a court order to have the majority of the cats removed from the yard and home because of his allergies, which were by this time, causing him severe asthma and even more serious skin disorders. Losing most of her cats was more than Miss Lacy could endure, and soon after the last cat was removed from her house, she suffered a heart attack and died. In her will, she left orders for all the money from the sale of the house and her artwork to go to the Humane Society and a no-kill animal shelter. She also asked that she be cremated with her best friend, Annie, the Raggedy Anne doll that she had for over seventy years.

After all the cats were taken away from Clementine Lace Grassley's home, the residents of the neighborhood began to see more and more mice and even large rats in their homes. What everyone failed to realize was that there was a large sewer drain that emptied into the back of Miss Grassley's woods and that her cats had held the mice and rat population in check for many years. Now that the cats were gone, the mice and rats were breeding like, well, mice and rats. Within months, the number of rats that emerged from the sewer had become more like a swarm of bees and they carried with them a large number of fleas. It wasn't long after their arrival that Miss Grassley's old neighborhood had to be quarantined due to an outbreak of bubonic plague. Several elderly people died before the quarantine, the effective extermination of the rats and mice, and the timely use of antibiotics quelled the disease.

The health department did not hide the fact from the town that Miss Grassley's neighbor had been the cause of this problem and everyone began to hate the man known as Melvin Vance Merkel. Because he was already severely immuno-compromised, he was also one of the few people that died from the plague before it was contained. No one who learned of his death was unhappy when they heard the news. The more familiar the town became with the neighbor and his behavior with the sweet Miss Lacy, the more contempt they had for the man.

Familiarity breeds contempt

Chestnut Drive

"Are you sure this is the right way? How in the hell do people who don't have all-wheel drive get up this damn road?"

"According to Google Maps, we are only about two miles away from the cabin. I told you we should have left the party earlier and not come up this road so late at night. We could've gone to a motel and that would have been fine with me. I've been on these roads around Ski Mountain before and they can be nasty at night."

"We left the party in plenty of time. I'm sorry my damn colon decided it had been ignored for too long and reminded me of its ability to bring destruction and ruin to all things ceramic. And before you start, don't say anything about the shrimp or the whiskey shots again."

"Honey, I didn't say anything about shrimp to you. And I enjoyed drinking the whiskey shots."

"Oh, hell, don't patronize me now. You complain about my drinking all the time, Jane. Tonight was no different."

"Honey, my name isn't Jane. I think that was the other woman you were with that stormed out of the party."

Bill looked over at the woman sitting next to him and tried to focus on her. The face of his wife moved in and out several times and was then gone, revealing the face of a young woman with dark red lips and eyes that seemed to glow green. She saw him staring at her and she smiled.

"Like what you see, big Bill? You told me you couldn't wait to get your hands on them back at the party."

He watched her grab her breasts and squeeze them, and remembered the all too familiar argument with his wife and then sitting down next to the buxom young blonde at the bar.

Oh shit, what have I done? Too late now, Bill. Might as well enjoy what's sitting there next to you. But what's her name? You know it isn't Jane, laughing to himself at the thought. *Juicy? Yeah, she does look like that could be her name. Hell, that's almost it. It's Lucy.*

"I do like what I see, Lucy. And why did you call me big Bill?"

"Because I made sure to check under the hood before we left," Lucy answered as she reached over and grabbed his crotch. The car swerved but Bill adjusted his steering and had the car back on the road when he looked over at the woman and smiled.

"Lucy. You can't do that while I'm driving. Unless you want me to stop for a minute right here in the middle of the road. Probably not too many cars on this road at this time of night. I think we could stop for a moment or two and be just fine."

"No, honey, I want more than a moment or two and I want it everywhere. We're just a mile away from the cabin. I can wait."

Upon hearing those words, Bill pressed his foot on the accelerator.

"Won't be long now; just another half-mile. Oh, and honey, are you sure you're ready to pay for all that this will cost?" she murmured.

"What?" Bill asked and turned to look at Lucy. Just as he did, he realized he had lost control.

"Oh fuck….oh fuck….NO…..Shit!!!"

The expletives reflected the knowledge that the wheels of the car had moved off the narrow asphalt of the road and were now momentarily suspended in the air before they landed hard on the forest floor. The car shook as if a tornado had grabbed hold of it and they found themselves unable to speak as the tree limbs smashed against the sides, top, and back of the SUV. The scratching noise that the limbs made against the metal of the car sounded like tortured animals before they heard the glass shatter and felt pieces of it fly into their skin and become embedded in soft tissue and bone. The car flipped several more times until it slammed up against a large boulder and stopped.

They were upside down and the driver's door was crumpled in. The bark from the large tree touched Bill, who was unconscious. A piece of glass was lodged in Lucy's left eye and her other eye had been scratched by a tree limb and was now blurry with tears that burned.

"Fuck you, Bill, you son of a bitch. Bill, damnit! Talk to me! Don't you sit there and be all unconscious and shit. Wake the fuck up and get us the hell out of here!

"God damnit, I can't see. You dumb shit, do you hear me? Don't sit there not moving and not answering me. I've got a piece of glass in one eye and another one in my fucking shoulder and my other eye has been scratched with something and burns like hell. I don't remember anything in Health class that told me what to do when there is a piece of fucking glass in your eye," she screamed. "I swear, if you have fucked up this fifty thousand dollar face and hundred thousand dollar body, there will be hell to pay. So, wake your pussy-ass self up and tell me what to do with this piece of glass that is sticking out of my eye!"

"You need to know how big it is," Lucy heard Bill whisper.

"Bill, you dumb son of a bitch. It's big. That's all I know. Get your ass together so you can get me out of this damn car."

"I've felt better."

"What's that? I don't remember asking you how you feel as I don't give a shit. Do you know where we are, asshole?"

"I suspect Hell, based upon the way I feel."

"Not yet, ass-wipe. Not yet. Tell me, can you move? I want to get out of here!"

"Maybe. When the car quits spinning."

Bill could feel something wet dripping down his cheek; he knew it was blood. *Well at least I don't have to worry about anything being in my colon anymore*, he thought. *Unless maybe blood. My ribs and abdomen really hurt. Damn. This is the first time I hope I did shit on myself.*

My head hit the windshield he thought and he knew he had lost consciousness but he didn't know for how long. His eyes blurred and he felt dizzy as he turned his head toward Lucy. He closed his eyes for a moment, then gritted his teeth as he reopened them and tried to focus. He thought he saw the glass protruding from her eye like a tip of a spear before a bright light caused him to blink.

Is that a light or is that something going off in my head? God, my head feels like someone is trying to twist it off of my neck. I bet I have a concussion.

"Lucy?"

"Yes, asshole?"

"How bad are you hurt? I thought I saw something in your eye before I was blinded by a white light. I don't know if that's a real light or just something in my head."

"I'm hurt bad. Are you deaf as well as dumb? I do have a piece of glass in my left eye that feels like it's in my brain. My right eye is fucked up too and really blurry. I don't know if I have any broken bones because everything below my waist feels numb. I can move my left hand but not my right arm and my stomach hurts like a son of a bitch. So, on a scale of 1-10 with 10 being fucking bad, I am about a 50, you piece of shit!"

The bright white light returned and Bill asked Lucy if she saw it, He realized that was a stupid question as soon as the words came out of his mouth. *She's got glass in one eye and the other is blurry, remember?* But surprisingly, she responded.

"Yeah, asshole. I see some sort of light but it's like looking into the sun. I can't see what the hell it is."

Before Bill could reply, the light moved over to his side of the car and began to talk.

"Lord a mercy, folks. You two look to be in a world of hurt. But, don't surprise me none that you run off that damned road, cause you sure as hell ain't the first two that done it. Did you see sumpin 'at skeered you, or was you two doing sumpin you shouldn't been doing?"

"No, I didn't see anything. I just ran off the road," Bill answered.

"Uh-huh. Been a drinkin' a bit much though, ain't you, cause I smell it. Reckon you had a tad too much to be drivin' on this here road. You shore as shit is lucky to be alive, though you appear to be twixt a rock and a hard place seeing how the car is pinned agin that big ole boulder. No sir, it ain't good at all."

He didn't really just say that, did he? Bill asked himself. *What kind of country bumpkin is this guy?*

"Look, Mister. Are you going to be able to help us? I think my friend Lucy is hurt pretty bad and I've got some busted ribs and I'm feeling pretty dizzy."

"Damn, son. I wouldn't have come down here if I didn't think I could help you. As I see things, I reckon the only thing I can do is try and remove this here tree that's butting up against this here door a yourn. That boulder the car is wedged up agin ain't ever gonna move. Well, not unless this is Revelations, Chapter 22, and the ground is about to open up."

Oh shit. A damn Bible thumper from the backwoods. I am screwed.

"But I came prepared. Got my chainsaw with me. When I hereah crash like yourn, I always grab my chainsaw and come a-running. I figure I might need it and damned if it don't seem like I always do. I reckon I got a sixth sense bout dat type of thing. People around these parts call me Lou by the way. And when they holler out my name, I always come a running."

As Bill listened, he realized Lou sounded crazier and crazier.

"I don't mean to be a sceering you folks, but to be honest with you, you both appear to be up to yore ears in cow shit. Mister, I can tell you rite now, you got busted ribs from that twisted steering column brushing up agin em, and probably have a concussion by that cut on your head and the bump that's ah stickin outta yore head like a horn. And you did say you wuz dizzy. And there's glass everywhere in your body and dat lady of yorn. Missy, dem eyes of yourn are ah mess. Plus, your legs and right arm are ah might twisted and your stomach looks fuller than an old tick on ah coon dog's ear."

"Lou, enough with the diagnosis. We need your help. Can you help get us out of here?"

"Oh, my God! My stomach hurts! Oh my God, it hurts so bad…..Oh my God…oh shit….uh……….."

"Lucy! Lucy! Stay with me, Lucy. Don't close your eyes, Lucy!"

Again, just as he said that Bill realized how absurd his comment was considering the state of Lucy's eyes.

"I don't think she's ah going to do much talking rite now, Mister, and to be honest with you; that's probably good and bad. Good that she done passed out 'cause I think the way her body looks, if she was awake the pain would be unbearable. Bad that she passed out 'cause that probably means she's got nerve damage and by the way her gut looks, she's got ah lot of internal bleeding. She may not have much longer."

"God dammit, Lou. Do something!"

"I'm going to ignore that nasty tone ah yourn, cause I know you ain't in the best of shape and mite be ah bit worried 'bout the missus. But ifn you remember, I didn't have to come by here at all. Hell, you could have just used your cell phone to call an ambulance."

God damn. That crazy son of a bitch is right. I don't need this idiot working on us when I can get professional help, Bill thought. He reached into his pocket and pulled out his cell phone only to see that he had no service.

"Fuck!"

"Yeah, I was afraid at mite be the case. No service, huh? It's real hit or miss out heer, but ya never know till you try. Like they say, ain't no point in beatin' a dead horse – but then it can't hurt either. Rite?"

What the fuck does that mean? I bet that damn asshole knew I didn't have cell service. Crazy bastard. But concentrate, man. You need this old coot to help you. Concentrate on that now.

"Sorry, Lou. You're right. You're right. I'm really worried about Jane…I mean Lucy. Just help us, please."

"Like I said, I brung this here chainsaw and I reckon I can start cuttin' away this here tree for ya but I'm not sure you're ready for the price you'll have to pay in getting out of this mess you find yoreself in."

"Damn, Lou, you really want to talk about money now? Hell, just cut the damn tree!"

"There you go agin with that unpleasantness in yore voice. You know, you got choices. Reckon you could jest start ah praying and call on the Lord for help and hope he sends someone around to help ya. Like they say around these here parts, an empty wagon makes a lot of noise."

This son of a bitch is bat-shit crazy. I don't know what the hell he is talking about but you need his help. Just get his help, Bill. Praying isn't going to help now. Focus and get him to get you and Lucy out of the car no matter what he wants to charge you.

"Okay, Lou, okay. I'm sorry. Just help us, please. Lucy is hurting really bad. I can hear gurgling sounds coming from her body. I'll pay whatever it costs."

"Yes sir. I hear those awful noises too. Don't sound good, do it? All right, just close yore eyes fer a minute while I start a-working on this here tree."

Bill heard the chainsaw start and felt small bits of sawdust flying into his face. After about ten minutes there was a crack and he felt a thud as the tree fell to the ground. When it did, the pain reverberated in his body and he screamed.

"There now. Got that old tree down. Now let me see about this door. Dang if it ain't wedged in tighter than an old winder in wet wood. We're going to have to pull ya thoo this here winder. Watch yourself now, I'm gonna knock out the rest of the glass."

Bill heard the shattering of glass and then nothing for a moment before Lou spoke up.

"All right, now that's done, I'm gonna cut you loose from yore seatbelt. I can't stop you from falling some agin dat steering wheel, so be ready cause this is gonna hurt like ah sumbitch."

Bill felt the tug on his seatbelt and then he felt free for a second before his stomach and chest fell onto the steering wheel. The pain was unbearable and he screamed again. Just before he passed out, he heard Lou say, "Did you know, Bill, that a worm is the only animal that can't fall down?"

Bill woke up at the University of Tennessee Medical Center. A policeman was sitting in his room and a nurse was tending to several IVs that were in his arm.

"Hello, Mr. Reynolds. My name is Sophia. I'm your nurse for this shift. That man in the chair is Officer Hesse. You're in the University of Tennessee ICU with major internal and external injuries. Do you remember what happened?"

"We were in a car accident. Where is my wife? She was hurt bad, is she okay?"

The policeman walked over to the side of the bed. "Your wife was here earlier to check on you, Mr. Reynolds. She stated she wasn't in the car with you and based upon the condition of the car, we know that is true as she would have been dead."

Fuck. That's right. We argued. She left the party.

"Oh, yeah. So, how's that other woman?"

"Other woman?"

"Yes. I think her name was uh…uh…it was Lucy. Yes, that was it. Lucy."

"Mr. Reynolds. There was no other woman at the scene of the accident. Did you hit someone when you were driving?"

"No, damnit. She was in the car with me. She left with me. Her name was Lucy."

"Mr. Reynolds. There was no one in the car with you or that left the party with you. You drove off the side of the mountain which isn't surprising considering your blood alcohol was point four-two. That's five times the legal limit in the state of Tennessee. You had no business getting behind the wheel of a car, period. Yet, somehow you survived and crawled out the window. Even so, we have no idea as to how you sustained those injuries and survived."

Like someone had turned on the tv in his mind, Bill watched the rerun of the night before when he and his wife were at the party. He heard the argument with his wife about his drinking that had occurred many times before and then heard the bet he made about being able to drive to the cabin. He remembered his wife saying that was a stupid bet and that only a drunken idiot would tempt fate or the devil as he watched her walk away and he went back to the bar. He screamed as he looked down at his body when Officer Hesse asked him the question.

"Can you explain to us why you don't have your right arm and leg? They look like they have been cut off with a chainsaw and then cauterized so you didn't bleed to death. They weren't anywhere to be found and we searched for hours. We thought maybe an animal had done this, but the cut was too clean. We didn't see any bite marks or any tracks and we were there at the scene of the accident within fifteen minutes after it happened."

Bill closed his eyes and saw the face of Lou and heard him laughing. He feared he would see that face and hear that voice for a very, very long time. Perhaps even for eternity.

Cost an arm and a leg

Bring in the Clowns

"Well, Chester, what are you going to do with all your free time once the school year is over? No more teachers, no more books, no more teachers' dirty looks, huh? School won't just be out for the summer for you, come June - it'll be out 'For Evah!' Yeah, man! Sex, drugs, and rock and roll, huh, Chester?"

Chester smiled at the man that he had known and tolerated for forty-two years.

How in the world does he know so much about history? At times, I think his head is filled with nothing but booze from the weekend and some god-awful pornographic film he probably watched. But amazingly, it's not. He knows more about history than anyone I know. I suppose that's why I have tolerated his boorish demeanor all these years. We do have some interesting discussions about history and I so love that subject. It complements Literature in so many ways.

"Can you really see me at an Alice Cooper concert, Ernest? Perhaps Alice in Chains, but not Alice Cooper."

He laughed. "Good one, Chester. Didn't even know you knew Alice in Chains was a band. Pretty good movie, too," Ernest said as he winked.

"Please, Ernest. No details are needed. I understand the gist of the movie from the title. I don't know why you waste your time watching that trash. It is not good for society or yourself, you know."

"One of the greatest societal advances was prompted by sex, and by that, I mean the internet. Now, don't get me wrong.

Pedophiles are pieces of shit and should be hunted down and put away for the rest of their lives. But if it's two consenting adults - I'm pretty much okay with it. I do prefer man-woman stuff but I don't judge others if that's their thing. And hell, Chester, they have even found pornographic images drawn by cavemen.

"And I'm not being sexist when I say cavemen because sexual equality was not a topic for discussion during that particular period. You know, I think the first published pornography was in 1524 by some guy by the name of, wait a minute… it'll come to me. Marca.....uh…yeah, Marcantonio Raimondi. He published sixteen sexually explicit engravings done by Giulio Romano, titled *I Modi*. But only the rich could afford to see that stuff. It wasn't until the late 1800s, early 1900s, that Joe Blow, no pun intended, got to see sex acts on film - and then it was Katie bar the door."

"Ernest, your ability to recall historical events has always been extremely impressive to me, albeit their significance at times is suspect."

"Thanks. Got to admit, if I wanted to know anything about Literature, you'd be my go-to person. But, in all seriousness, what do you plan to do when you retire this summer?"

"I'm not sure I'll change what I do much at all. I still love to read. I guess I can wake up in the morning with a good book and sit there until dark. Well, I can't sit there until dark anymore. I do have to get up and pee a bit more frequently these days."

Ernest chuckled and nodded his head. "Yeah, I hear you, brother. Knock on wood; my plumbing still works pretty well. Just had a physical, and my PSA was normal and my urinalysis was clean. And just so you know, I still don't need the little blue pill. I can stand up and salute whenever necessary."

"Yes, I'm sure you can," Chester said as he smiled at his colleague, yet grimaced within his mind.

One thing I will not miss is his incessant references to anything sexual. I don't even really like being around him anymore. It disgusts me to think about him watching that repulsive filth, and God only knows what he thinks every time he sees some woman pass by him. I don't need those images in my head, and in this case, absence will not make the heart grow fonder. It will only clear my head of this needless waste.

"Brother, you've got to do something more than just read for the rest of your life!"

"Is that so? I wasn't aware there was a city ordinance or federal law regarding that activity. Did I miss something?"

"Funny. You know what I mean."

"Yes. Yes, I do. I do have other interests and pursuits, Ernest. I love working in my garden. You've seen the flowers on my desk before."

"Yeah, I know. So that's it - books and flowers?"

"'A garden to walk in and immensity to dream in—what more could he ask? A few flowers at his feet and above him the stars.' That's from 'Les Miserables' by Victor Hugo."

"Not a big fan."

Why am I not surprised? "I also have my volunteer work. It means a great deal to me and I look forward to having more time to devote to it and to refining my painting skills."

"You never told me you did volunteer work? What do you do?"

"I read to those who are no longer able and have no one to read to them."

"An old folks home?"

"Yes, though I wouldn't call it a home. It's more like a repository for society to store those that they can't kill outright, and allow the residents to die a slow inhuman death."

"Yeah, had a grandmother in one of those places. It was awful. But she didn't know if you were there or not. Do you really think they can hear you reading to them?"

"'Music is like a dream. One that I cannot hear' - Ludwig van Beethoven. By the time he composed his Ninth Symphony, he had been profoundly deaf for almost ten years. I don't know what they hear or don't hear, but I suspect they hear much more than anyone in this world will ever know. I believe their brains take them into another world, one that we only imagine exists beyond the clouds."

"That's beautiful, Chester. Maybe I can go with you sometime."

No. That won't happen. I will not have the coarseness of your human depravity near them. But, calm down. You know he wouldn't actually do it. Just go along with his statement for the time being. Soon he will be gone and forgotten.

"Perhaps, Ernest. Perhaps."

"Well, that bell says I need to go teach some of our 'leaders of tomorrow.'"

"You say that in jest but some of them will indeed be the leaders of tomorrow."

"God help us if that's the case with this next class. Well, there might be one. But it's all I can do to keep them from falling asleep after lunch. I think some of them may have done drugs at lunchtime."

"So, you just let them sleep?"

"Yeah. Better to let them sleep than get into a fight with some drug addict I just woke up that will be filmed by everyone in the class and make me out to be some sort of ogre. I just don't need that shit. I've only got two more years to go and then I will be off to the race track, fishing, Vegas - wherever and whenever I want to go."

Another reason for me not to like being around you. Why can't you connect with the students? You are teaching them history and it's a fascinating subject.

"What are you teaching this class right now, Ernest?"

"This is my freshman class, so we've just finished the Revolutionary War period and have started studying the War of 1812. Funny how that war was branded as such. It wasn't just a war that lasted a year. The damn struggle went on for thirty-two months, which was longer than the Spanish-American war and our involvement in World War I. Did you know the Battle of

New Orleans took place two weeks after British and American envoys signed the peace treaty, although Madison and the Senate didn't ratify the treaty until about a month later?"

"I could sit in on that class and be thoroughly entertained, Ernest. Such an interesting period in our history. Did you know the Brothers Grimm published their first book, 'Kinder-und Hausmarchen' in 1812? And Jane Austen wrote 'Pride and Prejudice' in 1813 and 'Mansfield Park' in 1814 and 'Emma' in 1815, though it was dated 1816. Not long after that war, one of my favorite books ever written was published by Mary Shelley in 1818, 'Frankenstein.' Absolutely brilliant writing. Two very amazing young women for their times. Well, let me clarify that, for any time period, considering what they accomplished."

"I didn't know all that, Chester, but I'm not surprised that you do. You're right, it was a fascinating time and a very interesting war when you know how it got started and what occurred during it. Not only did we get our National Anthem from it, but we also got Uncle Sam. A military supplier named Sam Wilson in Troy, New York packed meat rations in barrels for the soldiers. They were told the U.S., stamped on the barrels, stood for 'Uncle Sam' Wilson, who was feeding the army. That name stuck to signify the U.S. government, but the white-bearded guy didn't appear until World War I."

"I wish I could sit in on your class, but with everything I'm trying to get done, I just can't. Also, I just don't understand how the kids could be asleep with all of the fascinating history that you share with them."

"Drugs, Chester. Drugs and maybe girls. See you later, friend."

Sex, drugs, and rock and roll. Yes, I hear you. And fortunately, I won't have to hear you refer to me as a friend much longer.

"Good afternoon, Ernest."

Chester sat in the teacher's lounge and finished his tea. He had a thirty-minute break after lunch before his next class so he wasn't in a rush to leave. He opened "The Colour Out of Space," an anthology of short stories by H.P. Lovecraft, and began reading where he had left off last evening. He got lost in the words as he knew he would and only his phone alarm pulled him from the book. But back in the classroom, he embraced his role and began discussing with his senior class the themes of good and evil in early American Literature, studying the works of Nathaniel Hawthorne and Edgar Allan Poe. There was always a vigorous discussion among that particular group of students and it made him remember why he had become a teacher so long ago.

His final class of the day was sophomores and he had spent the entire year with them studying the early English authors of influence, focusing on those he enjoyed such as Shakespeare, Wordsworth, Keats, Dickens, Browning, Bronte, and of course, Austen and Shelley. He made sure to include all those regarded as influential within the literary world, but he did not go into much detail on those poets and authors of which he was not a fan, such as Chaucer, Lord Byron, Burns, Yeats, Tennyson, Milton, Donne and Mary's husband, Percy. Nevertheless, if a student showed interest in any of those authors, he was still more than willing to discuss their works because he never wanted to dissuade a student from pursuing literature of any kind.

It still troubles me that Mary married Percy. She was so young, just 16 when she married him. Of course, you have to admit it wasn't uncommon for a girl of 16 to get married in that period. Regardless, I don't care for his work or his socialist and atheist views. But we all make mistakes when it comes to love, I suppose.

On the way home, he always stopped at the grocery store for some fresh fruit and whatever necessities were needed at home. He much preferred to do a little shopping each day, rather than do a long drawn-out day of it on the weekend, which would take him away from visits with his elderly friends or working in his garden, or reading.

Funny how Ernest didn't even ask me if I would be enjoying time with a girlfriend when we talked about retirement. I just realized something. In all this time we've been teaching together he has never asked me about a girlfriend. Mr. "I don't care what consenting adults do" doesn't want to ask me about it because he thinks I'm gay. What would that matter, Ernest, you damn Neanderthal hypocrite? Granted you have a greater mind than those beings, but I suspect your sexual intellect is very similar to those brutes.

It must be because he doesn't understand the concept of commitment. I can't remember if he's been married five or six times. He is truly a crude man. Really, why have you put up with him all this time? There's only one answer. It's the historical knowledge that he retains somewhere deep within that cave-like crevice of his brain. You so enjoy hearing him talk about history and you have had some very stimulating conversations over the years. But those are coming to an end and I don't think you will miss them one bit. No, I am sure you won't.

At home, he unpacked his one bag of groceries and placed the beautiful Golden Delicious apples in a bowl and the milk and fresh vegetables in the refrigerator. He carried the bowl of apples downstairs to his office and put them on a table next to his stereo. He admired the full room mural of the blue sky and clouds, which one of his girlfriends had inspired. He felt her presence in the room each time he looked at it and he often talked to her. At times he could hear her response as if she was still there.

"Good evening, Phyllis. I hope you are well this evening."

"Hello, Chester. What beautiful apples. Golden Delicious?"

"Yes, dear. They certainly look nice, don't they?"

"Yes, they do. By the way, isn't the sky just beautiful today? Does that cloud over there look like a little cocker spaniel to you?"

Chester didn't think it looked like a dog at all, but he knew why Phyllis would think so.

"Yes, dear. It does look like little Albert. He was such a good dog. I'm sure he is just floating by to say hello to us and to let us know he's doing well."

"He was a good dog, wasn't he? I don't think I'll ever stop missing him."

"Nor I, my sweet. Nor I. After dinner tonight I may read 'Shiloh' again. It's such a beautifully written book."

"It's a very emotional story, Chester."

"Yes, my love it is, but all true love stories command unbridled elation as well as sorrow."

Phyllis's voice disappeared as he said that. Again, he understood why.

He retrieved his paintbrushes and sat down in front of the table in the corner and began working on finishing his latest balloon sculpture. It had taken him years since he had met Phyllis to perfect the process. But now, twenty years later, everything was as beautiful and as well planned as a hot air balloon ride.

Once he confirmed the person had no one else and would not be cremated, he retrieved the head after it had been embalmed and placed it in the casket. No one ever checked to see if anything was missing before the coffin was placed in the grave. He was as meticulous and skillful as a watch repairman in peeling the skin from the head and completing the drying and tanning process. He removed the brain and eyes in the next step, replacing them with cotton and glass eyes that looked as if they had been cloned, before finally sewing the skin back onto the skull.

All the seams were well hidden by hair or by his natural painting ability which he had refined through many years of art classes that focused on portraits and the human body. When his balloon sculpture was finished, he placed a scarf around the neck and tied a long ribbon that matched the color of the eyes around the scarf, and allowed it to hang down exactly sixteen inches. He then carefully attached the tribute onto a hook that seemed to disappear into the clouds on the ceiling and allowed the head to float within the beautiful sky that had been painted onto the walls.

He always permitted himself several minutes to admire the finished product and almost gloated as he looked at the others that complemented the new arrival. They all looked lifelike as they floated like balloons within the clouds. He knew no one else had ever accomplished what he had done because human skin was so difficult to work with and preserve. As he finished his latest creation, he pulled the ladder from the closet and positioned his latest girlfriend on the ceiling.

"Phyllis, Donna, Ann, Peggy; I'd like to introduce you to Beckley. Isn't that just a wonderful name? I thought it was and asked the staff about it when I was first introduced to her. Appears that her family was from West Virginia and she was named after the town where she was born. Pretty name, don't you think? I must get to that town one day. I have always wanted to go to West Virginia."

He heard everyone say hello to Beckley and he smiled.

"I'm thinking I should show everyone how beautiful everything looks down here, don't you agree, Phyllis?"

"You do realize you will be labeled a freak, or a lunatic, or perhaps even a psychopath? I don't think that's such a good idea."

Chester thought about Phyllis's response as he stood there and looked up at his creations.

After a moment, he replied. "You're right, dear, they wouldn't understand, would they? I am sure those like Ernest would just make a crude reference to everything I have accomplished. 'Life, although it may only be an accumulation of anguish, is dear to me, and I will defend it.' What beautiful words by Mary Shelley, don't you think, ladies?"

Have your head in the clouds

Abracadabra

Some say the dislike for each other began in high school but it actually started much earlier, although only one of the two knew exactly when. The other one believed it was just something that developed over time but that wasn't what occurred. No, the animosity arose the very first day the two individuals met. Funny how something as simple as a bag of Oreo cookies at break time could generate such anger, but it did. Probably because the reason for this hatred had as its genesis an emotion that existed long before the most famous book in the world had that title.

Jealousy is a primordial emotion that both people and some animals, particularly dogs and primates, possess. It was present with the first humans and still exists today, although some are better at controlling that emotion than others. Unfortunately, the jealousy that began when Steven and Justin first met became a long-lasting resentment that festered into an uncontrollable rage.

Most boys and girls in their first-grade class had more than Steven, and though it had always bothered him, some other switch went off in Steven's brain when he saw Justin with the bag of Oreos that day. Other children had brought cookies to school before, homemade oatmeal or chocolate chip, but no one had ever brought store-bought Oreos. So, perhaps it was the fact that Justin's family could afford to buy Oreo cookies, and no one else, especially Steven's family, could. Perhaps it was the fact that Justin had shared his Oreo cookies with the classmates that sat around him that day and did not offer any to Steven. Perhaps it was because Justin gave one of the Oreo cookies to Emma Sue, the prettiest girl in the first grade, and made her smile.

Scientists state that envy occurs when one person lacks something that another one has. Jealousy requires a social triangle and arises when someone perceives a threat to a specific relationship. Justin and Emma Sue were not old enough to be considered boyfriend and girlfriend, but Steven did not like the way Emma Sue laughed that day or the way she looked at Justin from that day forward. Steven did not like the way that Emma Sue and Justin laughed and smiled all the way through high school, and he hated the fact that she did indeed eventually become Justin's girlfriend.

Justin never knew it as they grew up, but Steven always remembered that very first day with Emma Sue and the Oreo cookies. And though they never had an argument or fight, Steven detested Justin. The only thing that kept Steven from getting into an argument or fight with him, was knowing it would destroy any chance he had of ever becoming Emma Sue's boyfriend. So, Steven took out his frustration on many other young men, both in and out of school, hoping that he might get his chance one day with Emma Sue if he just waited and posed as a friend to both. And just as he had envisioned, when Justin went off to state university and Emma Sue stayed home to attend the local community college, the relationship between the two high school sweethearts began to wane.

By the time Emma Sue graduated from the community college as a nurse, she and Justin were no longer dating. Though still friends, Justin had a keen interest in getting away from the town where he grew up and wanted to see the world, and Emma Sue did not. She preferred to stay in the same small rural community, close to her family and the mountains that she had grown to love. They had fights about their future many times and came to realize the relationship could not withstand the constant bickering. For the sake of their friendship, they decided to go their separate ways.

After they stopped dating, Steven began to let Emma Sue know of his interest in her. She had never really considered Steven as someone she would date because he did have a reputation for having a short temper, but he had always been very nice around her. So, she convinced herself that those rumors about him getting into fights were just that - rumors. After all, he had a steady job and reputation in the community as a good mechanic, and she always had a soft heart for "strays," so she agreed to go out with him.

Steven was not a good influence on Emma Sue. He frequented the local bars where he was well known and feared, and Emma Sue began to enjoy getting "high and drunk" with the gang. She enjoyed the way others looked at her in the bar with Steven. She could see in their eyes the same things she had seen in her classmates' eyes when she and Justin walked together in the school halls. Plus, there was something else that excited her. She recognized that the men in the bars wanted her but were afraid of what Steven would do if they said anything to her that even suggested their interest, and she could tell the women were envious of their relationship. Both of those new feelings made her feel special and helped her forget Justin.

For the next several years, Steven and Emma Sue saw each other almost daily. Emma Sue slowly started to understand that the rumors of Steven's temper were not simply rumors. She saw him beat up several guys at the bar who were looking at her in what he thought to be a disrespectful way. For a brief moment, she found that display of testosterone to be chivalrous, but she did not like it at all when that same manner of anger was projected onto her after they got in the car.

He slapped her and accused her of enticing them. Even though she denied it, her protests were unheard. And despite the fact she knew Steven was very jealous, she sometimes did things just to provoke him. She would pay for it later, but she enjoyed having that power over him. Her close friends advised her to leave him but she told them she wasn't worried about him. No matter how bad things got, Steven always took extreme measures to make it up to her. She told herself she was happy, even though it took longer and longer for the bruises to heal.

It was during the Thanksgiving holidays that Steven and Emma Sue walked into their local hang-out and saw someone familiar sitting at the bar. It was Justin. Emma Sue ran to him, calling out his name. Justin stood up and embraced his old friend. It had been several years since he had seen her or even talked with her as he had been out of the country studying in Europe and North Africa.

Emma Sue was still a beautiful woman, but Justin could see that she had changed. He suspected the make-up she was wearing was hiding some long nights and other reckless behavior, but he didn't say anything. He wanted to ask how she was but before he could, Steven came over and asked him what had brought him back to the little town that he had been so eager to leave.

Justin smiled and said that he had come home to see his mother who was not doing well. Though Emma Sue looked surprised, she really wasn't. She knew Justin's mother had been sick and had been meaning to go by and check on her, but just never had. She looked away for a moment and wondered why she had never done that. When she turned back and saw Justin's face, she realized the answer. His mother would have reminded her of a past she had tried to forget, and seeing that past now right in front of her made her feel sick.

She excused herself to go the bathroom for a moment and then kissed Steven on the cheek and asked him to order them all some drinks. Steven smiled at Justin when Emma Sue kissed him and told her that he would be glad to as he put his arm around Justin's shoulders and asked him what he wanted to drink. Justin said a beer sounded good, so Steven told the bartender to get him and Emma Sue their regular drinks and to bring his good friend a beer.

Emma Sue had composed herself when she came back to the bar but still needed some tequila courage before she could sit down and talk to her old friend. After several shots, she and Justin were deep in conversation about his mother and his travels. Another hour of drinking seemed like minutes to Emma Sue but felt like several hours to Steven. He had moved over to the pool table as he had nothing to say and wasn't inclined to converse with Justin. And the longer they sat there and talked and laughed, the angrier Steven became.

It was hard for Justin to believe that Emma Sue was with Steven and when he asked her how long they had been together, he was even more surprised by the response. He tried on numerous occasions to steer the conversation away from himself and toward her, but she would not let him. He didn't need Steven to come over to the bar and hit him in the head with a pool cue to understand why she didn't want to talk about her relationship and life. The persistent stare from Steven, which was both callous and threatening, told him everything he needed to know.

But he wasn't afraid of Steven. He was scared for Emma Sue. He finally got a chance to ask her if she was happy and she nodded yes, but he saw the tears start to form in her eyes and he reached over and hugged her. As she wiped away her tears, her brain ignored the numbing effects of the alcohol and allowed its cathartic attributes to surface. She admitted that she was jealous of everything that he had seen and done and often wondered if she had made a mistake by breaking up with him. Justin slowly pulled out a plastic bag that contained several Oreo cookies. The smile on her face seemed to glow as she looked at Justin and heard him say that he had been hoping she would come by.

Steven simmered as he watched Emma Sue and Justin smiling and eating the Oreo cookies. Everyone except Justin and Emma Sue heard the pool cue snap in his hands like it was a twig. He took a deep breath before he marched toward the bar because he knew if he didn't, he would be arrested for what his mind and body told him he needed to do to Justin. In a very stern tone, Steven told Emma Sue that they needed to leave as he had an early morning the next day. Justin could tell that she didn't want to leave but he also knew he had to be very careful about what he said next.

He told Steven that he would be glad to get an Uber for Emma Sue, but she jumped up and stared at Steven before turning back to smile at Justin. She told him that it was wonderful seeing him again but they did need to leave. She kissed Justin's cheek and whispered in his ear that she missed seeing his turquoise eyes every morning. Justin feared what would happen to her if he said or did anything else, so he simply nodded and said he'd see her before he left town and sat back down and ordered another beer.

Steven seethed as they drove home and when they got inside he began to show Emma Sue how stupid she was for trying to make him jealous of her old boyfriend. He hit her twice in the face and then shoved her to the floor and started to strangle her. She clawed at his eyes and scratched one of them so badly that it bled before he let go of her. While in the bathroom to take care of the bleeding, he heard her yell at him that he should get used to having sex with blow-up dolls again because it would be a cold day in hell before he ever touched her.

Steven yanked the medicine cabinet off the wall and then walked back to Emma Sue who stood there, daring him to do anything. He told her that she was pretty stupid for a smart girl, and punched her so hard in her stomach that she lost her breath. Before she could regain it, he hit her across the chin, knocking her unconscious. He left her lying on the floor, slammed the door, and got on his motorcycle to head back to the bar. When he arrived, he checked to make sure Justin was still inside. Upon seeing that he was, he smiled and then went over to the unlit side of the building to wait. After about thirty minutes, Justin came out of the bar and just before he got to his car, Steven ran over and smashed his head with a tire iron.

Steven struck him over and over with the tire iron until Justin dropped to the ground, where he continued to kick him in the face until it was a bloody mask. He bent down on one knee next to his body and plucked his left eye out of his face with the tire iron. The eye rolled over onto the gravel parking lot and Steven smiled.

"I don't guess either of you will ever see or just plain understand, huh?" Steven asked as he laughed and stood up. The last thing he thought about was the Oreo cookies as a large semi-tractor trailer came speeding down the road and spit a wad of gravel into Steven's face. One large rock embedded into his temple and another one wedged against the bridge of his nose, twisted into his eye, by the last act of his hand. As he fell to the ground, his right eye popped out and rolled toward the unattached blue orb that awaited it with a lifeless stare.

See eye to eye

Banc Giefan

"What time will they be arriving?" William asked as he opened the door to the basement.

"I think around 8 p.m.," his wife answered. "I just hope they don't run into a lot of traffic. There will be so many people on the road today. This damn pandemic has just made everyone ready to get out and visit with family over the holidays."

"Language, Mother. Language."

"I know, I know. I'm just anxious to see them. It's been over a year. I'm allowed a little spice in my words, considering all that's transpired, don't you think?"

"Yes, but please try and refrain from using those words around the children," William said as he turned on the light and started walking down the stairs.

"I bet they've heard worse," Sarah mumbled to herself as her husband disappeared into the basement.

William opened the door at the far end of the basement that led into the corridor to the mortuary. It was convenient to have their house so close to their business and this access was extremely helpful when he wanted to avoid the bad weather that was not that uncommon in their location. The city wasn't called the "nation's icebox" without reason.

He smiled when he remembered the reporter talking about International Falls setting a record low of 45 degrees below for January 31.

"Been colder," he said out loud as if someone was walking with him. "And I had two funerals to do that day. Didn't stop us from doing them either. We come from hardy stock, us Minnesotans. Those two who had a showing that day were both in their nineties. 'Weather don't mean much unless you allow it to mean much,' is what my father always said. Look forward to seeing you later, Dad. Wish Mother was still with us."

William entered the elevator and pushed the "up" button and when the doors opened, he was at the back of the funeral home where the crematorium and the embalming rooms were located. He was glad there were no funerals today. He needed some time to catch up on his paperwork and had been trying to get his office reorganized for several months now. He walked down a long hallway and past several locked doors before he came to the main part of the building. "I think I can get a lot done today," he thought and then looked at his phone.

"29 degrees. Heck, Mother and I can go swimming later if I can get everything done," he said as he smiled and opened the door to his office.

He sat down at his desk and thought about the fight that led his son to pack up and leave home. Though he didn't regret anything he said, he wished he hadn't used the words with such an angry tone. His son had a right to live his own life and make his own mistakes. He still believed he was making a mistake getting married before he finished college and he certainly didn't like his idea of becoming a writer, but it was his life and he needed to accept it and move on. He hadn't even expected to see him over the holidays but was glad that he was coming and he hoped he had the ability and opportunity to say he was sorry.

Sarah busied herself in the kitchen making the pumpkin and apple pies that everyone expected from her each year. "I may put a little bit extra spice in both pies, William," she said as she turned and looked around to make sure he wasn't there. "Goodness, Sarah. Why are you so jumpy? Holidays, I suppose. Oh, you naughty girl! You know it's not just the holidays. You know Aubrey and Ela have a surprise, don't you? Yes, quite a surprise!" she said and once again looked around to make sure that William wasn't around. She smiled as she thought about the look he would have on his face when he learned the news that Ela had given birth to their first grandson.

It was close to five o'clock when William looked at the clock on his wall and realized he needed to get the meat out of the refrigerator in order to have it cooked by the time his son arrived. It had been marinating for three days now in his special herb and garlic oils and the aroma of the meat was intoxicating. *This may be the best one yet,* he thought as the pulled the large metal pan out of the refrigerator and shoved the door closed with his hip.

Sarah heard him coming up the basement steps and opened the door for him. "Oh, William, that smells delicious. I'm so glad you decided to make that for Aubrey. It's such a nice gesture on your part and I'm sure it will not be lost on our son."

William just nodded and placed the large pan in the oven. "Did you say they were arriving at eight?"

"Yes, about then. I told them we would have dinner ready when they got here."

They. It still didn't sound right. He gritted his teeth and took a deep breath. Sarah could see the tension in her husband's face and knew she needed to say something.

"You know, William, Aubrey reached out to us about coming back here. I had nothing to do with it. He wants to come home and see us. That is a good thing. Ela is a good woman and will be a good wife to him. I'm sure of it. I hope you can see that when they get here. I think you'll be very happy when you see them together."

Especially with their little surprise package, she thought to herself as she forced herself not to snicker.

"You're right, Sarah. I've thought about that a lot today and you are right. I'm happy Aubrey and Ela will be celebrating Banc Giefan with us. It's a celebration of family and I do realize they are family, Sarah. I will not lie to you. It has taken some time for me to accept that, but I will be welcoming. I promise you I will do that for you and our family."

Sarah hugged her husband. "Thank you, William. Thank you."

William said he was going upstairs to clean up. "Put on that Old Spice with the pine scent that your father used to wear all the time. Will you do that, William? I think that would be appropriate for tonight. I know it will make it feel like he's here with us celebrating."

William nodded and smiled as he leaned over and kissed Sarah on the cheek. "See you in about twenty minutes."

It was five minutes before eight when the lights flashed against the front window of the house. Sarah ran to the window and pulled back the curtains as the car pulled into the driveway. She was so excited she almost peed on herself as she called out to William, who was in the kitchen basting the meat with some herbed butter.

"William! William! Come in here. They're here. We should be standing here to greet them. Come here, hurry!"

"Sarah, it's not the King and Queen coming to our house. It is our son and …" He was unable to finish the sentence as he saw his son and his daughter-in-law come walking through the door. In Ela's arms was a baby and she was smiling as she looked at him.

"Hi, Dad. I know it's been a while since we talked but I thought we could put all that behind us now, seeing how some things have changed. This is your grandson, Aldis. Ela says he has your eyes and I think she's right. What do you think?"

William didn't move as Sarah took the baby from Ela's arms and brought him over to her husband. The baby burped and everyone laughed except William, who just stared at the child. Aldis gurgled and smiled as he looked up at the new face, and when he did William couldn't help himself. He smiled at the little boy and stroked his face gently with his index finger before Aubrey or Ela could warn him. Seconds later, Aldis turned his face toward the finger and snapped the tip of it off just beyond the nail.

The baby started choking as blood squirted onto its face. Aubrey grabbed the baby and removed the finger from his mouth, while Sarah took her husband's hand and held it raised over his head as she led him toward the kitchen.

"Come on, William. Let me wrap that finger in some cold bandages before you bleed all over the carpet," Sarah said as if she was talking to a child.

William smiled at his wife and then back at his son as he walked toward the kitchen.

"I seem to remember another little boy who had razor-sharp teeth as a young child. Bit things off before knowing what to do next if I recall. Is he okay, Aubrey?"

"Yes. Just some blood on his face. I have the tip of your finger if you want to go to the emergency room and try and have it sewn back on. They might be able to do that."

"Aubrey, it's Thanksgiving and 35 degrees below zero. I doubt there is a surgeon here in town who can do that type of delicate surgery and they are not going to be able to find one before the finger is no longer viable. Mother can get the bleeding stopped and then stitch it up and I'll be fine. Just take the little nub and place it on the counter in the kitchen. I'll take care of it later."

Thirty minutes later, William's finger was cleaned and stitched and wrapped in a bandage that looked like it had been done by a nursing professional.

"You see, Ela, here in this town, in this kind of weather, you have to be good at fixing your own injuries. Mother has become skilled in that art."

"Yes, I see that. Are you hurting?"

"No, not at all. I'll be fine. I won't even miss that little nubbin. Now, let's sit down and have a wonderful Banc Giefan! You are familiar with the feast?"

"Yes, Aubrey has told me everything about it. I am ravenous."

"Is that grandfather's thigh, Dad?"

"It is, son. It is the last of him. I've been saving it for a special occasion, made even more special by the arrival of my grandson of whom, eh hum, someone could have prepared me for by telling me about him much sooner."

Sarah just bowed her head and snickered.

"Anyway," William started and then excused himself. When he returned, he told everyone to sit down.

"I placed the finger in some hot water. We'll let it sit there and simmer while we eat and then I think someone will have his first finger puree on this most special of nights," William said as he looked over at Ela and winked.

Aubrey couldn't help himself as he reached over and grabbed a slice of the thigh that his father was carving. "Some things never change," William said as he laughed.

"I can't help it, Dad. Grandfather always had good taste. In life and in death," a comment that made his parents smile.

"I think it is time for a toast," Sarah announced as she lifted her glass. Everyone else at the table raised their glasses, except Ela, who was holding Aldis. William nodded his head toward them and began the blessing.

"Just as our forefathers and their forefathers and their forefathers, we share in the blessed nature of the flesh. What is born, provides sustenance, even in death, as it should be then, and as it should be now, and as it shall be always. Amen."

"Amen" everyone replied and began eating, telling stories about the father or father-in-law or grandfather, dependent on their relationship with the meal that they were now consuming.

Bite off more than you can chew

August 22, 2021

"Aren't you tired of this pandemic shit, Jackie?"

"I'm more tired of all this fricking work, man."

"I heered at, alrighty den."

Jackie laughed at Bill's impression of one of the elderly salespeople that he regularly conversed with at the Quik-N-Out where he bought gas.

"You sound just like him. Are you sure he ain't some distant relative of yor'n?"

"I'll kick at ass of yores if ya say at shit agin."

Jackie laughed even more at his friend's response. He could always make him laugh. He looked up at the calendar on the wall and realized the date was next weekend and that Bill would want to do something with him to celebrate. But that couldn't happen. Not this birthday. No, he had something else planned and Bill couldn't know anything about it. He had to start planting the seed now as to why they wouldn't be together this time.

"I think I might ask Karen out on a date. What do you think?"

"I think you'd be crazy not to, man. She's got the hots for you. All you need to do is ask and before you know it, she'll be wanting to go out with you all the time. I know it will be awkward at first, having her around with the both of us, but I'm sure she'll get used to it."

Jackie laughed again. "Yeah, uh-huh. You're right. It might get awkward, especially if we plan to take the relationship to another level. You do know about the birds and the bees, don't you?"

"Yes, but Jackie, you're not going to get anywhere taking her to an aviary or apiary. I mean the Scarlet Macaw is quite stunning and sure, you might get some real good honey, but I suggest taking her to the Big Mo' drive-in over in Monetta, after a really nice dinner. You know something like Taco Bell, not Burger King or McDonald's."

Jackie laughed and shook his head. "I appreciate the advice, Dr. Bill, but I think I'm up to date with the 'ins and outs' of a good date."

"Ins and outs. Nice one. Come on, man, let's finish putting these two computers together and call it a day. I'll buy you a beer, and maybe if you're good, a bowl of peanuts over at the Windsor Tap Room."

"Uh, aren't the nuts free?"

"Not for them, genius."

"Ahhhh. Got it. But yeah, let's get these things put back together and get out of here. I'm ready for a cold one."

The two friends completed putting all the components in their custom-built computers and closed up their shop.

"See you at the Tap Room."

"Yep," Jackie replied, thinking that would be an even better place to start the discussion about his birthday. After a few beers, it would be easier to explain to his best friend that they couldn't celebrate together. Not this year at least.

Bill was already sitting at the bar when Jackie walked in. The light from the wall sconces and the neon beer signs provided a soothing environment for the patrons and encouraged them to leave their concerns outside. A V-shaped frosted pilsner glass with the Budweiser logo on it was sitting in front of the empty bar stool next to Bill. Jackie smiled as he sat down and took a drink from the icy glass.

"Tastes good every time, especially after a long day of work."

"Yep, it do. Help yourself to the bowl of peanuts I ordered for you."

"Thanks, dude," Jackie took a handful and put a few in his beer, and started eating the rest.

"So, what do you plan to do for your birthday?" Bill asked.

Well, that didn't take long, did it? Jackie took another sip and tried to formulate his response.

"Like I said, I've been thinking about asking Karen out. Maybe a birthday date wouldn't be such a bad idea, if you get my drift."

"Oh, hell no, that ain't happening. A birthday b-j? What the hell, man? On the first date? Do you think you're living in a porno movie or something?"

"No, not that. I just thought she would think it was special. That's all."

"Well, how the hell is she going to know it's your birthday, Mr. Hefner?"

"You tell her."

"Me tell her? Oh, so I'm going on this date with you two. Okay, that makes sense. I'm in."

"Uh, no, that's not what I meant. I mean, I know we'll see her next week. She has to come by and pick up her computer that's in the shop. Well, she doesn't have to come by, but I'm pretty sure she will when we call and tell her it's ready. And you could just casually bring it up. You know, just say something like, 'so what do you plan to do for your birthday, Jackie,' and then I'll take it from there. I'll offer to help her load her computer in the car and then you know, just ask her if she'd like to go out."

"Jesus, dude. How many nights have you been lying awake thinking of this little episode, Ang?"

"Uh….um …"

"Okay, okay. But don't expect me to be there when she says no, even though we have spent our birthdays together for the past sixteen years. Nope, ole Barn won't be around to pick up the pieces so don't even ask. Don't even think of asking me 'cause, I will just nip it. Nip it in the bud. Speaking of bud, barkeep, over here please."

"Funny."

"I thought so. And now that I've had a moment or two to think about it, yes, I'll be glad to help you in this subterfuge."

"You're the best, Barn, just the best."

"Yeah, yeah. Now, I'll take my hamburger medium and I want a baked potato and salad with bleu cheese."

"Coming up," Jackie said as he tipped his glass toward Bill.

****

Karen came into the store on Wednesday. Though Bill made Jackie work for the planned conversation, he finally relented and began to question him about his birthday. Jackie acted as if he hadn't given it much thought while he tried to assess what Karen was thinking about the discussion. Just as he intended, Jackie carried the computer out to her car and talked to her for a few minutes, glancing back at the store a few times. He knew Bill was watching him and though it made him nervous, he continued to talk to Karen for a few more minutes before he came back inside.

"Well?"

"I've got a date for my birthday! And just as my good friend suggested, we're going to a nice restaurant and then we are going to the axe-throwing place downtown."

"Axe throwing? Well, nothing suggests romance is in the air like a good hatchet in someone's hand. Are you nuts?"

"Hey, it will be fun! I'll tell you all about it on Sunday. Well, maybe not all."

"Yeah. Just be careful she doesn't toss that hatchet into your nuts."

"Funny."

****

Jackie left his house at around six that evening and drove toward Lake Thurmond and Essie May Washington Park. Something in his mind and body told him he needed to be away from everyone because he was starting to feel very ill. He drove around the park to make sure no one else was there before he parked his car beside the swing set. He got out and sat on one of the swings and watched the sky. The moon started to emerge from the clouds as he gripped the metal chains that were attached to the seat.

The sound of the car speeding into the park startled him as it came up and parked next to his. He was blinded by the headlights for a second and fell to the ground as if he had been struck by lightning. He looked back at the headlights that were still on and the light enraged him. It seemed like he could feel every blood cell moving through his body. He felt hot, as if his skin was on fire and he began to dig his hands into the dirt. Then he heard a familiar voice as a shadow moved in front of the headlights and began walking toward him.

"Not feeling too good, Jackie?" Bill asked. "I bet your skin feels like it's on fire, doesn't it? You know, a blue moon is an infrequent phenomenon; roughly every two to three years, a 13th full moon is seen in a calendar year. But you know what? One is occurring today, August 22, 2021, on your birthday.

"I knew where you were coming, Jackie. I knew you were just pretending to ask Karen out. I heard every word of your conversation. I can hear snakes bend grass as they move along the ground. I knew you would come to an isolated place. I could smell you as I came toward the lake. I have a rather amazing sense of smell, as well as eyesight and hearing. But, you'll soon find out what I mean."

Jackie screamed as the bones in his legs began to break and reform. The ankle bone popped through his skin like a compound fracture and it felt like he had been drenched in hot tar. As he watched his skin melt away, he screamed one word -

"Leave!" When he tried to scream again, the noise that came from his throat was a howl.

"Don't worry, Jackie," Bill said as he grinned up at the moon. "I will be okay. After all, how do you think you became what you are now?" he asked as the hair on his body began to thicken.

Once in a blue moon

Edgefield

Lester and Earl "Skeeter" Byrd were brothers who had been making moonshine in Edgefield County, South Carolina for over fifty years now. They had learned the skill from their father, Robert, and his friend, Zebediah, moonshine-makers ever since they came back from World War II. And just like their father, when Lester and Earl came back from the war, they carried on with the tradition, which became even more important to them since their father and Zebediah had both died while they were over in Vietnam.

"You know, Skeeter, Dad was a man ahead of his time to cut in Zebediah fifty-fifty on the profits of this here liquid sunshine."

"What do you mean, Lester?"

"Zebediah was black, Skeeter. When dad and him come back from the war, it won't no good for a man of color in this part of the country. Them damn Jim Crow laws still kept a black man down but dad never paid much attention to the government, especially when they passed stupid shit laws like them. Of course, that might be a bit redundant on my part to say the government passed stupid shit laws. They sorta go hand and hand with one another. Dad was a good man and he knew a good man regardless of the color of his skin. He always treated Zebediah as an equal."

"You damn right, Lester. Government laws are redunceant."

Lester laughed at Skeeter's attempt at saying redundant but as he thought about what he said, he realized his pronunciation might even be more appropriate.

"And you's right about Dad and Zebediah. He treated him as a pardner. But you know, Lester, we did the same thing over theah in those damn jungles."

"Suppose we did, Skeeter. Suppose we did. But now that I've thought about it some, I get mad at myself for never standing up and saying anything to the white boys that said turd words about them colored soldiers. They didn't deserve that. I sure wish I had said something, Skeeter."

"Lester, that war was over for us in 1970. Fifty-two years ago. We were 18 and 19 years old when we got over in that God-forsaken shit hole. If we didn't use our shine skills over ere and smoke at shit some of them other soldiers had, especially some of our black friends, I don't think we woulda made it back with our head in the right place and our body holding it on. And they knowed the feeling in our hearts. I knowed they did. They said it to me on more than one 'casion that you and me weren't no white crackers. Don't you 'member at night we got stoned as shit with em and they called us honorary soul brothahs? Damn, we was fucked up from Sunday, but I remember it. I felt really good at night. Felt like we was all one. You remember at, don't you?"

Skeeter's retelling of the story jogged his memory and he smiled. He doubted he would be able to remember very much any longer, even with his brother's prompts. The headaches were almost unbearable now and were affecting his balance and vision. He had difficulty seeing at all sometimes, and his memories were becoming shadowy images that only brought him frustration rather than solace.

"Yeah, Skeeter. I remember that now. Thanks for reminding me. That was a special night. But you think we made it back here sane? I still have nightmares almost every night."

"That's cause you don't listen to me and think this here shine will take yore pain away. It's good and all, I give you at. But it helps to have a little of this here weed to help accentualate the feeling and help keep them nightmars bottled up."

Lester laughed again at Skeeter's pronunciation, though again, he wasn't sure the word he used wasn't just as good as the real one.

"You know, Skeeter, I told you a hundred times before; you can't be smoking that shit when we're cooking a batch. You damn near killed us twice cause of some leaks. If my nose hadn't smelled them fumes and you had lit up a joint, there wouldn't be enough of us left to bury."

"I knowed it, Lester. I don't do that no more when we're cooking. I promise I don't. But after we's done, then no promises. You should try it after we git done with this here batch."

"Don't know if I care to, Skeeter. I admit it did help over there in that damn jungle. But now I don't like it that much. It makes me a bit jittery and it seems to make me remember the bad things instead of forgetting them. I'm haunted by the war. Reckon I always will be."

"Maybe you need some pills to go with the shine? Some of those morphine pills. I forget what they call them…oxen…"

"Oxycontin, Skeeter. And I don't want none of that shit. The damn Chinese are lacing all that shit with Fentanyl in order to kill Americans. Damn communist sons of bitches."

"Lester, you're 74 years old. You done had prostate cancer, lung cancer, and colon cancer. I don't think them pills are gonna kill ya. Shit, I'm not sure anything is going to kill ya. Like ole Zeb said, that shine inside of us protects us from all sorts of bugs and shit."

"Skeeter, dammit…. Zebediah wasn't referring to cancer. He was…." and then Lester stopped in mid-sentence. Perhaps Zebediah was referring to cancer even though he eventually died from liver cancer. And he knew Zebediah's medical issues painted his brother's reflection. He was just too fucked up to see it through his yellowish-orange bloodshot eyes. He was surprised his brother hadn't even noticed his orange skin. Hell, he probably thinks it's just a bad sunburn of some sort, Lester thought as he shook his head. Plus, they had been out in the woods for about a week now and there would have been no reason for him to look in a mirror, even though that was seldom done anyway because his brother was not a friend of soap. He also understood his brother's bulging stomach did not reflect fat. He was aware that it was filled with poisonous fluid, but he knew Skeeter had missed that warning sign too and probably just assumed it meant he had consumed more boxes of Little Debbies than usual.

His brother had not even bothered to ask him how his last doctor visit went and he was now glad that his mind didn't allow him to worry about things like that. No, they had been out in the woods ever since he got back from the doctor's office and learned the undeniable results of his Cat scan and MRI. They had made it back to those woods that they both loved and connected them to their past. Lester wanted to have at least one more good week with his brother and that had now been accomplished.

"How the hell do you know he weren't talking 'bout the cancer?"

"Cause drinking moonshine every day ain't good for your body, Skeeter."

"Says the 74-year-old man that's been drinking moonshine since he was 14. That's fifty-some years."

"Sixty years, Skeeter. Sixty years."

"You always was better at numbering than I was."

"Yeah, a tad better. Hey, I see a drop coming off that coon pecker. Time to check it out."

"Hell, yes, Lester. Hell, yes, I see it!" Skeeter ran over to the thumper keg and let the mason jar fill up before he tossed the poisonous methanol that came out first onto the ground. He replaced the mason jar with a clean one under the steady flow, bent down, and started rubbing his hands.

"Now we's cookin, Lester. Damn ole coon bone. Reckon our pecker bone is too big to use, huh?"

"We ain't got a bone in our pecker, Skeeter. Most mammals don't."

"Huh?"

"Our pecker is just muscle and blood vessels and a tube that leads to your bladder, which in my case, seems to have a mind of its own."

"We aint got no bone? Then why do they call it a boner?"

Lester saw no reason to argue as he smiled. "You make a good point. A real good point. Why don't we smoke a joint and celebrate this batch?"

"Why, hell, yes! Now you talkin, brother," Skeeter said as he pulled a joint out of one pocket and his lighter out of another.

"I got to admit, Lester, I had a joint earlier this morning while you slept and I is stoned."

Lester just smiled and nodded and knew that was why Skeeter didn't smell the ethanol fumes that surrounded them. He grabbed his brother's hand and watched the spark that was spun by the flint create a flash of light that suggested a segment of the sun had settled onto the ground for just a few seconds and embraced the two old brothers in arms.

Birds of a feather, flock together

English Mountain

It was the tenth day of the tenth month of the tenth year of the pandemic. I know because it was my fifth birthday, though technically, I wasn't five years old. I was, if one desires to think in the old ways, sixty-five years old. But that's the old way of thinking about birth and death. Since I died, I don't use that method to calculate my age, nor do many others. All time is now measured in pandemic time and the moment in which you "arose from the bed."

So, this was the moment I did that five years ago. The antiviral drug they put in my veins saved me. Just like that, I was no longer some alien life form whose chest moved up and down with every "ussssh" and "fussssh" sound of the ventilator. I had regained human form and I could breathe on my own. And believe it or not, I wasn't some frail, atrophied skeleton. They kept my body full of nutrients and vitamins, better than I would have if I had been making meals for myself, and the bed had exercised my muscles.

Once I woke up, I could talk (although with a raspy voice due to the ventilator being in my throat for so long), and I could even walk. At first, walking required some assistance but after a few laps around the unit with a nurse, I was moving along by myself. It was amazing and truly a rebirth. After the doctor saw me and listened to me breathe, and answer some questions – primarily, name some animals and do some simple math and division - I was told I could go home. Home. Can you believe it? After five years on a ventilator, I was going home.

Of course, along with that feeling of relief and happiness, the word "reality" came flying into my ears in the form of questions that the discharge nurse began to ask.

"No, my wife is dead. She died a year before I came to the hospital because of the goddamn virus. My children are dead too. I wasn't that upset when I got the virus as I thought I would be dead soon too and join them."

She let me vent a little while longer and then asked if I had a way to get home. I told her that unless the hospital had towed my truck away, it was still in the visitor parking lot. I drove myself to the hospital because I lived way out by English Mountain in Cocke County, over fifty miles from the medical center. As I said that to her, I began to wonder why I even went to the medical center, considering that I really just wanted to die. I reckoned that question would bother me for some time, but for now, I was ready to go home and see what my farm looked like.

She said the truck should still be there and gave me my keys and wallet which they had kept for me all this time. I smiled and started to stand up, and that's when the nurse said if I had a few more minutes that she would like to talk to me a little longer. A few minutes? Hell, I just had been born, I thought. I had all the time in the world, so I said yes and sat back down on the edge of the bed.

The nurse told me that things would be a lot different on the outside from the time that I came into the hospital. I wasn't sure what that meant and I began thinking she was about to tell me that we all had to wear space suits now, or that the sky was red and orange, or maybe there wasn't a sun anymore; then I heard her calling out my name. I told her I was sorry for becoming lost in thought for a moment and she said she understood and I had no reason to apologize. She added that there were therapists in the hospital who could come up and talk to me, if needed, to help me "adjust" to the fact that I had essentially been dead for five years.

Of course, she didn't use the word dead. She said "asleep," as if I had gone into hibernation or some kind of deep sleep you see in a sci-fi movie where the astronauts are lying there in their glass pods as they journey light years into space. I have to admit when I heard her use the word asleep, it sort of pissed me off, but before I expressed that feeling, I looked into the tired face that was smiling at me, and I could see that she was just doing her job.

Her face looked tired but her eyes projected sincerity and empathy and I realized that person, that nurse, truly cared and had probably gone through ten years of Hell and I needed to be a lot more respectful toward her. I told her that I bet she didn't hear enough "thank yous" for doing her job and I wanted to take a moment to sincerely thank her for everything she did to help me and hundreds of others through all this shit.

Not that I should have been surprised, now that I've had time to think about it, but at that moment, I certainly didn't expect to see her break down when I said those words. She didn't stop crying for several minutes and I was starting to wonder if I should call the therapist she had mentioned earlier to come speak to her. But she soon stopped and sat down on the bed next to me, took my hand, and said "Thank you."

Ain't that some shit? She was thanking me just because I said something that we were all taught since we were children to say. She was the one that had been working her ass off for probably sixteen-hour shifts, without any days off, and she was sitting there thanking me. So, I did what I should have done when she first came into my room. I introduced myself and held out my hand. She told me her name was Shelly Claiborne and I told Shelly Claiborne that it was my pleasure to meet her and though I appreciated her concern about a therapist consultation, I didn't think I was going to need one, at least for now. She smiled and patted my hand and wrote down a number on a piece of paper and said to call that number if I did need one in the future. I told her I appreciated that.

She added one more thing before I left the room. She told me to not be shocked when I drove home to see a lot less traffic on the road. She could tell by the expression on my face that I had an unspoken question and she proceeded to answer it. Half of the world's population had died since the pandemic started ten years ago. Those words took the breath from my lungs and I staggered back onto the bed. Shelly caught me and steadied me as she got me a glass of water. I tried to process those words and I felt Shelly's grip on my hand tighten.

After I finished my water, I said that I would be okay. I told her that I had come in here without any family left and I hadn't expected to come out of here alive, and though it saddened me to hear about all the deaths, I would come to terms with it in time. I pulled out the piece of paper she had given me a few moments before and told her I would probably give this person a call eventually, but right now, all I wanted to do was go home. Shelly said she understood and hugged me as she walked me to the elevator.

I will have to say Shelly was right, even though I doubted she would be at the time. The old red Ford F-250 was right where I left it. I can't believe I even remembered where I parked it but I walked right to it. It was sitting there at the top of the parking deck, next to the elevator. I don't know why I was shocked that I found it because it wasn't a huge feat of mental prowess. I always parked next to the elevators at the top of the parking decks. The inside of those decks made me a little claustrophobic so I always parked at the top in the same general area each time I used them. Regardless, I felt pretty good about my success and when I put the key into the ignition and the truck started right up, I screamed out the window like a madman. I looked around as soon as I did to make sure no one came running as I realized I shouldn't be hollering like that in a hospital parking lot. But no one came, so I began driving down the twisting tunnel toward the exit and told myself that I was going to write a letter to Ford when I got home telling them about the reliability of their truck.

Hell, they might want me to be part of an ad campaign I thought, and then laughed out loud. I couldn't imagine how they would frame that message.

"When you are sick and dying of the virus and need to get to the hospital, drive a Ford. It will be there, waiting for you should you wake up." Yeah, I didn't think that was going to be that good of an ad after all, but that still wasn't going to deter me from writing a letter to the company. No sir. I was going to do that.

As I drove down Highway 441 toward Sevierville, it did feel like it was a very early Sunday morning. There was hardly any traffic and I almost wrecked several times when I thought I saw my family members standing along the side of the road, waving at me. In fact, I saw more than family members. There were ghosts everywhere and I just had to tell myself over and over, they weren't actually there. It was just trauma from waking up after five years and it was affecting my mind. The ghosts did not go away until 441 became 411, which was still about thirty miles, so at least no more damn construction had taken place over the past five years I said to myself.

And then I shook my head as I thought about what I had just said and realized what was usually a source of frustration and prompted many curse words from me, was now a telling sign that the world had indeed changed and left me speechless. It was a sunny day but it was not a pleasant drive and I patted my pocket to make sure I had that piece of paper that Shelly gave me. I figured I might need to use it much sooner than anticipated.

There was no one around as I turned onto Connor Springs Road. The road to English Mountain wasn't well-traveled anyway, but it did get busy during the summertime as tourists flocked to Pigeon Forge and the Smoky Mountains. I drove several miles and turned onto Connor Springs Loop toward my farm, passing Price Road, where I knew of an old man, Mr. Seymour, who had a farm there. At least he had a farm there five years ago. So I stopped and turned down the road to see if he was still there and danged if I didn't see the old "cuss" out in the field driving his tractor.

I was not a friend of the man because he was prone to beating his animals and I didn't care for any person that mistreated an animal. I said something to him about it once and he pulled out a twenty-two and shot at my feet, so I never did say anything to him again. I should have called the police but folks that lived on English Mountain didn't call the police. So I didn't do anything and just avoided going down that road. I thought that perhaps this damn virus might have mellowed him a bit so I rolled down the window on my truck and waved and hollered "Hello" at him. He looked over at me and threw me a "bird." I just sat there for a moment and wondered why mean sons of bitches like him didn't die.

I watched him put some hay down for his horses, and as I was driving away, I saw one of the horses stumble and fall to the ground. *Shit, that son of a bitch will kill that poor animal* I thought and I put the truck in park and got out. I yelled at the old bastard not to hurt that horse and that I would take care of it. But before I could get over to him and the horse, he took out a whip and started beating it something awful before I saw it stop moving. I thought it was dead, but several moments later, the dang horse got back up on its feet. What I saw next, shocked the shit out of me. The horse shook its head once, snorted, and then attacked the old man, biting off his arm. The old son of a bitch could run pretty fast, but with all that blood spurting out of his arm, he couldn't run far. When he fell to the ground, the horse walked over to him and bit his head off.

I didn't know what the hell was going on, but I knew horses didn't eat people, so I jumped back into my truck and drove home as fast as I could. I didn't bother to turn off the truck as I ran into the house. When I went through the kitchen toward my gun cabinet, I saw that my shotgun was sitting on the table; a note tied to the trigger with a piece of thin wire. It simply said, "Shoot their head." I grabbed the gun and ran outside just in time to see the horse galloping toward me. I emptied both barrels into its head and without any semblance of a head remaining, the horse fell to the ground. When I went back inside, I found another note that said, "If you saw the first note, then burn them." So, I grabbed a bottle of George Dickel and a can of gasoline, and went outside and set fire to the horse. I sat there on the porch with George to make sure the fire didn't get out of hand until all that was left was a pile of sad-looking ashes.

I found out from some of my other neighbors that the virus had affected the horses in a very different way. It was my neighbor that lived one farm down Carson Springs Loop that had left the note for me on the table just in case I ever came back home. He told me that the virus killed the horses whenever it "got hold of them," but when it killed them, it turned them into some sort of zombies. I told him I appreciated the timely and neighborly advice and thought about old Mr. Seymour. He learned the hard way that it was never a good idea to beat an animal. Doing that now just pissed off horses and these days, they could be quite something to deal with when they were feeling poorly. I called the therapist several days later and set up a series of appointments.

Beat a dead horse to death

Closets

I think I've been afraid of closets ever since I was old enough to be in my own room. It didn't matter that my parents opened the closet door ten thousand times showing me that no monsters were there. Just because they physically moved all the shirts and pants and shined a flashlight in the dark corners, and let me lift boxes and move shoes around, didn't mean the monster wasn't there. At least for me, it didn't.

It was always there in my mind. And if it was there in my mind, it might as well have been there in the closet, because my mind made it just as real. Perhaps even more so. At least if I could have known that the monster was a noisy mouse that we found during our investigations or even a large spider that I somehow heard moving atop my shoes, maybe I wouldn't have been haunted by the monster that I saw. It was silver with eyes so dark that you never saw them until light revealed they existed. It had at least a thousand legs, with a large mouth like a pair of pliers that kept opening and closing and a scorpion-like tail that I was certain was poisonous. When I slept, it was always there in my dreams, chasing me through my backyard and house until I woke up in a cold sweat.

I eventually stopped telling my parents about it, but I never stopped seeing that hideous creature in my dreams. My dreams were so vivid because the door to my closet was, I believed, a door to other dimensions where nothing was as it was in our world. The skies were orange or red or black and always had some kind of green sun. The ground was usually a shade of blue, and seldom green unless it was some type of water that bubbled and smelled like the sewer. The trees were never brown, but various colors of the rainbow and always had strange purple spiny fruit hanging from their limbs. The fruit smelled good and may have tasted good, but you would have sliced open your hand if you tried to touch a piece. And regardless of what world I stumbled into when I opened the closet door in my dreams, that creature was always there.

It could never catch me though. I was always able to outrun it, especially if I happened to be in the world with the bubbling green sewer water. I became quite good at running just along the edge of the water and inevitably, the creature would allow several of its legs to fall into the green substance and I could hear it make a noise that sounded like a high-pitched squeak as if a hundred creaky doors were all opening at the same time. I would look back and watch its legs dissolve. But that wouldn't stop it. Once the legs disappeared, it would just start chasing me again. But because its body was now out of balance, it could never come close to me and always ended up falling into the green substance and melting like an ice cube in boiling water.

I don't know how I knew it, but somehow I sensed that if the monster ever stuck its tail into your chest, you would die. I just knew the poison in that tail would enter your heart and would stop it from beating. Unfortunately, my fears were realized when my grandfather died because I saw the monster that night.

It came out of the closet while the family was downstairs. My grandfather was sick and sleeping in bed. I heard the monster's legs tapping across the floor, and I yelled out, "No!" and ran upstairs. As I opened the door, the black eyes of the hideous thing were looking right at me as it stuck its tail straight into my grandfather's chest. And if a monster could smile, it smiled that night before it ran back into the closet as I screamed.

My parents and uncles and aunts all rushed into my grandfather's room. My uncle, who was a doctor, checked my grandfather and just shook his head. Everyone knew what that meant and I later learned from my parents that my grandfather's heart had just given out. I started to tell them I knew why his heart had given out but I didn't say anything. I knew they wouldn't want to hear what I had to say or believe me. Out of respect for my father who was so sad, I simply said I was sorry and tried to comfort him.

Once my grandfather died, I realized that monster wasn't ever going to go away, so I needed to find a way to keep it from hurting other people, including myself. I knew the green sewer water could burn it, but I feared that substance would burn me too. But one night, when I was in the world that had an orange sky, I found what I needed. The silver creature was chasing me as usual and when we ran into a forest that night, I soon noticed that the ground was covered in something that looked like pine cones. They cracked open as I stepped on them and a pine-smelling pink vapor arose out of them. I suddenly heard the monster emit another kind of screeching noise. As I looked behind me, I saw it running away from the pink vapor and I knew I had found the answer.

When I woke up that morning, I ran outside to find some pine cones. They weren't hard to find, since a large pine tree stood next to the house and one of the limbs scratched against the screen in my window on windy days and nights. I grabbed one and broke it open but I didn't see any pink vapor coming out and I felt very discouraged. But then I began to wonder if perhaps the pink vapor could only be seen in the "other" world. I knew there was only one way to test my theory and that night I did.

It was 2 a.m. when I heard my closet door open and I could see the brown sky and green lightning bolts, but I didn't get out of bed. I lay there and silently waited for it to come to me as I knew it would. I soon saw the glint of silver and heard the plier jaws open and snap shut several times. I counted to ten, sat up and twisted off pieces of the pine cone, put them in my hand, and blew toward the creature. Though there was a faint smell of pine, I didn't see any pink vapor, but it didn't matter, because the monster had paused. I twisted off several more pieces and blew again and this time I heard the monster make that screeching noise and then it was gone.

My theory was right. I couldn't see the pink vapor in this world but it was there in the pine cones nevertheless and the monster did not like it. From that point forward, I told my mother I liked having pine cones in my room, and she said that was fine. She liked the smell and look of them too, so that was how I was able to conquer the monster from ruling my life, even though I never stopped seeing or entering those other worlds at night. But I wasn't scared anymore and when the monster came for me, as it always did, I blew the pink vapors from the pine cone toward it and it always ran away.

When I was in college, my mother called and told me to come home right away because my father had a heart attack and was very sick. I arrived home just in time to run into the ICU where I saw a red sky in the room and the monster about to jab my father in his heart with its tail. I pulled out the pine cone I had in my coat pocket, snapped it in two, and blew as hard as I could toward the creature's face. The monster screeched and pulled away and disappeared into the red sky world, which went away with it. My hands were bleeding from the many pointed pine cone scales that had cut me but I didn't feel any pain. I washed my hands and held paper towels in them and I didn't leave my father's side until he got well enough to leave the hospital.

While he recovered at home, I told my mother that it would be a good idea to keep pine cones in his room and then showed her an article about the benefits of essential oils. I assured her that just having the pine cones in his room would be good for his long-term health and she thought it was a good idea. I took the semester off from art school to stay with them and there were several other times when I kept the monster from taking away another weak heart into its world. Eventually, the monster saw that the pine cones weren't going away and he realized trying to take my father's heart was too dangerous, so he quit trying. My father lived for sixteen more good years before he died of a blood cancer.

He lived long enough to see me have success with my painting and it made both my parents very happy. Apparently, within the art world, I was considered something of an artistic genius with my colorful abstracts of red and orange skies, blue trees, purple pointed fruit, and a multitude of green-shaded suns. I must admit, the pictures were very colorful and I didn't see the need to explain that I was just painting what existed in other dimensions. At least not until I met Alexandra.

I remember the first day we met. It was the thirtieth of April and I was painting a field of tulips in the park. I was so involved in my work that I didn't even notice she was there until I heard her mother apologizing to me. I didn't know what she was apologizing for until she picked up the little girl who was standing at my feet.

She said her daughter was normally very shy and didn't really like being around people, so it surprised her that she had walked over to me and stood there watching me paint. Her mother asked what I was painting and before I could answer, the little girl spoke up.

"Flowers, mommy. Flowers," and then she pointed toward the field of grass that had once been filled with tulips but were now just a few brown stems and some green leaves.

For me, though, there was still a bank full of tulips. Yes, they were oddly shaped and colored not of this world, within a pistachio-green sky and cerulean grass, but they were there. Interestingly enough, the little girl could see them too. Her mother seemed embarrassed by her daughter's comments as she couldn't see the flowers, but I knew at once that I had to help that little girl. I knew what she saw at night.

I smiled at the mother and told her the little girl was very sweet and I then introduced myself. I wasn't surprised that the mother didn't know who I was. I doubted that she moved in the same circles as I did, even though, I didn't really move in them either. I was just there among them, selling my "color visuals" for exorbitant prices. I asked what her daughter's name was and she told me it was Alexandra. I shocked her mother by saying that her daughter was right and that I was painting flowers, tulips to be exact. Her mother just smiled, backed away several steps, and began to look around the park, while holding dearly onto her child.

I knew what she was doing. She was looking for my nurses, as she probably thought I was doing some sort of supervised outdoor therapy. I began to laugh, which in hindsight, was probably not the best thing to have done. Thankfully, a fan of my work noticed me and came up to tell me how beautiful my painting was, and talked for several minutes about my art. As we talked, I could see Alexandra's mother begin to relax.

I thanked the young woman and told her the title of the painting was "Tulips Reimagined." She smiled and remarked again how beautiful it was and then asked if it was for sale. I replied that I wasn't sure yet but that if I put it up for sale, it would be at my gallery on 6th street. She nodded and told me that she would be "watching for it," as she walked away

The mother smiled at me when I looked over at her and I gave her my card and told her that she had a very special little girl as a daughter.

"John De La Jean?"

"Yes. That's my real name too and very seldom do people pronounce it correctly. They usually say Gene at the end. Did you study French?"

"In high school. I could get around in France but I couldn't carry on a serious conversation with a Frenchman or woman or umm, what do you say these days? I guess, uh, a French person. Oh, and my name is Sara. Sorry. I should have said that earlier."

She is still a little nervous. She doesn't understand how her daughter could see the tulips in the empty field. Honestly, I can't say that I blame her.

"Nice to meet you, Sara."

I bent down on my knees so I could be on Alexandra's level and introduced myself to her. I told her I was a painter and I thought she had a wonderful imagination. Imagination seemed to be the magic word for "talk" because as soon as I said that, Alexandra began to tell me all about everything that was in her room - her books, her coloring books, her dolls, her toys, her clothes, and the scary closet.

"Now, honey, I don't think Mr. De La Jean wants to hear about the scary closet."

She's embarrassed again. And scared. I have seen those eyes in a mother before.

"It's okay, Sara," I said as I looked up at her and then back down into Alexandra's eyes. "So, you have a scary closet?"

Alexandra nodded.

"You know, when I was about your age, I had a scary closet too. And my parents helped me make sure the scary closet couldn't scare me."

"They did?"

"They sure did. You want to know how?"

Alexandra nodded her head.

"Pine cones."

Alexandra knew at once what I meant. I could see it in her eyes. "Can we have pine cones, Mommy? By my bed?"

Sara looked at me oddly and I stood up and smiled.

"Your little girl will be fine if you do this, Sara. Trust me."

I could see her wondering what would be the harm of having pine cones in her daughter's room, especially if it made her nightmares go away. Then she smiled at Alexandra and said, "Yes, darling, we can get pine cones for your room."

"Sara, if you'll let me, there are a few of them just over there. May I take Alexandra over to the pine tree and pick out a few? You have my card and my art supplies. Believe me, we'll be in your sight the entire time and will come right back."

Sara was a little hesitant but Alexandra tugged on her pants begging, "Please," and she relented.

I walked slowly toward the pine tree with Alexandra by my side. I bent down and helped her pick out a few cones.

"You see a monster in your closet at night, don't you, Alexandra?"

"Yes, an awful giant silver thing with a thousand legs and a sharp, snapping mouth and a long tail and eyes as dark as my closet."

"Well, the next time you see it, just break off a little of the pine cone like this and blow. Do that in this world and in the other worlds that I know you can see. Do not worry about what the doctors say is or isn't real. Stay true to yourself, because only you know for sure what the truth truly is. When the creature is chasing you in the other more colorful worlds that you visit, you will see a pink vapor come out of the pine cones and it will make the creature want to run away from you."

"Yeah!"

"Yeah, is right, Alexandra. I call the pink vapor "The Doubt" because people never believed me when I was your age and told them about the monster. But, believing in myself saved me and I know if you continue to do that and use these pine cones, you will grow strong and be able to protect your family. Understand?"

Alexandra smiled and nodded her head.

"Good. And one more thing; this will be just our little secret, okay?"

"Yes, our secret. Now, will you show me how to paint the pretty flowers?"

"I can't teach you how to paint because I cannot teach you how to see. But, don't worry, sweet girl, your eyes can see the world of color that surrounds us. And one day, when the monsters come and you blow the doubt away, your hands will listen to your mind and follow your eyes, and you will paint beautiful flowers for the rest of your life."

Benefit of the doubt

Sshhh….

I first saw the man out of the corner of my eye, standing off in the distance. I didn't pay any attention to him for several minutes because there were other people in front of me asking about my work. They purchased several books, one that I signed for a granddaughter and one for a son. I thanked them for coming by and told them to let me know how they liked the books.

After they walked away, I looked up and saw the man again. He had come quite a bit closer and was staring in my direction. But I knew he wasn't just staring at me. He was looking at the picture of my friend in the make-up she did as an interpretation of a demon.

"It's a demon in one of my books," I said to him as I smiled. He walked closer and studied the picture for a moment longer before he glared at me.

"Mister, demons aren't nuisances. They're real and you shouldn't be inviting them into your home with your books or pictures."

"Shit," I said to myself. I didn't expect this type of reaction at a book signing. Then I remembered I was at an arts and craft show in a small southern town, and I was surely the only one there with a picture of a demon on the table. I wasn't sure how to respond, as I didn't want to offend or antagonize him into accusing me of being a blasphemer and yelling at others to "cast me from their presence" so I just said what I believed.

"There is evil in the world, that's true. There has been evil since the beginning of time, and my books just reveal the struggle between good and evil. It's a never-ending battle."

"But yous inviting the devil into your home by speaking about him."

"Well, I don't mean any disrespect but that's not at all true. I have a strong faith and I am not inviting the devil to do anything. I just write horror stories."

"You walk the path to Hell and I won't have any part in it."

"So, does that mean you aren't going to buy a book?" is what I wanted to say but I kept my mouth shut and watched him give me the "stink eye" a little longer before his wife, or sister, or sister-wife, came over and led him away; thankfully, without suggesting anything else be done to banish me from the premises.

Once he was gone, I turned to my wife and rolled my eyes. "Well, that was interesting. Be ready to pack up and leave quickly should you see some folks headed this way carrying torches."

"Funny."

"Hey, the witch trials didn't only happen in Salem. There were four people accused of witchcraft in 1792 right here in South Carolina, just because some cattle began to die. Funny, how it always seems to start because the cattle die. Anyway, the main witch, a Mary Ingleman, was accused of levitating people, transforming herself into animals, and even turning a young man into a horse so that she could ride him to a witch's convention to meet the devil."

"You're making that up. Is this in some new story you're writing?"

"No, not yet, but if I become a participant in the story, I may."

"Hah! No really. What happened to the witches and this Ingleman woman?"

"Well, I don't know everything yet, but as I understand it, Mary Ingleman practiced simple cures and used herbal remedies on the townsfolk - you know, 'eye of newt and toe of frog' sort of thing. So, she became an easy target when the cattle started dying. Supposedly the town was trying to avoid the hysteria of Salem, so, the residents quickly blamed Ingleman and her three neighbors for the deaths of the cattle. Of course, without any hard evidence. They were tried and convicted, then beaten, tortured, and burned, but not to death. Just singed a bit to get their attention. They also tried to kill Ingleman several times, including hanging her, but she eventually died of old age."

"Are you sure she wasn't a witch?"

"I don't know if she was a witch or not, but I'm leaning toward the idea she was just a convenient suspect who used herbal remedies and got caught up in scary superstitious fear-mongering. Hell, doesn't that still happen? Can you imagine what would have happened today if there were folks here selling crystals or Tarot cards? Shit. We could have seen the beginning of some new witch trials. Maybe even a few people levitated off the ground - unwillingly."

"You're letting your imagination run wild."

"That is something I cannot control."

"Yes, I know."

That night after the book signing, I did more research on Mary Ingleman. I discovered that the incident occurred in 1792 in Fairfield County. Mary was a German immigrant, born in 1714, so she was up in age when they accused her of being a witch. Some farmers said she lifted a cow and slammed it back on the ground, breaking its neck. She was accused by a local woman of putting a curse on her and her sister. Then her own son, Adam Free, swore that his mother had tried to take a cow from him, and when he refused, she put a spell on the cow so that the udders gave blood instead of milk.

I hate when that happens...

Then her grandson stated that she turned into a horse and took him to an apple orchard where she hit him in the head when he tried to get an apple. Wait a minute. Another story says she turned her son into a horse which she rode to see the devil. Hell, even back then, the media couldn't get the story right. She could also supposedly transform into a panther and stalk her prey.

Now, Mary, that would be pretty cool if you could do that. You'd be a superhero, not a witch. Let's see. Here's more... Philip Edward Pearson, a doctor at that time wrote: "...a court composed of witch-doctors..."

Witch-doctors huh? I wonder if I knew any of their ancestors when I worked at the hospital. Some of them were real sons of bitches. Anyway, what was I reading? Okay. Here we go...

"....of witch-doctors was held at the house of a Mr. Thomas Hill, five miles below Winnsboro. Four persons were tried, found guilty, and punished by stripes and burning their feet at a bark fire so that the soles came off."

How pleasant. That's definitely more than just a singe. Now, if they could only use that foot-burning process in Congress.....

Ingleman was later able to sue her persecutors and win a small settlement, though the fine was never paid. The men found guilty of the assault and battery - or the flogging and burning of the soles off of their feet - fled the area and were never found.

Hmmm...Mary's ghost is said to still haunt the Fairfield County courthouse. I can't say that I blame her. I wonder if I can find any pictures of the witches or the men. It was 1792 and a witch trial. Surely someone was there making a sketch or two for the paper. Damn. Here are some pictures of her house from 1970 before it was torn down. Wait - there is some sort of rune or symbol on the side of the chimney. Okay, okay. Hang on a minute there, Dr. Venkman. Read on. These types of runes were common and used for protection. Mary's rune was diamond shaped and called a Germanic Ingwaz, which was the rune for fertility, good fortune, and creative power. *Interesting though that the word "inglenook" which is Scottish in origin means chimney corner. Ingleman and Inglenook? Coincidence? Maybe.*

I found no sketches of Mary, but there were a lot of pictures of descendants on Ancestry.com. I couldn't see where they looked like witches, but then, would they really? I mean, Samantha Stevens didn't look like a witch. Endora, on the other hand...*Focus!* I didn't find anything on Thomas Hill either, but then I remembered her son, Adam Free, and wondered why his last name was Free. Ok, here you go. Per Ancestry.com:

Adam Free Sr. was born in 1737 on Hilton Head Island, British Colonial America. His father was Lawrence Frueh and was 27 at the time and his mother, Mary Ingleman, was 23. Adam married Eva Margareta Heinzelmann in 1772 in Fairfield, South Carolina.

Hell, he had 12 children; 9 sons and 3 daughters. I wonder if I can find any pictures of his family.

"Hey!" his wife called out.

"Whoa! Damn. You scared the shit out of me."

"Sorry. What are you doing?"

"Researching Mary Ingleman. Pretty wild stuff. Her own son and grandson accused her of being a witch. She was 78 years old when they did all that stuff to her. Found a picture of her house before they tore it down. Take a look. Pretty spooky, huh?"

"Wow! It was close to 200 years old when they tore it down. Dilapidated. Dirty. Out there in the county by itself. Of course, it looks spooky, especially when someone claims a witch used to live there."

"Well, the courthouse in Fairfield County says her ghost sits on the steps still awaiting justice."

"Of course, it does. How else do you get people to Fairfield County?"

"Okay, okay, good point. You're so good with this ancestry stuff, so help me here. I'm trying to trace the ancestors of Adam Free who had twelve kids and was the son who accused Mary of being a witch. Look at what I've found so far." As we looked through the pictures of the ancestors beginning in the middle 1800s, for some reason, I found them oddly strange. Then when we got to the 21st century, I froze as I stared at a picture and the picture stared back at me. I turned my head slowly to make sure my wife saw what I saw.

"Holeeee Shit! The man…..the man at the book signing…earlier today…"

"Well, speak of the ….

"Sshhh. Don't say the last word. He's probably listening."

Speak of the devil

Modoc

I live in Hell. Okay, it may be spelled Modoc and in South Carolina, but as far as I'm concerned it is still Hell. I found out that the origin of the name of my town was Indian; a tribe that was relocated here after the Modoc war which was in 1872-1873. The Indians were famous for defending their lands and for outwitting a larger, stronger American force of soldiers for several months by living in lava caves and fighting them from lava trenches. Now, I can't find where it says that in writing, but it doesn't take a genius to see that a tribe of people who lived in "lava" holes and fought from "lava" gullies, had to be familiar with Hell. Thus, I am confident that they found their new home in South Carolina very accommodating.

To make things even worse, I had just started working at The Chicken Shack. I was sixteen and my mother said that if I wanted money to spend, I would have to earn it because she was doing everything she could just to make sure that we didn't starve and had a roof over our heads. "I can't do everything for you, Joshua," I heard her say at least a hundred times. But I can't fault her at all for that. She did work very hard. She was a nurse in a small hospital, thirty miles outside of town, and sometimes she worked 12-hour shifts for seven days straight, which, taking into account her commute and the workload, always ended up being closer to 14 to 16-hour days. When she came home from one of those weeks, all she wanted to do was sleep for a couple of days, and I could certainly understand why she was so tired. So, I didn't give her any shit about me finding a job. I didn't feel like I had a leg to stand on considering what she was experiencing.

Because of my age and lack of experience, I figured that my best option for work would be at The Chicken Shack. The town of Modoc had very few options, though I never really considered the eight buildings, lined up evenly on each side of the state highway, a town. More like a settlement, I thought. After all, it was the home of relocated Indians just 150 years ago. Regardless, everyone else now called it a town, so I went with the flow. It did have access to cable and the internet, so I guess calling it a town didn't seem too inappropriate.

The Chicken Shack was one of the most popular dining options in town, but to be honest, there were only two choices. There was The Chicken Shack and there was a Mexican restaurant called El Taqueria. According to the words on the large picture window, El Taqueria had some of the best tacos in the state. In fact, the advertising said "Best Tacos in the State of South Carolina" in big green, white, and red letters. In a town of 1,176 citizens, according to the town marker just outside the city limits, who was going to question that statement? They could say whatever the hell they wanted and I think as long as the food tasted good and didn't make you sick, they would have no one questioning that claim. My mother and I had eaten their tacos. They tasted okay, but they did make me sick, although my mother was just fine. I just can't handle spicy food, so I didn't hold that against them.

I found it rather amazing that Modoc was home to other establishments that stated that they were the best at what they did. The Chicken Shack advertisement on its window said "Best Fried Chicken in South Carolina." I had to admit it was pretty good, but my mom and I got sick several times after eating there. I will get back to that in more detail in a minute. Bob's Tires had the best discount tires and retreads in the state. Tilly's Treasures had the best little antique store in the state. Shirley's Clothes had the best bargain for your clothing needs in the state. Harold's

Hardware had the best feed and seed store in the state. Walter "Wally" Wiggins was the best hometown lawyer in the state. And, Betty Lou and Buster's Convenience Store and BP station had the "lowest priced gas and the coldest beer" in the state.

To say the word "best" was overused and misused would be an understatement. Neither I nor my mother considered any of the stores that were in Modoc the best at anything. As I said, the chicken at The Chicken Shack was pretty good, but it was also too greasy at times and had made me and my mother sick. The tacos were okay, but seeing how my mother and I hadn't tried any others in South Carolina, and they made me sick too, we couldn't honestly say they were the best. (Not that I had a desire to try them elsewhere but I think you get the gist.) The tires were fine, according to mom, but she said they were far from the best. They were just the best she could afford.

I didn't know much about antiques but I had been in Tilly's and I seriously doubted that the best antique store in the state had an entire area devoted to birdcages and cereal box tops. I am still waiting to be proved wrong on that. The clothes in Shirley's were okay but, hell, they were just regular clothes. Mom said Walmart had the same clothes at better pricing; but it was too far to go to Walmart, which was an hour away. I didn't know much about feed and seed - but just how good could feed and seed be, I wondered? I guess if the vegetables and flowers grew and the cows and chickens ate the stuff, you could say it was good. But the best in the state? I don't think so.

Wally was the only lawyer for sixty miles but, again, I doubted he was the best hometown lawyer in the state. I would think the attorneys that practiced in the capital were probably better, and some of them were probably born right there in Columbia. Granted, with lawyers, that could be a discussion that might never end, so I just will say he wasn't and leave it at that. And I was too young to drink beer but the gas was reasonably priced according to mom and I had opened the cooler and felt the beer and I will say that it was damn cold. So, maybe, in all the stores in Modoc, the one store that might be able to get away with what they said was Betty Lou and Buster's. But no one else could. Uh-uh. No way. Case closed.

But I will add this. If the town really wanted a claim to fame and wanted to advertise itself as the best in the state, it could without a doubt, say it was the closest thing to Hell during the summer and produced more sweat per capita than anywhere else in the country. I was certain the only other place that came even close, might be Death Valley in California. I mean, its name has Death in it. And it has temperatures over 130 degrees, for God's sake! And yes, I am certain Hell is hotter, but besides those two places, Modoc was the winner and without a doubt, the winner in South Carolina.

In the summer, it was easy to pick out someone who lived in Modoc, and someone who was just passing through, perhaps to buy gas or get a cold beer or visit the antique store for some birdcage that a crazy aunt had to have. Visitors to the town didn't venture out of their air-conditioned cars for too long and if they did, you saw beads of sweat on their faces and sweat stains beginning to form on their clothes before they got the hell out of town.

If you were a local and if you were wearing a shirt, (because those without breasts often did not), the armpit sweat made deep circles on the shirt that extended to the bottom of it, and on really hot days, the entire side and back of the shirt were soaked with a circle of sweat around the neck and over the stomach. I am still surprised to this day that there were any overweight people in our little town because just walking in the summer felt like running a marathon. But, believe me, there were some big people in Modoc. And God forbid if they were big and had active sweat glands because no matter what they were wearing, they soon looked like they had been soaked with a water hose. Man or woman. It didn't matter. It was disgusting.

I swear, some of them just said "fuck it," and didn't even try and combat the sweat with antiperspirant and deodorant. And because the town was so small, you knew they were coming from one hundred yards away. I don't know how the salespeople waited on them. Perhaps they put Vicks under their nostrils like the morgue folks did for a really smelly floater, but I never asked and I never went and investigated. I just left that question unanswered and got the hell away as fast as I could.

That was another reason I picked the Chicken Shack as a place to work. It was drive-through only and I knew if one of those "smellers" came by, I could just close the window and then hold my breath when I had to open it to get their money and give them their chicken. Unfortunately, I didn't realize until I started working there that The Chicken Shack was another version of Hell that existed within the town.

As I stated earlier, I would get into more details about The Chicken Shack, and the first thing I can say is that it was appropriately named. It looked like a shack on the outside and, believe me, it looked like a shack on the inside, with very hot deep fryers and one big ass freezer. I had only been working there a day and I knew that if the people who came there to pick up food ever saw the kitchen where it was prepared, they would never eat there again. *No wonder I got sick* I thought when I saw the dirty oil the chicken was fried in. On that first day, I started to say something to the manager when I realized that the man had owned the place for twenty years. What was I going to tell him that he didn't already know? Yep, the answer was nothing and I knew the only thing I could do was call the health department to try to get some of these issues fixed.

My mother had enough to worry about so I didn't tell her about the problems I saw at The Chicken Shack and my plan to contact the health department. I thought she would be proud of me for doing the right thing. But the next day, I realized that doing the right thing was going to do little good. That was because I saw the owner and the health department inspector sharing a drink in his office when I got to work. I didn't realize he was the health inspector until he came out and gave the owner the health inspection form to hang on the wall and I saw the "92" score. And before I could say, "How in the hell could that happen?" I saw the owner give the health inspector an envelope and tell him, "Thanks."

I didn't have to be a detective to know what was in that envelope and I didn't have to be a rocket scientist to know how this place stayed open. Whiskey and money made the inspector "overlook" or "miss" some things. Like the often-broken temperature gauge on the freezer that the owner said he would fix, of course. Or the oil that smelled like it had been in the fryer for weeks that the owner said he would get emptied, cleaned, and refilled, which never happened. Or the many cockroaches that crawled out from behind the counter where we stored bags of food and condiments.

That's when I decided I would need to go higher up the chain of command. When I got home that night I read about the health code expectations and realized that the damn ratings were a joke. Reading the details of how the health department ratings were determined, I realized no one gave a fuck about what went on in restaurants. How else do you explain that a passing grade involved an acceptable amount of rat turds in the kitchen? We had them, and I'm sure we exceeded the acceptable number, but it didn't matter. Hell, nobody cares if that's the bar that's been set by the people who ensure that your food is safe to eat.

The next day at work I decided that all I could do was make sure that the place was as clean as I could make it, which made me a "target" by the owner. When the owner saw me cleaning, he actually told me to get to work, as if I wasn't working by cleaning up the damn place. But I should have known that's what the son of a bitch would say. Thomas "T-Bird" Burdy was one of those large people in Modoc that had said "fuck it" a long time ago and he smelled like chicken, sweat, and whiskey. Trust me, in no combination at all, is that a good smell.

Somehow, T-Bird deduced I had read the details of the health code manual as I was doing those things that needed to be done, like throwing away soiled paper goods, checking the temperature of the freezer, and cleaning out the rat turds and cockroaches. He actually asked me if I had read the manual and though I didn't answer his question, he just smiled and said, "You don't have to answer, boy, 'cause I know the answer."

He then grabbed a meat cleaver and snatched up some of the chicken we were frying and proceeded to mutilate those birds while telling me he doubted that the town would miss another drugged-up know-it-all teenager who just ran away from home. As he threw the parts into the hot fryer, the oil splashed up onto his hands. I knew it burned him because I saw the charred hair on the back of his bear-like hands, but he ignored the pain and just looked at me and smiled. He told me that if the health department ever got a complaint about his restaurant, he knew where to come looking and then he left.

He might as well have come over and kissed me on the lips and said, "I knew it was you, Fredo," because I felt like I had just been told my life was over by the Chicken Godfather of Modoc, and I wondered what I had just done. I had nightmares about being cut up and thrown into the fryer and being served to customers for several days after that interaction, but thankfully, they did go away and I was able to go back to work without too much anxiety.

Though I didn't think the other two people who worked with me were demons, one of them did exhibit demonic behavior, and I think both of them were prime candidates for getting to Hell one day. I am certain Junior (don't ask me who he was the junior of because I never asked and he never told me) never washed his hands after going to the bathroom, which in itself, should be a felony. You would agree with me if you saw his hands and smelled what he left in the bathroom some days.

What he did in the bathroom could probably be considered assault in some states, because that was the foulest shit that I had ever smelled in my entire life. I suffered PTSD whenever I saw him head toward the bathroom door that pretended to be white.

The silver lining, if there can be one, is I am sure the only reason we didn't have bugs in the bathroom was that they couldn't survive in his shit. Except maybe dung beetles. Maybe they could stomach it, but like the patrons at Chicken Shack, you took a chance of getting sick each time you ate something from there.

The other employee's name was April and she was the one that I said at times exhibited demonic behavior. April was stoned most of the time. On the first day we worked together she announced that she was a Wiccan witch and could cast spells on me or anyone else who pissed her off. I immediately told April that I would help her do her job when she was there at The Chicken Shack and she could smoke all the dope she wanted and I wouldn't tell T-Bird. That made April happy. I wasn't real sure what a Wiccan witch could or could not do, but the fact she worked and ate at The Chicken Shack whenever she got the munchies and never got sick, indicated to me that she had some sort of connection to the supernatural and I didn't want to fuck with her or it.

But just like Junior's shit, as I said, every cloud has a silver lining and the silver lining within the nuclear mushroom cloud of The Chicken Shack was threefold. First, it ensured that I would never work in the food industry in any permanent capacity. Ever. Second, it ensured that neither I nor my mother would ever eat anything again from The Chicken Shack, saving us both from periodic episodes of abdominal distress. Third and best of all, it ensured that I would find a way to do whatever I needed to in order to make good grades in high school and find a way to go to college.

My mother and I realized that most of the job training at the Technical College was not suited for my skillset and that my best bet was to go to college. I was very good at math and solving complex problems and figuring out how to do things on the computer, so we decided that getting a degree in computer science would be the best plan for me. But, she also told me that I would have to get my grades up and try to earn a scholarship because there was only so much she could do to help me pay for tuition.

Unfortunately, this was not going to be easy for several reasons. One was that I had never done well in school before now and two, I wasn't doing well now. I had certainly not been a model student prior to the pandemic, and now the "at-home learning" process was not working well for me. I wasn't good at learning on my own. It wasn't that I was dumb or incapable of learning. Far from it. I was actually quite smart. My teachers knew it. My mother knew it and I knew it. But the problem was, I had not ever accepted the fact that I had a learning disability.

The teachers told my mother that I suffered from what they called an "Insatiability disorder," or as they liked to refer to it, I was an "M n M" child which stood for "me, now, and more." According to my teachers, I was often dissatisfied with their responses, was persistent regarding my needs, and was distracted by my constant desire for new things and attention. Now, again, you have to look for the silver lining here.

From a positive perspective, I was future-oriented, but as a result, chronically restless. I was bored easily and frustrated, and in the past, when that boredom surfaced, I was prone to stir up trouble to avoid it. If you had a list of descriptions that had ass in it, I had been called it at one time or another. Asshole, check. Smartass, check. Pain in the ass, check. Badass, well no check if you asked others, but I sort of considered myself one.

And now, staring at a computer, instead of acting out, I just muted the teacher and went off and did something else. Again, on the positive side, I do have a perpetual hunger for new and novel activities. But because of my acting act out at school, teachers and students labeled me as a troublemaker and my grades suffered. Now my grades suffered because I wouldn't participate in the zoom class and just didn't pay attention.

I do have to admit when they first gave my mother that candy label, I didn't help things by saying that was just a bunch of psychological bullshit.

"God. if that ever got out to the rest of the students that the teacher called me an 'M n M,' I would never hear the end of it," I screamed at my mother when she first told me. Now, looking back, I realize, everything they said was true. But that day I was told, it made me so mad that I just stormed out of the house and rode my bike into the country, not sure where the hell I was going. I was just riding along when I saw a bull all alone in a pasture, and I knew I had to stop. After getting off the bike, I climbed over the fence and yelled at the bull, and started throwing rocks at it to try and make him mad.

But the bull was old and not concerned with a few pebbles that probably felt like raindrops bouncing off his tough hide. He snorted a few times and pretended to charge toward me. He watched me jump back over the fence, snorted once more (which I was sure was bull for 'fuck you"), and then he headed back down a long creek that disappeared between two large ridges.

Well, that was helpful I thought sarcastically. But as I was riding back home, I realized it actually was very helpful. That bull just taught me that the world doesn't give a shit about what I do and unless I changed, that's the way it would always be. So, when my mom and I talked later and she told me that I would have to improve my grades, I didn't run off like I did the first time. I just apologized for being such a pain in the ass in the past and said I would work my butt off for the next two years to graduate with an A average. I knew I could do it and my mom knew I could do it and she said she was proud of me for saying I would work my butt off. (She didn't like using the word ass).

And that's when I showed off my problem-solving skills to her. I told her that I was still inclined to get bored with some of the stuff they taught over these zoom sessions, so I asked my mom to talk to my teachers and request some special assignments and additional work for me that would help me get into college. It was like I just told my mother that I had won 50K on a dollar scratch-off. She jumped up and grabbed me and told me that was a great idea and she was proud of me for thinking that way.

The teachers thought it was a great idea too, and several of them even said that I could work on those other assignments if I got bored during the zoom sessions, provided I didn't mute them and was able to participate in the current learning module for that day when necessary. I told them I was cool with that and I wasn't worried at all. As I said, I was good at multi-tasking so having my mind on multiple things at the same time was just a challenge for me and I loved it. Within just four weeks, I had turned my C's into A's and I knew I could see a way out of this Hell hole one day.

But you know, just when you think you have it all figured out, life has a funny way of punching you in the gut. It happened at The Chicken Shack several weeks after I started making good grades. I was working the evening shift with April and it was a Saturday, which meant it was going to be busy as Hell. But this Saturday was busier than usual. I told April that even though she was slightly impaired I needed her to focus on the orders as I tried to fill them. She mumbled something I didn't understand and sounded like either "sure" or "curse you," but she did indeed speed up her work. Thankfully, T-Bird hadn't been by in a while and he didn't usually grace us with his presence on Saturday night because it interrupted his drinking schedule, so we got everything finished by 9 p.m. and were able to close the window and call it a night.

Of course, closing the window just meant we didn't have to sell any more damn chicken. Now, we had to clean up the place and that was always a difficult job, especially with April who wasn't that handy with a broom - which I found odd since she said she was a witch. But that evening, I told April if she would sweep the floor, I would mop it and clean all the countertops.

I knew she would go for that because she hated the mop and cleaning the countertops with some substance that T-Bird got from his health department friend. It was probably illegal in most states but I liked using it. You had to wear gloves and a mask because it was so strong and bad for your lungs, but I figured it killed every germ known to North America and I felt like I was actually making the place safer. Maybe twenty years from now when I start growing boobs or a tail, I might think differently, but for now, I was good with using "Germ-Away."

Like I knew she would, April agreed to what I suggested. Her eyes quivered when she mumbled and then she just stared at me or through me; I wasn't sure which. But after a moment, she blinked and started sweeping. When the countertops were clean and she had the floor swept, I told her that I was going to the back of the store to get the mop and bucket. Surprisingly, she said she would stay and help me. Stranger things have been said to me, so I just nodded and got the stuff, and started working.

As I did, I realized April's idea of helping was watching the mop go around in circles on the floor, but I didn't care. She did give me a little break and cleaned a two-foot diameter circle really well. I finished the rest and told her it was time to go and that I would check the freezer and lock up. Once again, she looked at me with those strange eyes. She wasn't moving so I just said I'd see her later and went to the back. I was in the freezer when I heard the door close and lock and I realized what April must have heard me say was "lock up the freezer" because that is exactly what she did.

As I've mentioned, the equipment at The Chicken Shack was not reliable, especially the freezer. There were times when even T-bird realized that the chicken in the freezer had not been kept cool enough and he couldn't sell it without causing a city-wide event that would probably get the attention of his health department buddy's boss and reporters from across the state. But it had been repaired recently and now the damn thing was zero to negative three degrees every day. I know, because I was the one recording the temperatures; you know, for the "health inspector." And now I was inside a 10 x 12-foot container that was minus one degree Fahrenheit, wearing a short-sleeved shirt and jeans, surrounded by frozen chicken parts.

I was familiar with what Hypothermia was and I knew that at this temperature, I could probably survive about thirty minutes in there with what I was wearing. I felt for my cell phone before I remembered that it was sitting on the countertop next to the cash register. "Fuck!" I yelled and then I realized I needed to problem solve and problem solve quickly. The first thing I did was yell April's name and "Help!" over and over and bang on the door. After doing that for several minutes, I realized April was probably gone and I was wasting precious time that I needed to use more wisely in order to survive.

I then noticed the peeling rubber around the edges of the door and thought that perhaps I could pull it off and wrap the pieces around me. They would provide good insulation, perhaps even enough to help me survive longer if I could use them along with some large cardboard boxes to protect me from the cold. There was always duct tape around the store and I saw a big roll of it in the freezer, so I began to pull the rubber from around the door and wrap it around my bare arms and body, fastening it in place with the duct tape.

Because the door was old, the rubber came off fairly easily and I was able to get quite a bit to wrap around my arms and stomach. Now, I just needed some cardboard. Some large boxes would work well, as I could get underneath them and protect myself from the cold. Perhaps if I did all that, I could at least survive until my mother came looking for me when I didn't get home by 11 that evening. That would mean I would have to last an hour or maybe ninety minutes in this temperature. With all the rubber padding, and with more cardboard taped over the rubber, and putting myself under a cardboard box, sitting on layers of cardboard, I thought that might be truly doable.

I smiled when I found several large boxes in the corner of the freezer. One of them would be perfect for the shelter and the other one would be perfect to tear down and use as a floor to sit on. The boxes were marked "Frozen Chicken" and someone, probably Junior, had written "shit" in black marker next to the word "chicken." I began laughing and then I thought, *Hey - Junior is not that clever*. When I opened the box, I jumped back and fell against the shelving, knocking several boxes of frozen chicken to the floor. I didn't know who had written "shit" on the box, but I now knew it wasn't Junior. I was positive it was whoever stuffed T-Bird into the box. I didn't have to check to see if he was dead. The bullet hole in the middle of his head and the fact he was stuffed in a box in the freezer labeled "Chicken Shit" told me he was very dead.

I wasn't really surprised once I got over the shock. I had seen him paying the health inspector money several times and I had also heard that T-Bird liked to gamble. Apparently, he wasn't much better at gambling than keeping his damn restaurant clean, and then it hit me. I was fucked. There were only two big boxes in the freezer and that son of a bitch was in one of them and I couldn't use it. It was a fucking crime scene now. As I began to check for other cardboard boxes that I could use, I heard the door open. My jaw dropped when I saw April standing there pointing her finger at me and laughing.

I really wouldn't have cared if it had even been Junior standing there pointing one of his disgusting fingers at me, I ran to her while some of the rubber and cardboard wrapped around me started popping off, wrapped my arms around her, and told her I loved her. She looked at me like I was mentally unstable and jumped back and asked me what the fuck I was doing, and added that she wasn't "that kind of girl." I told her that I thought I was going to die in the freezer due to hypothermia and she got those "googly eyes" again and just stared at me for a moment before she whispered into my ear.

"Bet it was as cold as a witch's tit in there," she said. I had heard that saying before, but this was the first time that I believed someone really knew how cold a witch's tit actually was and I just nodded. I didn't care that she knew that particular information or that she had whispered it into my ear after I had just told her I could have died. I just picked my phone up off the counter, called 911, and told them to come to The Chicken Shack because there had been a murder.

Funny, after I said that to the police, they didn't act like that was strange and just said they would send an officer over as soon as they could. When I thought more about that later, I realized they were probably always expecting that call. After hanging up, April looked at me in a puzzled way and I told her about T-Bird. She started to go in the freezer and I told her not to as it was a crime scene. She just shrugged her shoulders and went in anyway.

I shook my head as I watched her go over and look at T-Bird because I knew it probably didn't matter. I knew April wasn't the one who shot him. If she had had the desire to kill him, I don't think she would have used a gun. And then it hit me and I laughed out loud. I bet old T-Bird would get a lot of ribbing in the place where he was probably residing now. Moments ago, I had almost frozen to death but now just being back out of the freezer for ten minutes, I had to shed my insulation as quickly as possible because it was still hot as hell in the store. And considering it was hot as hell here and probably even hotter in T-Bird's new home, and the fact that he was found dead and entirely frozen, I had to laugh. Yeah, that headline just wrote itself.

Cold day in Hell

Madness

The ghosts have not been as discrete in making themselves known to me as they once were. At first, it was just a drawer that I would find pulled out in the kitchen, or a cabinet door left open, and to be honest, I didn't even consider it to be strange when they began to occur more frequently. But after some time I started to find my car keys (which I always put in a little bowl next to the door) out on the countertop, on the kitchen table, or even in the bathroom sink.

And then before I could simply attribute everything to old age and declining memory, I started to hear the noises and I began to truly question what was happening. I heard drawers being opened or "clinking" sounds in the middle of the night while I was reading a book in my bedroom. Upon investigating the cause, I would find multiple kitchen drawers pulled out and find my keys in an even odder place like a coffee cup in the cabinet or the sink. One night, I even found them behind a locked Stickley display cabinet in the kitchen. That's when I knew. It wasn't just old age and forgetfulness. My house was indeed haunted by ghosts.

Now, when you hear people say that, your first inclination is probably to think either the person is crazy, or if they aren't crazy, they are suffering from some mental disorder such as depression or anxiety brought on by some type of trigger. Very few believe the disturbance is created by a ghost and I don't blame anyone for thinking that way. But I can promise you, I am not crazy and I can tell you there were and are ghosts in my home. I can also tell you I was never afraid.

I was never afraid because, in the beginning, I just wanted to think it was my granddaughter playing a prank on me. I could hear her voice in my mind yelling, "JD lost his keys again, Grandma!" and then that laugh of hers that always made me smile. My granddaughter called me JD, not grandpa or papa or pawpaw or any of the other "grandpaw-ish" names. She called me JD because my best friend had called me JD, and I wanted the two of us to be best friends from the first moment I held her in my arms. I have to admit, when she was old enough to call me JD for the first time, I wept tears of joy and I never got over that feeling whenever she talked with me. Just her calling me that name created a bond with us that I hoped would last forever.

So finding my keys misplaced and remembering my granddaughter running around telling Grandma was just a wonderful memory, nothing scary at all. I could see myself chasing after her and tickling her into submission when I caught her until she returned my keys. And then we both laughed out loud and I could remember thinking that my granddaughter was a smart little thief. She knew she could not only be chased and tickled until she couldn't laugh anymore, she could bribe JD into giving her some ice cream before he got the keys returned to his hand.

So, at first, the fact that I heard those noises or saw the drawers opened or keys misplaced didn't bother me. It comforted me since my family was gone. My wife, son, daughter-in-law, and granddaughter were all gone. And no matter how much I tried, I couldn't remember why they had died and now visited me as ghosts. I knew the inability to see the 'why' must be my brain stopping me from shutting down. Severe trauma has a way of erasing what you experienced and I didn't want to push it. I was afraid if I tried too hard to remember, I would crumble into pieces from what I saw. That's what scared me more than the ghosts. I was terrified to go further into my mind to find the 'why.' So, I didn't. I decided I would be content to live with my ghosts.

The house was very lonely without my wife and granddaughter running around it and I also truly missed my dog. I do recall that my dog died of old age, four years after my granddaughter was born. I kept telling myself I was going to go down to the pound and get another dog but I just hadn't done it yet. And now that the ghosts had begun to come around, I couldn't bring myself to do it. I was afraid all of the ghosts would fade away if I got a new dog because they would see that I wasn't as lonely anymore, and I couldn't accept that. I know that doesn't sound rational, but rational thinking and seeing ghosts are probably incompatible within the sane view of the world, so, I lived with my ghosts and they slowly became bolder in making their presence known.

I found a bag of my granddaughter's favorite potato chips open on the sofa one morning, even though I was sure I put them away before I went to bed. I noticed several Oreo cookies, my granddaughter's favorite, laying on the floor of the pantry several days later. Yes, I had eaten a few of them in the middle of the night but I was sure I didn't drop any. I would also find half-eaten Little Debbies in the pantry. I never ate only half a Little Debbie in my entire life but this was something my wife did all the time.

My wife loved to eat half of a cookie or cupcake or any kind of sweet, and for some reason, it would drive me crazy. I complained about it all the time and she would say, "Don't worry, I'm just saving the rest for later." Now when I found the half-eaten sweet, I just smiled. I didn't care. I knew she had been there and had left me a "hello" in the pantry or on the countertop.

One night the sound of an opera playing on the TV woke me up and when I went into the living room to investigate, I saw "The Magic Flute" playing. I am not a huge fan of opera and I never watch it on tv, but I did remember that was the first opera I saw my daughter-in-law perform. It's funny. It had been recorded on the TV and was replaying. I sat and watched a little of it and didn't delete it. *Maybe she would want to play it again another evening* I thought and I was fine with that if she did.

Another day not long after the night at the opera, I was reading a book out on the back porch and I heard the stereo come on. It was the Dawes recording of "Paranoid" by Black Sabbath that they had done at the LOCKN festival. My son loved the group Dawes and had made that recording for me as a Christmas present. I turned the music up and sat there thinking about him and how wonderful that memory felt and then something even stranger happened. I realized I could remember that Christmas and much earlier ones, but I couldn't remember any others after my granddaughter's first Christmas.

Details of earlier Christmas seasons were crisp and clear and I could remember every other holiday and birthday and anniversary, but I could not remember a Christmas beyond my granddaughter's first one. I knew my mind was telling me something. But as I tried to remember, my head started to ache and I felt dizzy so I stopped. I understood that my body was once again trying to stop me from hurting myself, physically and emotionally, so I didn't pursue it any further. But I was also now acutely aware that something had happened at Christmas that had to do with making my family into ghosts but I couldn't find the answer. I was afraid to find the answer.

After that experience with the Dawes album and the headaches from trying to remember Christmas, my ghostly encounters became even more intimate. That's when I started to see the ghosts. At first, they were only shadows moving out of the corner of my eye and when I turned to look, there was nothing there. I didn't think much of it as we have all had that happen to us a thousand times; so even with the noises and open cabinets and such, I still didn't worry about seeing a shadow. I even remember telling myself the shadows were probably created by the sun coming through the windows of the house at certain times of the day and didn't give it another thought.

Later, though, I began to see faces in those shadows. At first, they weren't clear and distinct and were only there for a second before they were gone. When I blinked my eyes and refocused, I found that I was actually looking at a picture on the wall, or a vase, or even my ceramic cast of John Wayne. I would smile and realize my mind was helping me to see faces that I wanted to see. That first time I saw John Wayne staring back at me, I thought I could hear his voice telling me, "Whoa, take 'er easy there, pilgrim," as if he was talking to me like he did to Jimmy Stewart in one of my favorite movies of all time, "The Man Who Shot Liberty Valence."

I remembered my wife when I thought of that movie. We loved watching it. Okay, okay. I loved watching that movie and my wife liked it, at least the first two times she saw it. But on the third and fourth and fifteenth times, she just tolerated it, doing something else while I watched. Later on in years, when the movie came on and perhaps I closed my eyes for a moment somewhere just before the big gunfight, she would switch it over to one of her favorite soap operas that she had recorded and watch them while I napped. It didn't matter. I enjoyed what I saw up until I went to sleep and I certainly enjoyed the nap.

But then when my granddaughter came along and was old enough, I got her to watch that movie with me and she loved it. Well, as much as a five-year-old could like an old western. Not only was she a good thief, but she was also a good actor. She told me she loved the movie, while also suggesting this was a good time to make a grilled cheese sandwich. And then told me when it was a good time to make the popcorn, and after the movie added, "To top everything off, we should have an ice cream sandwich, pilgrim." She always made me laugh when she did that John Wayne impression for me and my wife. And then she would giggle and laugh and I would laugh so hard I almost cried. God, I missed that laugh.

Over time, those faces in the shadows began to linger even longer. I would catch them out of the corner of my eye and when

I turned around, I would see my granddaughter's face smiling at me for just a second as she sat on the sofa. Or I would see my wife looking up at me from a book, or my son or daughter-in-law glancing up at me from their phone or computer. Now, they were no longer shadows coming through the window at a particular time of the day. They were the faces of my family reaching out to me. Logically, I knew trauma and grief could make you see all sorts of things. But I didn't want to think about this logically. I wanted to see the ghosts because I felt like there was a reason they were reaching out to me now. At first, I was sure it was just my family's way of comforting me because they knew I was lonely. But then, I began to see other images that were not meant to bring me comfort.

I first saw the image of my son looking at me from outside a window. He was trying to say something and as I got closer his mouth opened like he was yelling and he seemed to be trying to catch something before he disappeared. That image bothered me, but I saw something worse as I was shaving the next morning. My wife's face was looking at me from over my shoulder in the mirror. Of course, as I turned around, she was gone, but when I looked back in the mirror, I saw her again and there was blood dripping from cuts all over her face. I closed my eyes and screamed. When I reopened them she was gone, but I could not get that picture out of my mind.

That evening it was even worse. In the middle of a dream, I could hear my granddaughter laughing one minute and then screaming about the lights the next. I woke up in a cold sweat and fixed myself a cup of tea and sat down to read a book. Reading eventually put me to sleep, and I remember feeling much better as I slept. My wife was whispering to me and I could feel her hand on my shoulder but when I woke up, all I could see was blood covering the pillow and I jumped out of bed. I didn't get any more sleep that night and stayed up watching TV trying to forget what I had just seen. As I was flipping through the channels, I saw that "The Man Who Shot Liberty Valance" was on. It was toward the end of the movie when Jimmy Stewart and Vera Miles were coming back to say goodbye to John Wayne who had died.

I looked around the room and I knew this wasn't a coincidence. I threw some water in my face to make sure I wasn't dreaming. I could feel the water so I knew I was awake, but what were those awful images telling me? The bloody images of my wife and my son seeming to yell at me. My granddaughter screaming about the lights. And now, this movie. John Wayne was dead. Was that them telling me goodbye? Was that them telling me they died because of me? "What is it?" I screamed.

Suddenly, I began to remember all of the Christmases. I could see them. I remembered going to Gatlinburg for the holidays and my granddaughter talking about all the lights downtown and so many fudge shops. I could smell the fudge. I know it was Christmas Eve because my granddaughter made a comment that Santa Claus should be able to find this place a lot easier than where we lived since it was closer to the North Pole. I could hear our laughter and I could see her giggling.

And then the lights exploded and I heard her scream. I was holding her and I could feel us falling into lights that seemed to explode like the stars had collided in the sky. And then everything went black. I tried to call out but I couldn't hear my voice or theirs anymore. *Was this what death looked like* I wondered? I thought maybe it did for someone who had killed their family and I began to cry. But then I felt something touching my hand. I couldn't see what it was, but it felt gentle and then it gripped my finger.

I heard noises again, but this time they were beeping sounds and I wondered if was in an arcade. But I knew those weren't the sounds from a pinball machine. They weren't all "bing-bing-bing." They were an occasional beep, and then another same-sounding beep, and then another of the same kind of beep. Suddenly, there was my granddaughter's voice as I heard her ask my son, "Is JD waking up now?" and then I saw them. They were standing next to my hospital bed and smiling down at me. And I smiled back as I felt the tears streaming down my face.

My ghosts had saved me. They had helped me form new neural pathways around the hemorrhage that had caused my stroke on that Christmas Eve when I fell into the Christmas tree. That's why I couldn't remember any of the Christmases, but my ghosts had helped. They did everything they could to make me remember. The blood and cuts on my wife's face were not on her face, they were on mine. The lights exploding and my granddaughter screaming were from the bursting LED lights and the blinding light within my brain that was due to the bleed.

My family wasn't dead. I wasn't dead. According to the MRI the next day, I would make a full recovery. The physician said it was amazing how my brain had formed the new pathways in only three months. He had never seen it happen that quickly before. Over time, yes, but not like this. I wanted to tell the doctor how to ensure that happens for other people too, but I was too tired at the moment to tell him anything. All I could do was smile. But one day in the future, I would tell the doctor that seeing ghosts was not a bad thing that suggested you were mad. They were a method for finding your way home.

Method to my madness

Cursed

I always found her to be a bit peculiar. At least, that's the word I used with my wife when she told me her aunt was coming to visit us for the weekend. I told my friends she was an "odd bird" and asked them to check on me sometime Sunday just to make sure I wasn't in the hospital or dead or something because strange things always happened when she was in town.

Okay, I hear you. We all have that "eccentric" aunt or uncle and we just put up with them. I can even hear some of you saying eccentricity adds a bit of spice to life. The people who say that are probably the same ones who will eat a ghost pepper just so they can say they tried it, even though they won't be able to taste anything after that for a month because the damn pepper was so hot it burned their taste buds into ashes.

And you know what? If she was just eccentric, meaning something like she wore polka-dot shirts with striped pants, and a different colored shoe on each foot (which she did, by the way), I would agree with you. I don't mind that level of eccentricity. What I did mind, feared, in fact, is that I believed she was some sort of cursed being. And I'm not the only one who thought that. I'm not even the one who suggested it when a dead squirrel fell out of the chimney onto the fire the first time she visited us. I didn't even say anything disparaging about her when a large pine tree fell onto my car the second time she visited. It was my wife's family that claimed she was cursed.

They told me her side of the family came from the old country - and by old country, they meant Ireland - and that they had a history of being involved in strange behavior. Supposedly, and this was according to my wife's father, Aunt Brona's grandmother, and mother, were considered to be some type of witches over in Ireland. If not for the fact that they were well-versed in herbal remedies, they would have been killed on numerous occasions. But the people that they helped always came to their rescue.

"Her grandmother supposedly died by falling off a cliff, and the mother and father left Ireland soon after that," my father-in-law said and then continued, "You don't have to see the writing on the wall to know why they left Ireland after the old woman fell off a cliff, now do you?"

"How old was she when she fell off the cliff?" I asked.

"Not for sure, but I think close to 101 years old."

Now, you have to understand, I was being told this story before I experienced most of the stranger things that have happened during Brona's visits to our home, so I just thought this was one of those old tales that gets passed down from generation to generation without much investigation as to what truly happened. I didn't really consider a 101-year-old woman falling off a cliff that strange. Actually, I was surprised a 101-year-old woman was walking at all, much less near a cliff. And the fact she fell? Well, who couldn't say that an old woman like that didn't just lose her balance and fall? I sure as hell couldn't but I didn't say that to my father-in-law. I just let him tell me the stories because they got more interesting the more I heard.

According to my father-in-law, Brona's parents came to America where her mother had little Brona almost a year after arriving. They settled in a coastal town in New Jersey called Cape May, which I told him I knew of it as I had been there before. I always considered the town frozen in time a bit with all the Victorian-style houses, most of them restored to their original beauty. There were a lot of those "herbal remedy" and "new wave healing" stores in that town too. So, living there fit right in with the story, I thought as he went on.

"Brona's mother, Fionnuala, became very successful with her store of herbal remedies, crystals, and such. Her husband, Eamon, made a fortune with some gold coins that he brought over from the old country, which were worth quite a bit of money. He used them to buy some prime real estate on the beach and made even more money. Some say that didn't just happen by luck, if you get my meaning."

"Yeah, I hear you. Witchcraft and skullduggery of some sort," I said to myself as I nodded in agreement.

"Well, as Brona grew up, all sorts of wild stories started to pop up in the town where they lived. Brona and her father were swimming in the ocean one summer along with hundreds of others. A white shark appeared out of nowhere and attacked a man and his wife who were in the water right beside them, but the shark didn't touch them."

"And?"

"Don't you find that strange?"

"Sounds lucky to me."

"Exactly. Then, several summers later, a flock of seagulls attacked some people on the beach. But not Brona or her mother Fionnuala, who were there at the time."

I admit I was still trying to interpret the shark story so it took me a moment to respond to the tale about the seagulls. "Were the other people who were attacked possibly feeding the seagulls?"

"Not sure."

"So, you're saying that Brona caused the seagulls to attack the people that could have been feeding them?"

"If it quacks like a duck and looks like a duck, then it must be a duck, huh?"

"Or a seagull."

"Exactly."

At this point, if my father-in-law drank, I would have considered him drunk, but then the stories began to make more sense. If sense is the right word when you are becoming convinced that someone is cursed.

"When Brona was ten, she and her neighbor's child were flying kites. They were running down the street where they lived, which was the road next to the beach, and their kites got entangled in electrical wires. Well, the child she was playing with was electrocuted, while nothing at all happened to Brona."

"Oh my gosh, was the child killed?"

"No, he survived but now whenever a thunderstorm happens, he starts doing an Irish jig and speaking in Gaelic."

"Gaelic? And I don't suppose he was Irish and learned it as a young child or perhaps later in life?"

"Boy was born and raised in America. Parents were from Africa."

"Okay. That is rather odd."

"Cursed, I tell you. When she attended her senior prom in high school, Brona was the only one present who didn't get food poisoning."

"The only one that didn't get food poisoning? The *only* one?"

"Yep. And that's not the strangest part. That same evening, just before everyone got sick, a bunch of toads got into the school and disrupted the dance."

"Are you sure about all of this? I mean…" I couldn't finish my sentence before my father-in-law showed me the clipping from the newspaper about the food poisoning and the toads at the prom.

Damn, I thought. Shark, seagulls, electrocution by kites, not to mention a child with no known knowledge of Irish customs, doing an Irish jig and speaking in a foreign tongue, Gaelic. no less. And now public food poisoning and toads. Yeah, he was making a pretty good case for the fact that Aunt Brona was cursed. But then he put the nail in the coffin, so to speak.

"If you recall, I used to have some llamas on my land. They were good for keeping the grass trimmed and I liked having them around. Well, you'll never believe what happened once when

Brona was here visiting. She came out to see me in the barn where I was working, and I swear, if a gust of wind didn't follow her in and knocked several hay bales out of the loft which hit one of my llamas."

"Broke its back, didn't it?" I asked.

"Had to put it down. I loved that llama. She was a good one. Gave them all away after that incident."

The straw that broke the camel's back I said to myself. Only in this case, it was a llama, but still….

From that point on, I had my own stories to tell about Aunt Brona. I dreaded each visit because I never knew what was going to happen. I just knew it was going to be something miserable. And I was right. Toilets blew up. Refrigerators stopped working. And you remember that dead squirrel that fell out of the chimney? Several years later when she was here celebrating her sixty-eighth birthday, another one did the same thing, except it wasn't dead when it hit the fire. Just stunned. When it realized it was on fire, it jumped up and dashed through the living room and out the patio door, just as Brona came in from smoking one of her strange cigars.

Damn squirrel set one of the chairs on fire and if it hadn't jumped in my pool, it would've probably set my woods on fire. After I doused the chair with water and went out to check the backyard, I found the squirrel in the pool. I retrieved the squirrel from the water with my five-foot pole that had a skimmer net attached to the end of it. Somehow that process resuscitated the damn thing and it shook its head, scooted down the pole, and jumped over my head as it darted off into the woods.

I got a pretty bad bump on my head and was fairly sure I had a mini-concussion because when that squirrel was scampering down the pole, I was falling backward. It scared the shit out of me and I fell onto some large rocks that surrounded the pool. When I opened my eyes, my wife and Brona were standing over me. My wife was asking me if I was all right and Brona said, "He'll be fine," and offered me some special herbal tea that would make the dizziness and blurred vision go away. Later, as I was sipping that tea, I realized I hadn't said anything about being dizzy or having blurred vision. *Son of a bitch*, I thought. *Cursed was putting it mildly. Hell, she was a witch.*

That evening at dinner, I studied Brona's appearance. Besides the odd clothing, I now saw the image of a woman that looked like one of those really old pictures you saw in an early 18th or 19th-century building, while you were on vacation somewhere, which you went into because you thought you should since you were in that town, and as my wife would say, "We may not ever be back here again."

She was that woman hanging there on the wall in a cracked oil painting and ornate frame. You know, the one with a gold plate beneath it denoting who the person was; and of whom, 99.9% of the people viewing the picture and reading the plate would make the same comment - "Hmmm" - and then move on to the next room and picture. The tour guide or "caretaker" (if there was one present) at that historic building would probably want to tell you about the person in the picture, and if not, sometimes the little gold plate might have a few words about them denoting they were of some distinction or infamy. That was who Brona was and I could see it now. Her face had that same nondescript quality about it that you noticed in those oil paintings, only now, instead of being uninteresting, you could see what that historian or little gold plate meant by saying the person was unique in some way.

My wife had a few pictures of Brona as a child and she just looked like any other light-haired child in a black-and-white picture. But as she got older her face had certainly changed and taken on that "historical oil painting quality." Of course, none of those old pictures ever had a man or woman in it with her hair color. The hair in the oil paintings was always blonde or black curls of some sort on a woman, and the man was usually wearing a type of white wig. None of those descriptions would fit Brona. Her blonde hair was never simply blonde. With each year, it took on a new hue of some sort, like purple, or blue, or pink, that for some reason seemed subtle in nature. I never could understand how a small streak of vermillion, coral, or magenta in someone's hair was understated, but somehow it was with her.

Brona didn't come back to our house for quite some time. It was another seven years before we saw her. but there she was - wearing yellow and blue striped pants, a pink and black polka dot shirt, a purple beret, with a cigar hanging out of her lip - standing on our porch announcing that she had come to celebrate her seventy-fifth birthday. Though it had been seven years, I could see no difference in her face at all. *Just like the oil painting,* I thought. As she walked in, I noticed the narrow tangerine streak in her hair. But, considering it had been seven years and it was a special birthday, I didn't say anything inappropriate; I just welcomed her to our house.

Later that evening, I walked outside to take Brona a drink, her favorite Irish whisky that my wife always kept in our liquor cabinet for her. She wasn't sitting by the waterfall, where my wife said she would be and as I looked around and called her name several times, I heard her voice calling back, "Up here!" When I looked, I saw her about forty feet up in the air sitting on a very large sweetgum tree limb. I was speechless and she yelled down to me that I needed to close my mouth or a bug would fly into it, and like a robot, I did what she said.

Now just so you fully understand why my mouth was an invitation to bugs for a moment, this was a seventy or eighty-year-old sweetgum, probably two feet in circumference. There were few limbs on the bottom part of the tree that you could even reach, much less climb onto, and then up into the tree. And yet, a seventy-five-year-old woman was sitting on a limb, approximately forty feet in the air. I knew I had to go get my wife so that she could see this for herself or she wouldn't believe me, so I left the whiskey on the ground for Brona and said I'd be back in a minute.

I didn't hear her say anything to acknowledge me. I just started to walk away as quickly as I could, without it looking like I was trying to run-walk. Before I could get the sixty yards back to my garage, I heard something behind me. When I turned around, Brona was standing there with the drink in her hand.

"How?" was all that I managed to say as she emptied her glass and replied to me, "How what?"

I pointed toward the tree and said, "How did you get up the tree and how did you get down the tree?"

She answered, "How do you think?"

I knew it didn't matter what I said. I could have replied, you flew, you levitated, you climbed - any of those responses- and she would have just smiled and maybe winked at me. So, I said them all, and guess what? Yep, she smiled and winked at me. She then went inside and poured herself another whisky. I should have told my wife that her seventy-five-year-old aunt had just been forty feet up in a sweetgum tree that only a squirrel or a little anole lizard or perhaps some animal not indigenous to Georgia or even North America could have climbed, but I knew she would have looked at me like I was crazy. So, what did I say? Nothing. But I knew. And Brona knew I knew.

Later that evening when Brona went outside to smoke one of her cigars and have another whisky, my wife and I suddenly heard a bunch of squirrels running around on our roof. I looked at my wife and said, "If another squirrel comes down that chimney, you have no one to blame but your *'Aunt'* Brona," and got myself another beer. My wife just looked at me strangely and asked what I had meant by that and I said, "Your aunt is not an aunt."

Before she could ask me any more questions, Brona came in and asked what we were talking about and my wife told her I was worried about the squirrels on the roof. Brona winked at me again so that only I saw the wink, and then said she was too and poured herself another damn whisky before she sat down and began talking to my wife about the latest renovations to her home in Cape May. As I listened I began to ask myself some questions. Normal questions I thought anyone should be asking themselves if they weren't yet too intoxicated to have a conversation with themselves.

How could a seventy-five-year-old woman climb a tree like that? Did I even really see her in the tree? Maybe, I just thought I saw her in the tree? Maybe, she put something in my beer? So, are you suggesting she is capable of putting something in your drink to make you see things? No, she didn't do that. She hasn't touched my beer, has she? Nope, she hasn't. Okay. Rule the hallucinogen out. So where does that leave us? It leaves us with a seventy-five-year-old woman in a tree. Perhaps she has really strong legs and arms. I don't know if she works out or not. She's in good shape for a woman of her age. But that first limb is eight feet up in the air. That's a hell of a first move. Wait a minute. You said shape. Yes, that's it. She's a shape-shifter. She can change into a lemur when she wants to or perhaps a giant squirrel that chases all the other squirrels onto your roof and into your chimney. Well, I think that went well. You figured it all out. Of course, you won't be able to tell anyone, but at least you now know the answer. I continued to drink beer that night until I was unable to carry on any more conversations with myself.

It was five more years before Aunt Brona came to visit again and none of the family had heard much from her until the day she arrived at our home. It was another special day in Aunt Brona's life. She was celebrating her eightieth birthday and I swear, that old oil painting face hadn't changed. There were several new colors in her hair but I wasn't exactly sure what to call them. There were shades of green, one dark and one light. I guess if I was looking at my Sherwin-Williams color wheel, I would say they were perhaps forest green and sea-foam green, but that's just my opinion.

For her birthday, my wife suggested I grill out Brona's favorite food, which was a pork loin. While it was cooking, we all sat by the pool with our favorite drinks. It was a hot day, so I grabbed a float and got in to enjoy the cool water and the cold beer. I don't know what caused me to think it would be a good idea to ask this, but it was probably the beer and the fact that the whole shape-shifting hypothesis was still bothering me; so I asked Brona if she had ever climbed up onto the roof of her house in Cape May to chase squirrels.

Not hearing a response, I then preceded to make things worse by asking her if she thought she could climb the large pine tree that was at the back of the fence, adding, "you know, like you did with that sweetgum tree out in the front yard five years ago?" I then tipped my beer toward her, and now that I've had time to reflect, I think that was like going into a zoo and suggesting that the monkey throw a turd at you.

Brona glared at me and I could see the oil painting picture of her face change. Now, the demure smile did not look coy in any way. Her mouth made what I would call a constipated grin and within seconds, several water snakes fell from the tree limbs that extended over the pool and landed right next to me on the float. I froze and could do nothing but watch them slither back and forth atop the water as they struggled to get out of the pool. I heard my wife scream and jump up when the snakes crawled out onto the stone deck around the pool before disappearing into the woods. I also noticed that Brona didn't move at all as she watched the scene unfold; she just continued to stare at me. When my heart regained a normal rhythm, I yelled at her that she needed to stop all this shit.

I told her she was making our lives miserable every time she visited and I was sick of it. And that's when the constipated look became a devilish grin and she winked at me again. She sipped her whisky and said she understood and would be leaving the next day. I could tell my wife was also disturbed by what had happened because she didn't say anything to keep Brona from leaving. I paddled over to the steps of the pool and got out and gave Brona a "gotcha this time" look, which again, in hindsight, was not wise.

Walking back to the house to check on the pork loin, I stepped on a copperhead and it just missed biting me on the foot by what I can only call a half-inch of discretion, an outcome which I think was born from my, up until this point, mostly friendly relationship with Brona. She even came over and grabbed the copperhead and moved it out into the woods, telling my wife (who looked on in stunned horror) that she didn't want anything bad to happen to us or the snake. Nevertheless, the snakes falling out of the tree and the copperhead was the bale that fell onto the llama's back for me. After Brona left the next day, I told my wife she was no longer welcome in our home. My wife hated snakes and had seen enough of her aunt doing strange things to not mount a defense, and she just nodded in agreement.

A month later, we received a letter from Brona's lawyer stating that she had died by falling off a cruise ship in Bermuda. Besides the very generous amount of 66,600 dollars that she bequeathed my wife, she also left her several paintings from her house in Cape May. My wife didn't think the amount of money that Brona left her was odd but the chill bumps moved up and down my spine as if something real was alive beneath my skin when I saw that number and those pictures. Thankfully, my wife didn't like the pictures and I convinced her that they belonged in a museum. And since we were fine financially, I suggested we donate the money to charity. She agreed and I knew I wouldn't have more nightmares than usual.

Six months after Brona's death, I was watching the National Geographic channel and they were talking about a new species of animal that had been discovered in Haiti. A distinguished scientist was being interviewed by one of the investigators for the scientific community and as the scientist talked, he said the animal he saw looked like nothing he had ever seen before in his sixty years of analyzing the flora and fauna within the Bermuda Triangle.

I quickly got on my computer and looked up Irish folklore and "creatures of mischief" and guess what? I happened to find a picture that looked very similar to the sketch the scientist was able to provide the reporter. The creature was called a jute and it looked like a huge black cat with large rabbit ears that arched upward. It had dragonfly wings, long fingers and/or toes on its four legs, and a long hairy prehensile tail. Though there was no little gold plate under the picture, it did say, "According to Irish legend the 'jute' likes to create misery and havoc."

The scientist could call it a new species or a new creature but I knew it was old. And I knew it had another name. I was fairly certain that he could call his new animal Brona and he would be 99.9% correct in doing so. I didn't tell my wife about any of this. I just understood that her aunt was not dead and that she was indeed a different breed and was, like my father-in-law suggested, "cursed." But, I would make a distinction about the idea that she or her family, were cursed. I would suggest the curse simply hovered around them and affected everyone *but* them. As time elapsed, I began to think that cursed may have been way too strong a term, but regardless, I understood that a person's life would be changed if you met a Brona or "The Brona." And whether you described her or those creatures like her as cursed, or mischievous, or just some type of miserable creation, I knew for a fact that those types of spirits enjoyed being around others.

Misery loves company

Cold

He came to the building on time and got a cup of coffee before sitting down. He didn't know anyone there and could sense that everyone knew he was attending that night for the first time. Thankfully, no one started a conversation with him. Most just acknowledged his presence with their eyes, but a few nodded toward him, without smiling. According to his knowledge of proper etiquette in these types of settings, he was not required to reciprocate in any way.

He followed his doctor's instructions and sat down and listened. After a few words of encouragement and reminding everyone to be respectful of each other, the doctor asked if anyone wanted to speak or share anything. A young and very muscular man with long sideburns and bushy, brown curly hair, said he wished to talk about his most recent experiences. He started by stating that he wondered if his type of haircut would be appropriate to be called an Afro considering he was white. He added that after going back and forth in his mind several times debating the issue, he determined that it would be perfectly fine and that calling his haircut an Afro wasn't racial. It was just a haircut.

Suddenly, as if several chapters of the book had been skipped, he began talking about how he understood what he was doing was hurting his wife and children and he knew he needed to stop but couldn't find the strength to do so. The person next to him said the fact he was there at the meeting was proof that he did have the strength to change (without ever asking him what he was doing to hurt his family) and he just needed to keep trying. Everyone nodded and a few clapped and the man with the brown Afro smiled and thanked them.

The doctor then asked the man who had just spoken if he had anything else he wanted to say and he said no, he was done for the evening. The doctor thanked him for sharing and then announced they had a "newcomer" to the group and looked over at him. He knew from the doctor's coaching and advice what he was supposed to do now, and considering everything he had just heard, he felt a little more at ease and began to talk.

"Hello, my name is Torrance, and uh…I guess I am a sex addict."

"Hello, Torrance," the group replied in unison.

"I uh… well, I don't 'guess' is the right thing to say. I do have a sexual addiction. My roommate has told me I have had one for quite some time. I finally sought some help from the good doctor here, and he asked me to come share my story tonight. So that's what I'm doing. And if I get off track or say the wrong thing, forgive me. I am very uncomfortable talking about all of this."

"You are in a safe space, Torrance," the doctor said as he smiled. "No one here will judge you. Everyone here has a sexual addiction and is here seeking help and support from others. I think you will sense that compassionate environment as you go along."

"Yeah, dude. We're here for you," the man with the brown Afro added.

"Thank you, Gerard, for saying that," the doctor replied. "Now, Torrance, you can continue."

The guy's name is Gerard, huh? I wonder if that's his real name. I should've been listening. Why is everyone staring at me? Oh shit, the doctor just said something to me, didn't he?

"Go ahead, Torrance, when you are ready."

That's why they're staring at you. They're waiting for you to speak. Time to speak up, Torrance.

"Well, like I said, my roommate said I needed to seek help 'cause I'm out with a different woman, just about every night. Usually one-night stands, sometimes we hook up for a couple of nights, but never more than two."

"I hear you, Torrance. Been there," Gerard said.

"Gerard, remember the rules of the group," the doctor stated.

"Sorry, Dr. Pendyke. I was just, well never mind. Go ahead, Torrance. Like the doctor has said, we're here for you."

"Thank you, Gerard. Again, I ummm, well, I work as a histotechnologist and I don't meet a lot of people in my job."

"A histo what?" Gerard asked.

"Gerard. Let Torrance speak without interruption."

"Sorry, Doc."

"It's okay. I hear that a lot when I say what I do. A histotechnologist works in the pathology department of the laboratory. We cut up tissue removed in surgery and prepare and stain it in a myriad of ways, for the pathologist to examine and determine if the tissue is okay. You know, if it's cancerous or not. I have a degree and am board certified by the American Society for Clinical Pathologists. That was a bitch of an exam. But I passed it and got a job right away in the local hospital.

"There are also histotechnicians working in the department but they don't have a degree or certification and can't do everything that we do. They're indispensable to the department though, and the two we have are studying to become technologists. But I guess I'm getting off track a bit."

"You are doing perfectly fine, Torrance. Letting people know what you do is good. It helps everyone see you in a more defined manner," Dr. Pendyke replied. "And as I said, but I feel this is worth repeating, this is a safe space. What is shared here, stays here."

"Good to know. I do feel safe here. I can look around the room and see that everyone's eyes seem kind and open to hearing what I have to say. Well, as I said, I am with a different woman every night and it's just not as fulfilling as it once was.

We don't have stimulating conversations anymore or do many things together. We just have sex. And sometimes it can be quite dangerous since there is the possibility of us getting caught and that would not be good for me personally, or professionally."

"Are you saying that some of the women you are with are married?"

"Yes. But they are always separated from their husband or wife."

"Wife? You are having sex with someone who has a wife?"

"Gerard, stop interrupting. It's perfectly fine for someone to be bisexual."

"I don't disagree with you at all, Doc. I love a ménage a trois myself. Like them so much, just talking about them makes me kind of horny."

"Gerard. First of all, you're here to help yourself control your urges, not think about how wonderful a sexual encounter would be, and brag about doing it in front of the group. You know that type of behavior would hurt you emotionally and hurt your relationship with your wife and children. You just said so, not ten minutes ago. Now, after Torrance is finished you can say whatever you want to say, provided it's helpful and constructive. But now we are listening to Torrance. If you cannot stop interrupting, I'll need to ask you to leave this particular session and come back another night."

"You're right, doc. You're right. I am sorry, everyone. Sorry, Torrance."

"Thanks, Gerard. It's fine by the way, you interrupting. At least it is with me. I see that the doctor is telling me it isn't by his eyes and well, he is the doctor, so you had better listen to him, not me. I know, I am rambling. I'm just nervous. Whew! Breathe, Torrance. Breathe. Excuse me, everybody, while I close my eyes and count to ten.

"Okay. Thank you. Well, like I was saying, we don't do anything except have sex. I guess that's what we both want. At least that's what her eyes tell me. I have to admit, it was a little awkward at first, but now we just get it done. And though I don't mind the coldness of the extensor digitorum, or trapezius or deltoid, there are other things that turn me off sometimes."

"The extensive what?" Gerard asked.

"Oh, sorry. That's the histotech in me. Cold feet. And the trapezius and deltoid are shoulder muscles."

"Oh yeah. My wife says I've got those. Cold feet, that is."

"Gerard. Please."

"Sorry."

"I enjoy the areola and nipple area, and the more adipose tissue the better, in my opinion. Sorry. I really like large breasts. And they make me hot as I massage them, but then when I go toward the bulbospongiosus and it's cold, I can get turned off sometimes."

"Okay, Doc, I'm sorry, but I do have to interrupt. I don't know what he's talking about when he uses all of these medical terms. And we can't be supportive if we don't understand what he's saying, can we? What do you mean by a cold bulbosponge thing?"

"Sorry, Gerard. The bulbospongiosus muscle is around the vagina. You see, I suffer from necrophilia."

"Is that what they call it when you fall asleep all of a sudden when you're having sex?"

"No, Gerard it isn't. Torrance suffers from UAA."

"What the hell is that?"

"UAA is an acronym and denotes an un-living affinity addiction. It's a disease and these people need help like everyone else in this room. We must remain supportive and sensitive to those with different perspectives of their sexual environment - that same world we are all trying to navigate. Having a UAA is not cause to be shunned by the cold shoulder of society or this group."

"What the fuck? Are you saying this son of a bitch is screwing dead people?"

"Yes."

"Oh, hell no!"

"Now, wait a minute, Gerard. We need to help him find alternatives for his sexual addiction in a healing and therapeutic way."

"Bull-fucking-shit, Doc. This is no disease or addiction. I've been called many things many times, but this crazy son of a bitch has gone and made my hours of porn and kinky shit with hookers seem like a carnival ride. We all may have strong sexual proclivities, but no one in here is a fucking zombie like this dude!"

"Gerard. Zombies aren't real. Plus, they don't have sex with other dead people. They eat the brains of the living. Those words just don't make sense."

"Oh, really? Is this any better? You are beyond fucked up, you slimy piece of shit!"

"Well, technically yes. But from a psychological perspective, we all perhaps need to stand back and take a look in the mirror before we do something rash."

"Horse-fucking shit. There's a line that everyone in here knows you don't cross and this sick fuck crossed it. Don't need any more talking, Doc. What we need to do is remedy this problem real quick-like!"

"Now, Gerard… Now, people……" but no one heard Dr. Pendyke's words as Gerard jumped out of his chair and started pummeling Torrance.

Gerard had the body of an MMA fighter. Torrance did what he could to defend himself, but he could not stand up to the beating he was receiving. His jaw and nose were broken and he lost consciousness and suffered a concussion as Gerard and the others kicked him while he lay there bleeding and defenseless on the floor. Those that weren't kicking Torrance were encouraging the others to do so. All Dr. Pendyke could do was call 911 and pray that help got there before Torrance was killed.

The ambulance and the police arrived at the same time and they placed Gerard under arrest. After taking statements from Dr. Pendyke and others, the police decided to let Gerard go.

After several weeks in the hospital, and another week home recuperating, Torrance was driving to work for the first time since the incident. He suffered a cerebral hemorrhage and drove his car into a telephone pole at a very high rate of speed. He was declared dead on arrival at the hospital.

During the autopsy, the pathologist realized that the trauma and concussion he had suffered weeks earlier had probably led to the delayed cerebral hemorrhage but he did not include that in his report. He had learned from several friends in the police department what Torrance had been doing in the morgue. His report simply stated that Torrance died of a massive brain bleed and stroke and was dead before his car hit the telephone pole. He placed him on one of the cold metal trays and slid him back into the morgue refrigerator, making sure there were no other bodies in the other chambers before he closed the door.

Give someone the cold shoulder

Shenandoah Valley

It was August of 2021 and they were both tired of being unable to go anywhere due to the pandemic. And then he saw the article in a magazine about the "ten best small towns to visit" and knew what they should do.

"Look at this, Mary. A lot of these places are in the Shenandoah Valley. I've always wanted to go back there. I think it would be a lot of fun to visit these towns. Lots of history. Very interesting. What do you think?"

Mary read the vignettes about the towns. "I think it's a great idea. When do you want to go?"

"How soon can you be ready?"

"Seriously. We have to make plans for the dog unless you plan on taking her with us."

"No, I don't think we can do that this time. Let's see if our son can stay with her and go from there. I'd be happy if we could go in the next two or three weeks. You think that's doable?"

"Well, let me start looking at some hotels and call Andrew. This sounds like fun. I'm glad you saw that story," Mary said as she kissed Jack on the cheek.

A week later, Mary had put together a possible itinerary and began showing Jack the route and some of the places that they should visit.

"This Blackburn Inn is in Staunton, Virginia, basically the town where we would start our trip through the valley. I know you're going to want to stay at this hotel. It was built in the 1800s and was the Virginia Lunatic Asylum for 150 years. After that, it was a prison for a while before someone turned it into a hotel."

"You're kidding! A lunatic asylum?"

"Yep. Here – look at the pictures.

"Damn. Even when it was a lunatic asylum it looked like a nice place."

"Yes, I'm sure it was just a wonderful place to go. I say that sarcastically, but they made a real effort to be more humane at this facility. Not sure what all they did in there but it was a beautiful building and the grounds are remarkable. They have renovated the inside, most of it anyway. But the exterior is pretty much the way it was almost two hundred years ago. Pretty cool, huh?"

"Yes, very. You're right. I'd love to stay there. What else is in Staunton?"

"Very large civil war cemetery and Mary Baldwin University - I know you'll want to get a t-shirt from them. Their team is called the 'Flying Squirrels.'"

"You know me all too well."

"Yes, and sometimes that worries me."

"Funny."

"I thought so. But let me tell you what else I found out. Staunton was a vital transportation crossroads in the Shenandoah Valley and the Confederacy sought to utilize and protect its infrastructure and wealth from the Union forces. Stonewall Jackson used the town as one of his headquarters and it served as an army depot, quartermaster and commissary post, and training camp. Union troops targeted Staunton for destruction for over two years and finally broke through and destroyed the railroad, but a lot of the old buildings from the civil war period survived. The bank of the Confederacy is still intact there. Here's a picture of the downtown area and you can see the bank and the store across the street."

"Nice old bank. And that building. Boy, looks like you stepped back in time."

"I guess in a way you have. And get this, on summer weekends they close the main streets downtown to car traffic and turn it into a pedestrian-only area so the shops, restaurants, and bars extend into the street. That's pretty cool too. And smart."

"I agree. Blackburn Inn, Civil war cemetery, Mary Baldwin University, downtown Staunton. Check. What's next?"

"Well, I'm not too sure about most of the other small towns we'll be passing through. We'll just have to wait and see what they offer as we drive through them. But the next place we'll stay is called Winchester. It's at the other end of the valley. The town has a pedestrian mall with shops and antique stores. Lots of Civil War history in Winchester too. The town changed hands 46 times during the Civil war. Can you imagine? And like Staunton, it was also Stonewall Jackson's headquarters and was the home of George Washington's office from 1748 to 1758 and, hold on to 'yore cowboy hat,' it was the home of Patsy Cline."

"I'm 'Crazy' over Winchester, Virginia. Get it?"

"Yes, I get it, Patsy."

"Well, it sounds like you pretty much have the trip planned out."

"Yeah, more or less. As I said, I'm not sure what we'll see in some of those smaller towns, but Staunton and Winchester should be pretty nice. I think we can go next week if you're ready. Andrew said he could come and stay with the dog."

"Great! Thanks for planning all that. General Jackson would have been proud of you. Looking forward to our trip. It will be great to get back out there in the real world again. It will feel like things are normal for a change."

The following weekend, Jack and Mary headed toward the Shenandoah Valley. The drive was beautiful and the six hours passed in what felt like half the time. Arriving in Staunton, they drove past the Civil War cemetery and saw signs for Mary Baldwin University.

"We will know where to come tomorrow," Mary said in a cheerful manner. They soon arrived at the Blackburn Inn and it was even more stately than the pictures suggested.

"Look at this place! It looks like a luxury hotel."

"I know! The grounds and the large old trees are beautiful. And those fountains in the front are original. They have kept them going for over 150 years. Hard to believe."

"Crazy. Well, let's go check in and then we can go downtown. We'll ask the reservation clerk about restaurant ideas." They parked the car and followed the signs that pointed toward the front desk.

"I bet these wood floors are original. Beautiful oak. Sort of a weird feeling in here, don't you think?"

"No, Jack. No ghosts are watching us check in. I knew you would say something like that."

There was no one present in the small room where the check-in desk was located, so Jack hit the little bell on the countertop.

"Don't do that, Jack. I'm sure that's just for ambiance."

"Well, don't be too sure about that," Jack replied because just then a young man in a red bow tie came from around the corner.

"Good evening, folks, and welcome to the Blackburn Inn. Checking in or trying to get away?"

"Huh?" Mary said.

"Good one, uh…"

"Lucius, sir. It was my great-grandfather's name."

"That was a good one, Lucius. We're checking in by the way. Though I did catch this one trying to get away. She may need a straight-jacket. She can be rather feisty."

"Yes sir. I can see that. I'll see what we can do. Do you have reservations?"

"Yes, Jack Taylor."

As Lucius looked at the computer Mary pretended to examine the décor of the hotel while she scrutinized Lucius. He was a tall, slender, nice-looking young man. His black hair was well-groomed and he had very dark brown eyes. The gray suit with the red bow tie and red vest was a nice touch. But there was still something about him that made her feel creepy. *Damn it, Jack. Now you have me seeing ghosts,* she thought as she heard her husband asking about the hotel and downtown.

"Well, the hotel dates back to 1828, when the state of Virginia dedicated 80 acres to building the Western Virginia Lunatic Asylum. Doctor Francis Stribling was primarily responsible for its design. He was one of the founders of the American Psychiatric Association and was a proponent of what he called 'moral treatment.' From what I know, I think we need more people like him in the profession.

"The architect for the building was Thomas R. Blackburn, who was a protégé of Thomas Jefferson, himself a noteworthy architect. The cupola on the building is original and still accessible if you wish to go there. I do recommend it, as it gives you a wonderful view of the grounds. After the asylum closed, it was a prison for a short time before real estate developers bought the complex in 2006. And after an extensive renovation, the Blackburn Inn opened in 2018.

"There is also a small art museum on the third floor. It's still in the early stages, but I encourage you to take a look if you do decide to go up into the cupola. We do recommend only a few people go up there at any one time since it is so old."

"Does that mean it's not safe?"

"Mary, they wouldn't let you go up there if it wasn't safe."

"No."

What the hell does that "no" mean, Mary asked herself. *No, it's not safe or no it's perfectly safe as long as you're not too big? Shit, he gives me the creeps, I don't care what Jack says.*

"I would recommend the Train Station for dinner. Excellent menu and is a local favorite. As for the downtown area, let's see, yes, you still have a few hours before the shops start to close since it is Sunday. I highly recommend it too. Lots of beautiful old buildings and homes."

"Thanks, Lucius, appreciate all the information. And we can just park over there on the side of the building, right?"

"Yes sir. Just come in through the side door and use the elevator to get to your room. Is there anything else I can do for you?"

"No, thanks, Lucius. You've been very helpful."

"My pleasure. Have a nice stay and don't let the bedbugs bite."

"Yeah. We won't. See you later."

On the way back to the car, Mary said. "Okay. You win. This is a creepy place and it is definitely haunted."

"What the hell are you talking about?"

"Lucius. Geez, Louise. He creeped me out."

"Lucius? What is wrong with you? He was extremely professional and helpful. All that history that he knows. Polite. Well-groomed. I really liked his attire. I think that was a 1920's wool tweed. He was perfectly dressed for this hotel. Talk about ambiance."

"There was something wrong with his face, Jack. And don't you find that a little off-putting to say 'don't let the bedbugs bite' in a hotel that is approaching 200 years old?"

"He was just playing the part. Good lord. Do you really think they haven't treated this building a gazillion times for bugs? Especially since, as you said, it is such an old building. They can't have that type of stuff get out on Yelp."

"Maybe. But there was still something wrong with his face. It didn't look right."

"Mary. He was a handsome young man. I thought you would love his brown eyes. You like men with brown eyes."

"Yeah, yeah. I see your eyes. No need to bat your eyelashes. Wait a minute. It was his mouth. Yeah, it was his mouth. It was out of proportion to the rest of his face. He had doll lips."

"Doll lips?"

"Yeah. Doll lips. Like those lips you see on those old creepy dolls."

"You mean the dolls that scare the shit out of you?"

"Yes."

"Okay, Mary Shelley. Now, who's seeing spooks? Let's put our luggage in the room and go downtown and check things out. If Lucius is hiding in the closet or under the bed, then we'll go find another hotel."

"You're hilarious."

"I am, am I not?"

"Now stop that, dammit. You're saying that just like him when I mentioned the cupola not being safe."

"Have you lost your mind?"

"Not yet."

Jack opened the closet in their room and tried looking under the bed but the mattress was sitting on a solid piece of wood. He did call Mary into the bathroom though and opened the cabinet under the sink and held out his hand as if to say, "See? Nothing here."

Jack walked into the bedroom and flopped on the bed. "Check it out. Very comfortable. Like floating on a cushion of clouds. Won't have any trouble sleeping tonight. C'mon," Jack said as he patted the open space on the bed beside him.

Mary laid down next to him and looked over and smiled. "It is comfortable, I'll admit that."

"See. Oooooh. Wait a minute. Damn. I feel real itchy all of a sudden."

"Ha-ha. Too bad you feel itchy," Mary said as she got up. "I was going to see how noisy this bed could get, but I guess we won't be able to do that now."

"Mary…"

"C'mon Jack. Downtown awaits."

Before they left, they walked through the hotel, going up to the third floor where they viewed the small sample of art. They saw the curved steps leading up to the cupola and the sign that stated a maximum of four people at any one time.

"Shall we?" Jack asked.

"Yes. I would like to see the grounds from up there."

"Listen to the steps creak and moan. You sure you want to do this, Mary?"

"I thought that was just your knees and you letting out grunts of old age."

"Hilarious. I hope my old arms can catch you should you start to fall through the windows or flooring of the cupola."

The cupola was indeed old and both Mary and Jack felt a little uneasy walking around in it, but the views were, as Lucius stated, spectacular.

"I wonder how many people have jumped out of these windows."

"Gee, I don't know, Jack. They didn't mention that in the brochure."

"Well, I don't want to be the latest. Let's head downtown while it's still open and then go get something to eat."

After exploring the historic city they found The Train Station restaurant that Lucius had suggested. The parking lot was full and Jack said that was a good sign so they decided to try it. Dinner was delicious and on the way back to the hotel Jack reminded Mary that Lucius, the young man with the doll lips, had recommended it. She nodded and said if he kept it up, he would never know if the beds in the Blackburn hotel squeaked or not. Jack didn't say anything else about Lucius.

The next morning, as they were having a continental breakfast in the small balcony café, Jack's back began to itch. Mary snickered as he scratched.

"I know what you're doing, but wait a minute. Lean over." She saw the red marks on his neck and said, "What the hell?"

"What is it? What do you see?"

"Little red marks on your neck."

"Do they look like the ones on your neck?"

Mary pulled a mirror from her purse and pushed her hair back and there they were. Small red marks on both sides of her neck.

"Is your back itching?"

"No, but my legs are. Especially around my crotch," Mary replied.

"Son of a bitch. Bedbugs! Well, we aren't paying for any of this! Let's get packed and get the hell out of here. We'll be talking with the manager before we leave."

They showered and examined their bodies which were covered with red marks. Jack said they would stop at a pharmacy on the way out of town. When they got to the reservation desk, Jack told the young female clerk that he would like to see the manager. Within a few minutes, a middle-aged man came out and introduced himself as the manager, and asked how he could help.

He said he had a complaint and the manager asked them to follow him to his office, where Jack began to explain about their bites and that they had bedbugs in the hotel.

"I am so sorry, Mr. and Mrs. Taylor. We do our best to keep this place clean but sometimes, well, it doesn't matter. We apologize and I want you to know there will be no cost for your stay with us. I would like to give you a $100 Visa gift card, just as our way of apologizing for the problems that were created by your stay here at the Inn."

Jack and Mary were both impressed by the manager's sincere apology. As the manager was getting the gift card, Jack told him how they had enjoyed the ambiance of the hotel and were sorry that this had happened.

"And that young man who checked us in. I wish I had employees like him. So polite and well dressed and informative. But you might want to tell him not to say, 'Don't let the bedbugs bite' when he checks people in."

The manager's face turned ash gray and he leaned back in his chair. He asked Jack to tell him what the young man looked like. Mary could see beads of sweat forming on the manager's forehead. As Jack finished the description, the manager pulled out a handkerchief from his desk and wiped his head.

"Are you okay?" Jack asked. "Do we need to call 911? You don't look so good."

"Yes, I'm fine. Will be fine. Excuse me, though, while I get some water."

The manager was unsteady as he started to stand up and Jack offered to get the water from the small refrigerator in the corner of his office. The color slowly started to return to his face as he drank a little bit. He sighed and then began to talk.

"I'm sorry for the scare I may have put into you by my appearance, but I am fine. Truly. But I'm afraid I must tell you that the young man who checked you in last night was not an employee of the hotel. His name was Lucius. He died in 1878 as a resident here."

"What?" Jack and Mary asked in unison.

"Lucius was a resident of the Western Virginia Lunatic Asylum. I think if you will look at those red marks on your body you'll see that they are not bedbug bites."

Jack and Mary checked each other's necks and noticed now that they didn't really look like bites. They looked more like small reddish-blue bruises.

"He was not a dangerous man but he was quite insane. His full name was Lucius Legarde. He came from a well-to-do family in Roanoke, Virginia. They say he was a bit precocious as a young boy but I believe that was just a kind way of saying he had mental problems that they could not resolve. The doctors said he suffered from thin upper lip vermillion syndrome. Some folks refer to that condition as doll lips."

Mary looked over at John and her eyes appeared frozen open.

"Lucius had a nickname when he was a resident here in the asylum. Many of the residents and some of the staff called him 'Beetlebaum.' He had a dog by that name and kept telling everyone that was his name, so it just stuck, so to speak. Appropriate name, I suppose considering that he had tiny lips and liked to go around and suck on people's skin. Especially when they were asleep. He was very good at always getting out of whatever room or device they confined him in, as I understand it."

"You mean these are…"

"Yes. I think the appropriate term would be hickeys, Mrs. Taylor."

She looked down at her thighs and wanted to scream.

"Let me make that gift card for $500. Would that be acceptable?"

Jack just nodded as he looked at his wife and wondered how many showers it would take to wash off the "Beetlebaum love bites." Several thousand ought to do it, he thought.

Crazy as a bedbug

Not a Greek Tragedy

Homer Jones was celebrating his birthday just as he celebrated most birthdays - by working, although he no longer worked from sunrise to sundown. When he turned seventy, he cut his work day to four–six hours so he would have more time for fishing. His nephew, who owned the cemetery where Homer had worked for seventy-one years, didn't argue for two reasons. One, he knew he would never win the argument, and two, and most importantly, he had promised his mother that Homer would always have a job at the cemetery as long as he wanted one.

"Elias Odysseus Bedlowe, you listen to me and you promise me now…..whuuuu…..if I give you all this land, the home, and the cemetery…..whuuuu……..that's been good to our family for now…whuuu…..on close to one hundred and sixteen years …whuuuu……you will promise me right now…whuuuu….that you will allow your uncle Homer…whuuuu…..to work here until he dies…whuuuu…..which he will…whuuu…. do…whuuu…I reckon…whuuuu….if he has a mind to…whuuuu…..which I figure…..whuuuu…..he does…. whuuuuuuuuuu, oooooohhhhhhhh," she said as he put her oxygen mask back on and took a deep breath.

"Yes ma'am," was all Elias said as he held his mother's hand. She was dying. They both knew that she probably wouldn't last through the night and was making sure she had every last thing done before she died. Ensuring her brother was taken care of was one of the first things she talked with Elias about when he was old enough to understand what she was telling him and would be one of the last things she talked to Elias about before she stopped talking; an action that Elias and every other family member, friend, or acquaintance would discuss after each said their version of, "I'm so sorry for your loss." Whether before or after the funeral and regardless of the setting, everyone would say after Penelope Jones Bedlowe was no longer present, "Death was the only thing strong enough in this world to keep Penelope Jones Bedlowe from talking."

Neither Homer nor Elias, her only two remaining immediate family members, would disagree with anyone who made that statement for they both knew it was simply the truth.

"Elias, did I ever tell you the story about your mother and me when we were just young 'uns?"

"Not sure, Uncle Homer, you've told me a lot of stories about you and mom when you were young."

"Suppose you're right there, son. You always had a good mind, Elias. Your momma knew it and I've known it for a long time too. You've done well with the business and I 'spect you will do well long after I'm gone. "

Homer smiled at that statement and then looked out from the back porch of the house, while a few distant cousins still lingered inside after the funeral. Elias waited for his uncle to tell him the story but Homer didn't seem to be there, even though the rocking chair he sat in moved back and forth.

"Uncle Homer?"

"Oh, yes …I was starting to say something about your mother, wasn't I? It's interesting how age becomes both an adversary and an ally to you as you get older and you look back into the past. Sometimes you want to remember a name or location and for the life of you, you can't. But then other times, the smell of newly mowed grass, the sight of a dilapidated old barn, or the sound of music or a particular song, can make you remember people and places that you hadn't thought about in years and can make you both sad and happy at the same time."

Elias enjoyed talking to his uncle and no matter when they talked, Elias always left feeling like he had learned something important. It didn't bother him that on this particular day, his uncle needed more prompting to finish a sentence, thought, or story. He understood why.

"What was that story, Uncle Homer?"

Homer laughed and got out a pack of Camel non-filter cigarettes. He had been smoking them since he was fifteen years old.   He pulled out the matching Camel Zippo lighter that Penelope had given him for his forty-fifth birthday.

"You know, Penelope gave me this lighter for my forty-fifth birthday. Said if I was going to continue to smoke, and it appeared to her that I was since it had been thirty years at that point, that I should at least have a good lighter. That way she could at least feel good about the fact that she was conserving trees by me not using wooden matches. Reckon I saved a lot of trees over these seventy-plus years, haven't I?"

Elias smiled as Homer lit the cigarette and took a long puff making sure to blow the smoke away from his nephew.

"You don't think my smoking contributed to Penelope's death, do you, Elias? Secondhand smoke is a real thing but I didn't ever smoke inside. Primarily because Penelope wouldn't let me, but I also know it's a habit that most people don't like, so I try and respect that."

"No, Uncle Homer, I don't think my mother suffered at all from your smoking. To be honest with you, some nights, I would find her sitting by her window watching you smoke. I truly think she not only enjoyed watching you, but she also enjoyed the whiffs of smoke that sometimes lingered around the window for a second before they disappeared."

Homer took another puff and then laughed, causing him to cough. Elias made sure his uncle wasn't in danger and then got up and got him a cold glass of sweet tea. Homer took several sips. "Thanks, son. I seem to be coughing a bit more these days.

Could be the smoke, I guess. Could be just from laughing too, don't you think?"

Elias nodded. His gesture suggested that it could be either, but he was certain it was the first thing his uncle said and not the last.

"You know, your mom; she used to smoke back when she was in her twenties. But she gave it up after she got married and was trying to get pregnant. She said she didn't want to stunt your growth and by the size of you, I think she accomplished that."

Elias laughed.

"What are you now, Elias, six-foot-five?"

"I'm six-one and I don't think I'll be growing anymore. At least height-wise."

Homer chuckled. "You know, that wouldn't surprise me at all about her sitting there in the window, catching a glimpse of smoke that drifted by just out of her reach. But she did have cancer and I have to admit, I do wonder at times."

"No need to wonder or worry. She was ninety-two when she died. She lived a good life. Mom loved you very much and so do I. We don't need to dwell on that at all. But you were starting to tell me a story."

"I was, wasn't I?" Homer took the last puff of his cigarette and dropped what remained of the cigarette onto the porch, and ground it out with his shoe.

"You know, for five years, my parent's friends didn't think I could talk."

"What?"

"Well, your mother started talking when she was two and I always liked hearing what she had to say. Seeing how she liked hearing what she had to say, I just let her do the talking. I figured I didn't need to say anything, since she said enough for the both of us."

Elias laughed so hard he cried and Homer smiled as he listened to his nephew. He had always believed it was good to laugh when a family member died. It meant you were remembering something happy about the person who was gone and he suspected that person would like that. He always thought it honored them if you could laugh on what was referred to as a day of mourning. He didn't like to mourn because he thought if a person had lived a good life, they would want you to celebrate their death and not be sad. After all, they would now understand the meaning of everything.

"Isn't that something, Elias?"

"What's that?"

"Penelope now understands the mysteries of the universe. Of life and death itself. I truly believe that happens when people die."

Elias wasn't sure what he believed but he knew how strong his uncle and mother's faith was and he didn't want to trouble him with his uncertainties today. Especially today.

"It's okay to have doubts, Elias."

He's still very good at reading people, even at his age, and especially on a day like this, Elias thought.

"I had doubts for a very long time, but after you bury enough people and you see so many people crying and laughing and celebrating the life and death of people, you know that there's a reason for that. People just don't live and die. They have a life and death is a part of that life. I just don't think that's the end. It would be depressing to me to believe that was the end. I think one day, you'll see it that way too."

"Maybe I will. I sure miss mom though and she's only been gone a couple of days."

"I understand and I miss her too. A lot of folks seem to lose themselves before they are no longer with us, but she was your mom up until the very last day. Up until the very last moment, really. She didn't miss a beat until her heart did."

Elias smiled. His uncle never missed a chance for a good pun even though he wasn't even sure he meant to make one at that time.

"You know your name Elias comes from the Hebrew Elijah and means someone who has a strong faith in God. I don't think your momma named you by mistake."

Elias sat quietly, thinking about what his uncle just said.

"You ever wonder?"

"Wonder about what, uncle?"

"Why we all have Greek names. That comes from your grandmother, Earlene. She didn't cotton to her name, Earlene Jones, that much so she named her children after what she had learned in school to be the first civilization of art, culture, and philosophy. She didn't graduate from high school but she was still smart and read and could quote Plato and Aristotle."

"I wish I could've spent more time with her."

" Me too. Funny, ain't it? Earl and Earlene Jones giving birth to Penelope and Homer Jones and then your mother finding someone she wanted to marry named Hector Bedlowe. Hector. If I didn't know she loved him so much, I would think she married him just for the name."

Elias smiled. *I can understand why you want to reflect so much today. I get it.*

"Earl and Earlene Jones. Sounds like a couple of country bumpkins -or even worse - cousins who married, doesn't it? But they were far from either. She only had a 10th-grade education and him a high school graduate, but they were both smart as whips. He had more people and life smarts than most folks and your grandmother had those skills too. But she also had book smarts, even though her education level would suggest she didn't.

"I can see now how her reading so much about Greek culture carried over to both me and Penelope. We loved reading about Greek and Roman mythology. Prompted me and your mother to become big fans of reading in general. We had some great discussions about the books we read out here on this porch, as you know."

"Yes, sir. I remember."

"I sometimes disagreed with your mom about the reason a character did something in a story just to see her try to convince me otherwise. Boy, I sure loved those talks. And danged if my reason for looking at the story in that contrary manner wasn't later determined to be the right way by both of us in the end. Ain't that something? Heading down a rabbit hole for the sake of conversation, and then ending up with the same opinion? I loved those evenings. Your mother never minded losing a discussion as long as you had a strong argument to support your position. You learned that from her. I see it in you when you deal with the business side of the cemetery.

"Your mom was a good woman, Elias. Good-humored. Good-natured. Friendly. Generous to a fault and trusted everyone until they gave her a reason not to. She learned to be a good businesswoman from your father and grandfather. Your father could sell a dog house to a cat owner. A kind and generous man too. I see that kindness and trust in you. Just like your mother had the best of her parents, I think you have the best of both your parents."

"I hope so, uncle. I hope I have some of my grandparents and uncle in my blood too."

Homer smiled at Elias. He lit another cigarette and watched the smoke float up into the sky for a moment.

"You were only one or two when they died, I don't remember which."

"I was just two when they died in that car accident."

"That's right. That's right. Your mother had you late in life. Not sure if she ever told you this, but she had several miscarriages and had just about given up hope of ever having a baby and then you come along. Oh, I remember how scared and happy she was at the same time. You know, she was forty years old when you were born."

"Yes sir. I remember."

"Yes, I suppose you do. Wish you could've known your father and grandparents more. Don't understand why a healthy man like your father had a stroke… and then that car just crossed the median headfirst into that semi-tractor truck …just don't make sense…"

Homer finished that cigarette and lit another and appeared to drift away with the smoke as he rocked back and forth in his chair. "Just don't understand it, Elias."

"I'm sorry. What?"

"I don't understand why your father and grandparents died that day and why your mother wasn't with them. She always went to the games with them when they went to Knoxville, but she just didn't feel good that day and even asked me if I wanted to go in her place. But I had already promised Horace I would go fishing with him. We were going to listen to the game on the radio while we fished. Which we did. Tennessee won that game. Beat Alabama, and it's always a good day when we beat Alabama. Didn't matter that we didn't catch one fish that day. I never laughed so much in my entire life listening to Horace tell story after story."

Homer finished that cigarette and put the little bit of flame out with his shoe.

"Seen a lot of things that don't make sense though in all these years. Tried figuring things out and pondered over words of great men and better thinkers than me and all I can get from all of that thinking and reading is that it just wasn't our time. Yes sir, it just wasn't our time. When it's our time, we leave. Until then, we stay. I suppose some people leave earlier than they should according to the way they live, but then others just leave and you're left trying to understand why. Penelope knows why now. I'm glad she understands now."

Elias looked into his uncle's glistening eyes and watched the tears flow down his cheeks. He reached over and put his hand on his uncle's shoulder and Homer patted his nephew's hand in return.

"You know, it was your grandfather that got this business started, during the depression. He had a lot of land and decided to use it for a cemetery and took out a loan to build the mortuary. He told me and your mom that people were always going to die and they would need someone to give them a good send-off and a good piece of land to live in for the rest of their life.

"I always thought that statement to be a bit of a contradiction but also worth remembering. Those were bleak times, the depression, and taking out a loan then was risky. I've met very few people who had that much foresight with regard to death, even though the general mood of folks at that time was what some people might consider to be mournful. Your grandfather had foresight because he knew that dead people needed a place to live. Dead people needing a place to live. Those words don't seem like they should go together but it appears your grandfather was right."

"Mom never told me that."

"That's a bit surprising but I suppose she had a million other things to think about after they all died and she had you to bring up. I couldn't help her as I didn't know anything about raising children. Heck, I was just beginning to figure out how to raise myself."

Elias chuckled. "What do you mean by that?"

"The war, Elias. The Korean War. I wasn't old enough to enlist in World War II but when the Korean War happened, my friend Horace and I enlisted in the navy. I think that's because we both liked to fish."

Elias wasn't sure if he meant that to be funny or not but he still laughed and when Homer looked at him, he did too.

"Yeah, it was a pretty stupid reason but it was a different time. Lots of concern about communism. Since we hadn't been able to help defeat the Nazis, Horace and I both decided we needed to be there to defeat the communists. Problem is, we didn't do that and that took a toll on us. War takes a toll on anyone who is unfortunate enough to experience it. "

Elias watched Homer finish his iced tea and asked if he wanted another one.

"Got anything stronger in there?"

Elias nodded. He knew what Homer wanted. His mother and his uncle had several Crown Royals in the evening after dinner most nights, more than several if there was a heated book discussion taking place. He would have a beer with them if he was home and not out on a date or with friends. It was always entertaining conversation even if it was mostly his mother doing all the talking with allowable interjections when prompted. He wished that he had spent more evenings out there on the porch with both of them.

He returned with two glasses of whiskey and they clinked their glasses together and took a sip. "You remember my friend Horace, don't you, Elias?"

"Of course. He was so funny."

"Funniest man I ever known. Kept me sane for the most part during the Korean War. We were on a cruiser during the war. At the Battle of Incheon. A battle the UN forces, the US, the Brits, and the Canadians won. But a lot of people were injured and died. Battle lasted four days. It took a long time for me to quit seeing parts of human bodies on the ship and in the water when I closed my eyes. My friend Horace never got over it. Affected him his whole life. That's why he took to drinking so much. He hoped it would help him forget but it never did. It just blurred his vision long enough for him to get up and go through another day.

"We were in the navy for six years. When we got back home, we didn't know what we were going to do. We just hung around for the most part, and then started helping your mother by digging graves for her. We didn't even ask to be paid even though she paid us. At first, me and Horace spent all our money drinking after work. I eventually quit doing it every night but Horace couldn't."

Elias got up and refilled Homer's drink without asking.

"Thanks. Did you ever hear the story about Horace and his cousin, Fredward?"

"Fredward?"

"Yes. Poor boy never had a chance with a name like that, did he?"

Elias laughed.

"Fredward Evers. Ran a moonshine still for a long time. Made good moonshine too. Me and Horace had quite a bit of it. But Fredward had to move that still all the time to keep from getting caught. One time he moved into an abandoned trailer park way out in the woods. Horace went out there one evening and told Fredward that something smelled really bad and he should move the still, but Fredward was either too drunk or too lazy to do it. Well, what Horace smelled was methane gas coming up out of old leaky septic tanks, and damn if not two days later, the whole place blew up. Horace said he couldn't believe what he saw there after the accident. There was Fredward shit everywhere along with a bunch of other shit. He then looked at me and took a long drink. He held up his bottle and said, 'Here's to a better fate than Evers.'"

Homer burst out laughing and Elias smiled but couldn't understand what was so funny until he heard the words in his head several more times. Elias finally got it and they both laughed for a long time, taking sips of their whiskey as they thought about the story.

"Horace was a good man even though alcohol killed him in the end. But he tried. Lord knows he tried, cause I saw him do so. At first, we both liked digging the graves because I think, even though Horace never said it, we felt like we were burying some of our grief from the war. Somehow like we were repaying those men that never had a proper burial. It was simple work but we knew it was important work.

"Sometimes we dug three to four graves in a day. That would keep you in shape and wear you out at the same time. How's that happen, you wonder? You figure you're in shape from doing a strenuous job day in and day out, so why does it make you tired?"

Elias didn't know if that was a rhetorical question or whether his uncle wanted an answer so as the pause continued, he replied. "Your body has a finite amount of energy, Uncle Homer. You need to replenish and rest your muscles and the balance of nutrients in your body or it just gives out. Now, robots on the other hand..."

Homer looked at his nephew and for a moment he saw his sister sitting there looking back at him and smiling.

"Yes, he's your son all right, Penelope. Good-looking man too, like Hector. Smart man like the both of you. Already looking ahead to the point where you can put some robot machine of some kind out there digging the ground. Surely possible, seeing how they have robots making cars today. Yes, that boy will be just fine, Penelope. Just fine."

"Did you say something, uncle? It sounded like you said my mother's name and then the words 'just fine'."

"Just thinking out loud for a moment, Elias."

"Horace quit working when I started using the backhoe. He came out there and spent time with me, drinking and telling me stories, but he didn't do much work after that. You do know what he called the funeral home and cemetery don't you?"

Elias answered, "No sir," even though he had heard this story many times.

"Spirit Airlines, one-way tickets only."

Elias laughed as much as the first time he heard his uncle say that and Homer laughed so hard he started coughing again. Elias ran in and got some water and paper towels for him. The paper towels turned pinkish-red as he coughed into them. Homer crumpled them up and stuffed them in his pocket so Elias wouldn't see, but he had already seen the blood today and many other times in the past month.

"You know, I buried Horace with a shovel. I knew he would want it like that. I'm just sorry that he turned into one of those folks that hung onto death more than life. But I pray he made amends before he left. People don't think about dying until they realize they are dying, but they should think about it long before that. Now don't get me wrong, you don't want to worry yourself to death about death, but you do need to think about what will happen to you after your body no longer responds to gravity."

"I understand, Uncle Homer."

"Yes, I do believe that, Elias. I truly do. Well, I guess I better go finish my work for today before the sun goes completely out of sight."

"Can you wait just one minute? I have something for you. I know that you don't like birthday presents but......well, here. I thought you might like this."

Homer took one last puff of the cigarette and then opened the box. The blue cotton short-sleeved shirt inside had "Spirit Airlines" embroidered above the shirt pocket with the name Homer stitched below.

Homer smiled and stood up and took off the shirt he was wearing and put on the new one.

"Well, what do you think?" Homer said as he turned around to model it, though it looked more like a broken mannequin had been moved from back to front as his body was so stiff and crooked.

"It looks perfect, Uncle Homer," Elias said as he hugged him.

"Thank you, son. Thank you for everything. You take care of things while I'm gone and I'll talk to you later." Homer picked up the shovel that was leaning against the porch and started walking away.

As his uncle disappeared over the hill, Elias sat down in the rocking chair and began to cry.

After Homer finished shoveling the dirt onto his twin sister's grave, he stumbled into a sitting position beneath the large cypress tree that overlooked the plot. He wasn't sure he could have done one more shovel full. He coughed several times until he managed to wheeze, "Happy Birthday," with one final "whuuuuuuuuuu, oooooohhhhhh." And as the breath left his body, he heard the words "better fate than evers" in his mind and he smiled as he lay his head back against the tree and closed his eyes one last time.

Better late than never

Pixie Dust

This is the story of my early childhood. Now, as I look back, I can see that in many ways, my life may seem like a fairy tale of some sort or one of those fantasy and adventure stories your parents read to you as a child. There were certainly many magical moments spent with the ones that I loved, but even so, one learns in all good fairy tales or fantasy and adventure stories, magic has a fragile nature about it, and as such, one must be prepared for those times when it is absent, and the darkness surrounds you.

It is in those dark moments, that one truly realizes whether they have the strength and courage to move forward and whether one can find the magic again. I faced those moments and I know now that by telling what happened back then, I can recapture some of the magic that occurred and keep it safe within me, and with each re-telling of the story, perhaps pass along some of that magic to others.

Now, I can't tell you how that magic occurred, or where it specifically came from, but I can tell you when it happened and how it happened and what it felt like. I don't think we ever understand how some of those magical connections are made, but we all know that they occur for a reason. I was lucky in that I discovered early on in life that I had a special ability to sense feelings in people and feel things in the world around me that others do not. Some of that, I am sure, was passed onto me by my mother, as we could, at times, see or hear what the other was thinking before any word was spoken. How that happened, I can't say for sure but without it, I know that I would not have been able to pass this story along to you.

Take hope from this story, because without hope, none of us can survive. Take love from this story, because without love, life has little value. And finally, take magic from this story, because without magic, there would be no reason to get up every morning and embrace the day that, in itself, is a story that remains to be written.

****

My parents thought I was a special child. Now that I have the inclination and the ability to look back, I believe most parents think their children are special. And though I am less of an expert in the divine nature of man and more of a believer, I am certain each parent who maintains that belief is correct. We may not all be born with the same talents or abilities, but I don't think that truly matters, neither in the beginning nor over time. What matters is that in the eyes of the parents and close family members, that child is indeed special.

Now, I can't say when it happens, or how it happens, but as we become less infant and child and more adult, some of us lose that special nature that is inside us. Just like silver that is not tended to on a routine basis becomes tarnished over time. I haven't been able to determine, nor am I certain I ever will while I am a member of this world, as to that moment when good becomes bad, and whether it arises from a result of the world around us or the way in which we see the world around us. But the fact is, some of us do change; so much, that what may have been bad and redeemable at one time, festers and becomes even worse and in fact, downright evil. I can tell you from my own experience, I have seen both the best and the worst in man.

It has been that way since the beginning of time and I suppose it will happen that way until the end of time. I can't say what will actually happen at the end of time for I will not be around to see it, but I am not worried. I will be okay when I am no more.

Just like most parents, my grandparents thought my parents were special. And by all familial standards and by all public perception, I think each one of them in their own way, was at one time considered to be a part of a perfect family. But history tells us, even pure perfection here on earth suffers greatly, and my family, like all others, did truly enjoy the wonderfulness of life, but also experienced sorrow and grief.

My mother's maiden name was Sarah Marie Packard, the daughter of Harold James and Jillian Packard. My grandfather, Papa P, established and owned Packard Iron Works and Packard Construction, and a whole lot of land within the town known as Bluff City, Tennessee. His wife, "Grandmother," loved to shop for clothes and antiques and, according to Papa P, "spend money." But as good as she was at spending money on herself, she was also generous with all her family and with those less fortunate.

There were those of a jealous nature who would on occasion refer to Bluff City as "Packard City," but thankfully, those with that misguided emotion were a small minority. The majority of those who lived around the town of Bluff City had nothing but kind words to say about Harold and Jillian and their daughter, Sarah Marie.

During her high school years, the name Sarah Marie Packard became quite well-known in the local community. My mother was the homecoming queen for all four years, the head cheerleader for all four years, and the Salutatorian of her graduating class at Daniel Boone High School. Some said she was beautiful, while some considered her "plain-looking" or only popular because of her money. That opinion was usually held by those who were subject to that misguided emotion I mentioned earlier.

Those who knew my mother well understood there was no puzzle to her true beauty. Her sky-blue eyes were full of wisdom and kindness, and her actions were never misled by them. She had a charitable spirit and the fact she had access to money was simply a convenient mechanism to ensure that those who had less, received more. I think she inherited that charitable gene from both her parents.

My father's name was Charles James Fulwider. He was the son of Joseph Edward and Patricia Ann Fulwider who owned Fulwider Wood Cabinets and Patricia's Pies in Piney Flats, Tennessee, which as they say in that part of the country, with regard to those two towns when my parents grew up, "I reckon no town was no more 'n a mile the way the crow flies."

(Besides the fact that they had different names, geographically, the two town's margins were less than five miles apart, so there wasn't that much difference between the two cities. And I say that, just so as I go along in this story, you will know that for all intents and purposes, when I speak of one area, I am speaking of both, or as they would say there, "bout both of 'em.")

Grandpa Joe was known as a master craftsman with wood and if you wanted the best cabinets for your home, you came to him, which my other grandfather did for his more expensive housing projects. People also came to him to have anything that was made of wood restored to its original condition. In all likelihood, these were items that "belonged to papaw or meemaw" in a lifetime or several lifetimes ago and had a great deal of sentimental value to the owner. Once restored, they often had a great deal of monetary value too. He built much of the furniture that was in our homes and taught my father and me, from an early age, how to work with wood.

Patricia Ann Fulwider, or Mammaw as I knew her, had the reputation of being one of the best bakers in the area. If you wanted a coconut cream pie for a special function or just because you liked coconut cream pie, you ordered one from her. She made about ten a day, but only on Mondays, Wednesdays, and Fridays. She made them all in her kitchen and by noon, they were all gone. Any pies she made on the weekend were only for family and special friends, and even if they were not coconut, they were still considered to be "the reason you had dinner" by anyone who tasted them.

It was also during his high school years that Charles James Fulwider became quite well-known within the community. He played on the varsity baseball team for all four years and led the team in batting average and home runs for three of those four. He grew four inches in those four years, and by the time he was a senior he was six-foot-two and had what they called an "outfielder's body." So, he moved from the infield to the outfield and played center or left field where he became an even better ball player.

Both his teammates and the opposing players knew that any ball hit up into the air wherever he was playing that day, was an automatic out. There were many foul balls that should have been foul and many home runs that should have been home runs, if not for my father's ability to track them down or extend his body beyond what seemed possible against tall fences that lined the perimeter of the field. He was also known for throwing runners out from his position in the outfield. Other teams quickly realized that a fly ball or a ground ball hit into his area was not a green light to advance or to take extra bases. He accepted a baseball scholarship to the University of Tennessee, but unfortunately, he tore the ligaments in his shoulder and elbow during his sophomore year at college and his playing days were over.

My mother met my father a month after she graduated from high school. He had just graduated from The University of Tennessee with a degree in mechanical engineering and had accepted a position with Packard Iron Works to help design equipment that would supply power to the plant in a more cost-effective and environmentally-conscious manner. They just happened to be with their fathers one day during a business visit between them about some cabinets for a new home.

Though no one ever said it was more than just a coincidence that they happened to be with their parents that day, I believe differently now that I've had time to reflect. I think that this was one of those magical connections in our lives that I alluded to earlier. Seldom do we recognize them at the time, but later in life, as we are reading the book that we created each day, we can see that chapter had somehow already been written.

My mother told me, "It wasn't love at first sight on that day, but it was certainly love after the second time I looked at him," and that always made me laugh. My father said he knew he was going to marry my mother when she made him laugh on their first date, and I never got tired of hearing him tell me that story. It will be one of those stories I will always be able to articulate, when other aspects of what I remember about growing up, become lost in those spaces of my mind that are irretrievable.

According to my father, their first date was a picnic on Papa P's farm. It was always called a farm, but there was very little farm to it. It was just a lot of beautiful land that had three big barns, where my grandfather stored large antique machinery and antique cars. There was nothing growing on the land of any significance, besides beautiful trees and flowers and a couple of rows of tomato plants that Grandmother insisted on having. I suppose it was called a farm because the land went on for as far as anyone could see from the road and the people that drove past it just assumed the cows and horses, or the four or five rows of tomato plants were probably part of a larger farm that was hidden from their view.

My father said, even though it was over ninety degrees on the day of the picnic, it was one of those summer days that you didn't think was hot if you were beneath the shade of a tree with the wind blowing. My mother had picked the perfect place beneath a grove of trees that looked out onto a sea of green grass and several creeks that crisscrossed through the hills below them. He told me that "the creeks created a noise that reminded someone who listened to them, that the world had more languages than any one man could master."

That was one of those phrases that I have never forgotten and when he was re-telling the story to me and he missed a word or two, I always reminded him of what it was supposed to be, and each time I did that, he smiled and said, "Oh, that's right." I understand now, that he omitted a word or two on purpose just so he could hear me correct him. It was a script that I think neither of us tired of reciting.

He asked my mother where their land started and where it ended and he said she pointed her finger toward the left and moved it to the right and said, "The land goes from here to there." Being an engineer, that response wasn't precise enough, so he asked, "Where?" as he looked toward the woods. She stood up and pointed toward the trees and the creeks and moved her arm in a 180-degree fashion and said, "From there to here." He thought he understood and said, "Oh, from there to there?" and she shook her head no.

"No, silly. From here to there. Not there to there. There to there would not be here, now, would it?"

My father looked confused and he said she rolled her eyes and then tried to explain the answer to his question. "If there is over there, you are indeed correct. But if you mean beyond there, you would be wrong."

"How far is over there?" he asked.

"Like I said when you first asked me, from here to there."

My father started to ask another question but he saw my mother smiling at him. He wasn't sure if it was the blue skies or her blue eyes but he said he sort of went blind for a moment and then felt a kiss on his cheek. His vision returned as soon as he heard my mother laughing and he saw her running down the grassy hills toward the streams. He ran after her, asking where she was going.

"From here to there," she said and then stopped and waited for him to catch up to her. As soon as he did, she put her arms around his neck and whispered in his ear, "From here to there, and there to here, it doesn't matter as long as you are there and I am there and I am here and you are here."

He never missed a word when he was telling me that part of the story and I know why. It was a fairy tale description of their first encounter with each other and one never forgets the first time you meet your true love in a fairy tale.

He said he understood "then and there" that he was going to marry that woman. I always loved it when he said that because it reminded me of something Dr. Seuss would have said in one of his books. I fully expected him to add, "and the bluffer banger sounded a bluffer bang sound when they realized what both of them finally found." But he never did and it didn't matter. I loved the story each time I heard it, even without the "bluffer bangers."

I'm not sure how many times he told that story to others, but he told it to me at least ten times when I was growing up and another ten times after I was grown. I never asked anyone else about the story even though I was sure family and friends of the family had heard it at one time or another. I didn't ask because I understood that as stories are told and re-told, important words or parts of the story are often forgotten or said in a different way, and I knew that would happen if someone else told me the story. I always wanted to hear the story the way it was supposed to be told, just like the way it's supposed to happen when you hear or read a true fairy tale.

My mother and father saw each other every day that summer, and just as many nights, and on September 1st, Sarah Marie Packard and Charles James Fulwider were married. As I was told by my grandparents when I was old enough to understand, the wedding was a grand event, with evidence they revealed from the Johnson City Press, the Bristol Herald Courier, and the Kingsport Times. Both of my grandmothers had clippings from each newspaper that they shared with me on multiple occasions, showing pictures of my parents on their wedding day and reading to me what the reporter had said about the couple and the wedding.

For those of you not familiar with East Tennessee, neither Bluff City nor Piney Flats is big enough to have a newspaper. Most folks in Bluff City or Piney Flats get their news from one of the three papers mentioned above, as Johnson City, Bristol, and Kingsport are larger, more metropolitan centers in that area of East Tennessee. If they don't get their news from one of those papers, they just rely upon whatever they hear at the farmer's market, feed store, local taverns, or from TV or the internet. (I say "metropolitan centers" but even as I write those words, I know there will be some strangers that will come through those aforementioned towns and scoff at the use of the term.)

My parents had no newspaper clippings of their wedding. When I once asked my mother why, she just showed me the framed picture of them on their wedding day and told me that was all they needed because they remembered every moment of the day. Considering my father remembered their first date on which he said he was going to marry my mother in such vibrant detail, I didn't doubt what she said.

I enjoyed listening to my grandparents read to me about the wedding, even though I heard it four different ways as each one recounted their version of how it unfolded and the newspaper clippings that they found to support their version of the story at that time. I know that the wedding took place on the farm in the exact spot where my parents had their first date. The reporters wrote that the setting looked like it had been "cut from a picture book," and that there were "over a thousand people there," and that it was a "grand event."

After hearing that number the first time from Grandmother, I asked my mom why so many people came. She just looked puzzled and said she didn't realize there were that many in attendance. But then she smiled and said her parents and my dad's parents had lots of friends and friends of friends and a lot of family spread out all over the country. And then she winked at me and said, "Plus, Grandmother likes to throw big parties," which made both of us laugh.

Exactly one month after getting married, my mother became pregnant. My grandparents and my father encouraged her to go to college, but my mother said she would pursue that endeavor after what she considered was "sufficient time becoming a mother and wife." It was during that time of her pregnancy, that my mother, who was once known as Sarah Marie Packard and currently known as Sarah Marie Fulwider, became known as simply Sarah Marie to everyone in the community. The reason was a simplistic change in her thinking, but appeared a tad pretentious to some of the "locals."

I never heard anyone call my mother anything but Sarah Marie as I was growing up. She didn't keep her maiden name as some women did when they got married. She thought Sarah Marie Packard Fulwider sounded like an heiress to some fortune who "jetted" all over the world. In truth, she was an heiress to a fortune but no one who ever met her would have known that. She knew when she married my father that she would always be married to him and she didn't find it necessary to be reminded of it by anyone calling her Mrs. Fulwider. She said she was more of a "Sarah Marie" type of person and liked the straightforwardness and modesty that was embedded in that simple identity.

She understood some people in town would think by calling herself just "Sarah Marie" that she was being snobbish or conceited, as if she was conferring celebrity status onto herself by such an act, like Cher or Madonna. But my mother never went through some formal process where she proclaimed in the paper or through a royal decree, in which there would be a lot of "wherebys and therefores" and then the pronouncement of the name "Sarah Marie" with a picture of herself or her coming forward from behind the curtains to a crowd of people.

She simply told people her name was Sarah Marie. Folks who met her remembered her name because my mother was the type of woman you didn't forget and so they called her that from that point forward. Her friends and family had always called her Sarah Marie, so that was never a problem for them. Even so, my mother still heard snide comments beneath the undercurrent of casual conversations, but she never let it bother her. She knew that those who truly mattered to her understood the basis of her thinking and that it was not meant in any way to dismiss her heritage or marriage.

She told me many times as I was growing up, that once she became a wife and mother, she felt like she had become the first non-professional actor to ever win an Oscar in her first and only movie. "Once I met your father, I knew what I was meant to be in life and that was to be a wife and mother, and I was so lucky to become both," she would tell me before kissing me on the forehead, usually after reading me a book or telling me to "sleep tight and don't let the bedbugs bite."

Yes, in my mother's way of thinking, becoming Sarah Marie brought less emphasis on her and more on her family and that was the way she thought it should be. She had gotten all the attention she needed in high school and though she enjoyed the accolades, she was truly humbled by them and at times uncomfortable being in the spotlight. She was a kind woman and always did things for those who had less than her. In all the years that I knew her, she never did anything that drew attention to herself ever again. She only acted as a woman who believed that everyone on the planet was the same and deserved kindness, respect, and a helping hand at times, and she made sure she always had one to extend.

My official full name was John Edward Harold Fulwider. At least, that was the name that my parents told the hospital to place on my birth certificate, but it was Mammaw who gave me my real name. When Mammaw held me in her arms for the first time, she said, "Oh, how I love my little Johnny cakes!" Mammaw liked to make and eat Johnny cakes, which if you don't know, are just pancakes with a little bit of cornmeal in them. From that point on, I was "little Johnny" or just "Johnny." I didn't mind. It could have been worse. Mammaw had a fondness for Twinkies too.

Soon after conferring the name of Johnny to me, Mammaw also told anyone who would listen that I was the "spitting image" of my father when he was that age, regardless of the age I was at the time she made that comment. And whether they all truly agreed with that assessment or not, I'll never know. But if you asked her, everyone could see the resemblance, especially when she showed them a picture of my father taken at about the same age I was during that particular moment of conversation.

Each time she made that comparison, Mammaw used the exact same words. "They's both just like a Reese's peanut butter cup turned inside out." It wasn't until I was five years old that I asked my mother what she meant by that comment and she told me that Mammaw was referring to the color of my hair having a peanut butter brown color and my eyes being a chocolate brown color, just like my father. I said, "Oh," and went outside and continued to play. Older now, I realize those were the early beginnings of my awareness of the colorful way Mammaw talked, and when I remember any of her "sayings," I always smile.

Her description of the resemblance to my father, said on numerous occasions, was the first time that I had an unspoken conversation with my mother. I am not sure how many times she had said it, but one day Mammaw said, "They's both just like a Reese's peanut butter cup turned inside out," while my father was standing there and I could see his face turning the color of a ripe strawberry and him shaking his head and rolling his eyes as if to ask, "Why is she saying that?" I then watched as my mother just smiled, ran her hands through my father's hair, and upon gazing into his eyes, I could see my father's embarrassment transformed into a smile, like magic.

My mother then said, "You are so right, Patricia Ann. Charley and Johnny's hair are the color of peanut butter and their eyes are that dark chocolate brown that is impossible for any woman to resist. No wonder I fell in love with your son. Peanut butter cups were always my favorite candy growing up and are still my favorite candy growing up."

And then she bent down and looked at me and ran her hands through my hair and though she didn't utter a word, I heard her say, without moving her lips, "I love you, little Johnny." And that's when I knew, that the second candy in that sentence was all about me growing up. I never forget that and from that point on, the special connection I mentioned earlier, was formed.

Mammaw seldom stopped with just the hair and eyes comparisons though. She also said my father and I had "perfect-sized airs" and for the longest time, I thought she was talking about our hair. But about the same time I learned what the peanut butter description meant, I learned from my mother that she was referring to our ears.

To a young child, being told you have perfect-sized ears means nothing. But as I got older and began taking notice of other people and even of myself, I asked my father what he thought about having perfect-sized ears. And that's when he said for me not to say anything to Mammaw, but he didn't think ears were perfect-sized on anyone's head, including his or mine. He added that he had never heard anyone except his mother refer to someone's ears as perfect and he thought they were just odd-shaped pieces of flesh on the side of people's heads that allowed them to hear. As I have had time to think about it, I realize my father was right.

In my entire life, I never heard anyone else ever say, "Now that person has some good-looking ears." Not even at the farmer's market, unless it was Mammaw describing me or my father to a friend of hers who was shopping there at the time.

Mammaw also used the "perfect" adjective when she spoke of either my father's or my nose and lips. According to her, we both had a "perfect-sized nose that wasn't so sharp it'd cut cheese and not so round that people would mistake it fer a button," and that our lips were perfect-sized for a male, "not too big and not too thin." And whenever she said that to anyone - friend or family- they would just nod and say, "Uh-huh" or, "Oh, yes, I see that now." I eventually asked my mother what she meant by all of that and she smiled and told me Mammaw just liked to use the word perfect when she was talking about her son or grandson. And then she would pick me up in her arms and look at me and say I was truly the spitting image of my father and that she was a lucky wife and mother to have two handsome young men in her life.

****

I was a very happy baby. My mother said she wondered if I had tear ducts for the longest time but when I became thirteen months old, she didn't wonder anymore. I'm glad I don't remember the exact details, but she said it was an awful experience when I got sick for the first time. When I was a little older and would catch a cold, she would tell me not to worry. "This cold makes you feel bad now, but in a few days, you'll be, as Mammaw would say, 'fit as a fiddle,'" and then she told me about the time when I had been very sick as a baby.

When I was thirteen months old, I had a Rotavirus infection which gave me a very high fever. I understand now that a high fever is a warning sign for anyone who is sick, and should it be extremely high or long-lasting, they should seek medical advice and/or intervention. I am also aware, having lived through it, that a high fever in a child makes parents very worried and as such, my mother and father were very frightened.

"The fever wasn't the only scary part," she went on to say, stating that the virus made me "poop and throw up all the time," and that worried her and my father even more. She said I cried a lot for almost ten days and scared them "terribly," but then she smiled and said they had two secret weapons to make that "bug" fly away.

The first weapon was something called Pedialyte, and she asked me if I remembered drinking that orange liquid. I nodded my head because as soon as she said orange liquid I did remember how cool and wonderful it tasted in my mouth. I still drink it today when I get sick. She then told me the second secret weapon was the car and she laughed when I looked puzzled. After they got me to drink some Pedialyte and it "stayed in my stomach," they would put me in my car seat and drive around, with one of them driving and one of them sitting beside me in case I got sick again.

"Every time we put you in the car, you'd be asleep within five minutes and always slept until you started feeling bad again. And it didn't matter how long or how far we had to drive; as long as you were asleep, we drove. And then when you woke up and started crying, we took you back home and you would get sick again. We'd give you a little more orange Pedialyte, and you would get a little better each time. Ten days later, you didn't have a fever anymore and you were smiling and laughing again. And that made us smile and laugh and cry a little bit too, but they were tears of joy because we knew you were going to be okay."

She then said that for some reason after that ordeal, a calming feeling came over her that told her no matter what life threw at me I would be fine. I remembered asking her if that calming feeling was like having a wonderful dream, and she said it was exactly like that and then looked at me as if I had started speaking in another language. When I looked into her eyes, for the second time I heard her tell me she loved me without saying a word, just like what had happened when Mammaw used the "inside-out peanut butter cup" description. Now, if I'm ever sick, I can remember that moment in vivid detail and see more clearly how strong that special connection was with my mother.

I don't think very many people would ever think that having a cold when you were growing up was a special memory but it was for me. Because each time I got a cold, I got to drink orange Pedialyte and have my favorite soup, chicken double noodle, with saltine crackers as often as I wanted. And, my mother always made me peanut butter cookies with M&Ms in them. As I got older, every time I saw those cookies in a bakery, I almost wanted to sneeze and pretend I had a cold.

It never bothered me that I sneezed a lot when I had a cold, or alternated between a runny and stuffed up nose, and at times coughed like Mammaw's cat when she was trying to get up a fur ball. Not only did I love what I got to eat and drink at those times, but my mother and I spent all day together watching the Cartoon Network or TV Land and when we weren't watching television, she would read me Dr. Seuss books until I fell asleep. We loved "The Andy Griffith Show" and "The Beverly Hillbillies." I even carried the love for those shows into my adult years because we both laughed so much at them. Mayberry reminded me of Bluff City and I can remember my mother saying in many ways they were similar, because the people in our town, just like in Mayberry, made us laugh and truly cared about what happened to each other.

I told my mother that Granny in "The Beverly Hillbillies" reminded me of Mammaw and my mother laughed so hard she cried. When she finally stopped, she told me that Mammaw wasn't as old as Granny and there really wasn't that much of a resemblance between them. She made me promise to never mention that to any of my grandparents or even to my father. And so I promised, but I could sense when she was watching "The Beverly Hillbillies" with me and Granny came on, she was thinking of Mammaw because she laughed even more at whatever she said or did.

****

I have come to realize within a family that loves one another, a child from day one to their fifth birthday can do no wrong. It is a period in their life when they are as close to being a member of royalty as they ever will be. When a baby smiles for the first time, it is as if an undiscovered Michelangelo has been found and family, friends, and even strangers are amazed and astonished whenever that smile is repeated. Once you add a laugh to the smile, you can expect to have your picture placed on the next stamp that the Post Office issues.

When you burp or pass gas, they laugh and say how wonderful it is. When you pee or poop on yourself, they clean you off and smile at you the entire time they are changing your clothes. And when you learn to go to the bathroom for the first time? Well, that is akin to Neil Armstrong taking that first step onto the surface of the moon. That simple act is talked about for weeks, and months, and generates an obeisance from your loyal subjects, for at least six months, or in some cases, if you are a late bloomer so to speak, for an entire year. Though I didn't understand it then, I certainly see the irony of it now as to why the toilet is called a throne; because when a young child ascends upon it for the first time, they are indeed provided the keys to the kingdom.

For the first five years of my life, I, like my mother, doubted the world could be much better. I realize that saying that seems sort of naïve considering I was a child for those five years, but looking back at those times, I truly don't know what could have been better. Without question, I had become the center of a universe that was filled with tremendous happiness and a sense of discovery within myself that led to even more happiness. It was indeed a magical time.

If my mother wasn't playing with me or teaching me something new, one of my grandparents was with me showing me something new and interesting. They talked to me about the land and the trees and plants on the land, about work, about food and how to cook, read me books, took me around the town and to the lake, and according to Mammaw, I was "jess like a sponge, soakin' everythun' in." And Mammaw was right, only I didn't feel like a sponge. I felt more like a royal alien of some kind, being shown all the best that Earth had to offer and it was spectacular.

Papa P took me to the places where he worked and I loved them all, especially seeing where my father worked and what kind of big machines he was designing. I particularly liked when my father showed me pictures on paper with lots of numbers and symbols and explained to me what they were, and then the same picture in life-size form made of all the kinds of different materials, and explained to me what they were and how everything worked together. And though I may have been young, I always remembered the way he or Papa P explained things to me.

Papa P took me to all his construction sites and believe me, work always stopped as everyone came out to see "little Johnny." Even as a five-year-old, I could remember names and faces and they loved it when they said hello to me and I answered, "Hello Mister Tom, or Mister Bob, or Miss Jean." It was on those trips to the construction sites and meeting with all the people that I felt a similar sensation that up until that point, had only been with my mother. Though they didn't speak to me without saying anything, somehow, I could always sense their feelings, especially when they had sadness within them. And whenever I felt that sadness or loneliness, I gave that person a hug and it always made both of us feel just a little bit better.

I remember Papa P talking to Grandpa Joe and Mammaw about it one day and telling them I had some sort of special ability to make people smile. Telling that to Mammaw was sort of like telling her what the temperature was outside because she acted like she already knew that as she took me in her arms and said, "Yes sir, my Johnnycakes has got sumptin special inside him, all right. Knew it the day he was born and we jess beginning to see all the specialness in that boy. Now, how 'bout a slice of coconut cream pie for all you young men?"

Of course, no one turned down a slice of Mammaw's coconut pie, so we all sat down and had a piece even if it was before dinner. Papa P brought me by Grandpa Joe's and Mammaw's home a lot after taking me to see his buildings and would make sure to comment on how I made someone smile, which always prompted Mammaw to offer us all a slice of pie. It didn't take me long to figure out that going to the construction sites also meant going by to see Mammaw and getting coconut cream pie. I learned early on that having a piece of pie before dinner does not ruin anyone's appetite. At least not in my family.

Grandmother enjoyed taking me around to all of her favorite stores and showing me off as if I was some sort of plaque or trophy she had won. I didn't mind it though because as a member of royalty, you have to get used to that kind of attention. As I got older I began to understand why she enjoyed that so much. I think it reminded her of doing something like that with my mom. She certainly enjoyed bragging about her daughter when the opportunity arose, and she made sure the opportunity arose quite often, and I think she just extended that way of thinking to me.

I knew she meant well and she loved buying me things, though she got into trouble several times with my mom for doing so. She just claimed it was her duty as a grandmother to spoil her grandson and she would continue to regardless of her objections. My mother didn't argue with her, because she knew each time Grandmother was in one of those fancy stores, she always bought something nice for a friend of hers, especially if they weren't feeling well or, as she said, "just needed a pick-me-up." Even so, after Grandmother left, Mom would ask me if it would be okay to give some of those toys and clothes to those who needed them more than me. I always agreed. It didn't bother me because I had that strange sensation come over me again like I had when I was with the people at the construction site with Papa P, and I always felt like I had made someone feel a little bit better at a time when they might need to smile.

Though I seldom, if ever, actually saw the children or parents who received the toys or clothes, I could somehow catch a glimpse of their faces as they emerged from a shadow for just a second and I could see their smiles. I didn't need to tell my mother that I could see them because when I looked at her, I once again could see those shadowy smiles in her eyes. That's when I became aware that the unspoken connection to my mother was growing even stronger and I realized for the first time, that sensing how someone felt without them saying anything was connected to the way my mother and I could communicate without saying anything. I wasn't sure what or how or why it occurred, I just now knew it did.

****

Grandpa Joe taught me how to work with wood in his shop, just like he had taught my father. He often made references to those times as he showed me how to use a file and sander, and how not to cut your finger off with a saw. I know now those times with me in the workshop brought back special memories for him with my dad. Memories are like that; they come into our minds at times when we least expect them and when we really need them. Whenever they come, they always evoke strong emotions, good and bad. If you're lucky, there are more good ones than bad ones, and if and when the bad ones do come forward, you have somehow learned how to make them go away. I have reached the conclusion that those who never learn how to make the bad ones go away can become truly haunted in life. Only with help was I able to avoid being haunted.

One of my favorite things to do was watch Grandpa Joe and my father work together in the shop after dinner. I could sit there for hours and watch them turn something that looked like it needed to be in the trash heap into something that looked like it belonged in an art museum. They always included me in part of the process, showing me when screws were better than nails and when wood glue was better than either. They told me about the difference between stain and paint and varnish and sealer and when to use which and how to sand the surface of the wood smooth, making sure I paid attention to the grain of the wood. After those nights in the workshop, I would come home and talk to my mom about what we had done, until my mind and vocal cords could no longer form a word.

And when the words stopped because my lungs told me I needed to breathe more and speak less, she would ask me if I wanted her to read to me before I went to sleep. And I always nodded yes and caught up on my breathing as I lay there and rested listening to the words that surrounded me like tiny little pillows. Watching my father and his father transform wood from what looked like something to burn into something to treasure was special. Listening to my mother read a book to me was something magical. We went to all sorts of worlds together, me and mom and Dr. Seuss. To this day, whenever I pick up a Dr. Seuss book I can still see and hear my mother. All of those memories bring me joy when something prompts them to reappear, no matter how old I get.

Sometimes, my father would read to me and my mom always gave him the same book to read. It was Dr. Seuss's "Fox in Sox." I think she did that on purpose because she knew how much we would both laugh listening to him trying to read it. That book befuddled my father, a man that could figure out how to make some of the most complex and efficient machinery on the planet. I am surprised I ever went to sleep when he read that book because my mom and I were laughing so much. But he didn't mind. It didn't matter to him that the book twisted his tongue up in knots. He enjoyed watching us laugh until he finally got through the book and said it was time to go to sleep. Man, I loved Mr. Knox and the Fox. Dreamed about them all night after hearing that book and had the best of times with both of them in their world until it was time to wake up and venture back into my own.

One of the reasons I loved being read to was because I had such wonderful dreams afterward. It didn't matter what the book was, it became a part of my dreams that night. And even from the age of three, I could remember whole sentences that the characters had said and the images on the pages. I was always a part of the story, interacting with the characters and even talking with them in rhymes that weren't in the book. It wasn't until years later that I realized not everyone had dreams like that.

****

My father once told me that he loved my mother because she was the kindest and most caring person he had ever met and the more I was with her, the more evident that became. It was impossible to not see the kindness in those eyes that reminded you of the cloudless heavens above. I never heard my mother say a harsh word to or about anyone; even if someone made cruel comments to her with me standing there as if they didn't see me or just didn't care what a small child heard. She would just tell me those people didn't really mean that, regardless of what they had said, and not to worry about people who have nothing good to say about you. "Forgive and forget, Johnny," she always said. Good words to live by even though I still haven't quite mastered the concept.

I don't think my mother and I ever went downtown, whether we were shopping, or just going that way, without stopping in the Goodwill store to drop off boxes of clothes. Sometimes they were clothes that I had outgrown, or my parent's clothes that she said just took up closet space, for the most part. On more than one occasion, though, I heard my father ask where a certain shirt was and realized the answer was "gone," when he saw the shrug of my mother's shoulders. Sometimes they were my grandparent's clothes, of which Grandmother had a lot. My mother said she had to be careful when she pulled something out of those closets because Grandmother was very particular about her clothing. But I never heard Grandmother complain. I think she liked my mother going in there and "thinning the herd" as Mammaw would say when she knew we were going up to

Grandmother's house to get some clothes. "Cause once thinned, she can restock," Mammaw would add and she and my mom would laugh. They didn't have to explain what that laughter meant. I knew Grandmother liked to shop for clothes.

Besides providing clothes to the Goodwill each time we went downtown, my mother also bought extra canned food whenever she went grocery shopping, and she dropped it off at the food pantry, every time before we headed back home. Not sometimes, every time. I saw her do it a hundred and twenty-eight times, so I am certain, saying she did it every time is the truth. She told me no one should ever go to bed hungry and that I should never forget that. I never did, and when I was old enough to buy clothes and food for myself, I did what my mother had taught me and always made sure I purchased extra for those in need.

I know it may sound like I am describing my mother as somewhat of a saint, and if saints do truly exist here on earth, perhaps she was indeed one. I am not able to give a definitive answer on that subject, but what I can say, with certainty, is that if there was a fairy princess needed for any story, my mother would have been the perfect model.

That's sort of funny, in a way, as I always thought my mother could have been a model, and based on how she was viewed and talked about in high school, I think others held the same opinion. If Mammaw said the features on my face and my father's face were perfect, then the features on my mother's face were more than perfect. They were pluperfect, which is a real word. I know that because my teacher told me so that I could use that word to describe my mother. It comes from the Latin phrase "plus quam perfectum" which means "more than perfect." Mom just smiled at me when she heard it and asked how I got to be so smart and I told her I thought it came naturally.

She laughed for days about that, considering I was just nine years old when I said it, but it just so happens my father was helping me at the time with reading the book, "The Acts of King Arthur and his Noble Knights" by John Steinbeck. There were some Latin phrases in the stories, and I asked my fourth-grade teacher one day how you would say "more than perfect" in Latin and she told me. My mother told my father how I had described her and he knew immediately what had occurred. He just whispered to me later, "I couldn't have said it any better."

Besides teaching me by example, my mother provided many lessons to me and on that day when she asked me how I got to be so smart, she told me that even if I thought I was smart, the smartest people in the world didn't go around showing and telling other people they were smart. They just did things that demonstrated they were smart without making others feel less smart. The smartest people of all were those that made others feel smart too by helping them learn. I got the message. Teachers are very smart people and my mother was one of the best. My respect for teachers grew even more after that lesson.

****

My fifth year of life was a year of great change and one that resides in the portion of my brain that is always visible whenever I want to view it. Though it could have become one of those memories that haunted me, my connection to my family was so strong that it became a component of inner strength and resolve, not only for me but for my other family members. They say that everything occurs for a reason but I am not sure who "they" are. I think "they" say that because "they" need to hear those words to help them cope with whatever happened. I cannot say everything happens for a reason because I have seen things occur that defy reason. I only know what I see, what I hear, and what I think. I pray a higher power will help me understand, and in the meantime, I learned from my family how to move forward.

Like the first four years of my life, it began as a year of wonder and magic. Perhaps everything seemed enhanced because I would be going to "real" school the next year after finishing Kindergarten. I am not sure. All I can say is that for almost twelve months, life was perfect. It was a magical fairy tale moment in time, made even more magical at Thanksgiving when my mother announced to everyone that I was going to have a little sister.

That was one of the best holidays I can ever remember and it was followed by one of the worst. All the joy that surrounded us on Thanksgiving and for weeks after, disappeared the week before Christmas. My mother went to the hospital and was there for a few days. I wasn't allowed to visit her. I stayed at Grandpa Joe's and Mammaw's house for those horribly long days and nights and had the worst dreams.

I dreamt my mother was trying not to say goodbye to someone. She didn't want to leave but had no choice. I could never see the person she was talking to, but I knew it was a girl because of the outline of her shadow. And though my father told me my mom was going to be all right, I could tell that he wasn't sure that was true. I knew he was having bad dreams too, so I never mentioned mine.

My father has never lied to me. Ever. And he didn't lie to me about my mother getting better and returning home. She came home two days after she went into the hospital and though she looked tired, she hugged me and told me she was fine. She sat on the couch by me and as I looked at her face, I saw little raindrops hanging onto the corners of her sky-blue eyes as if it was one of those days when it rained while the sun was shining. She clutched my hands in hers and told me that I wasn't going to have a sister yet. "It just wasn't time."

When I asked what that meant, she said, "Sometimes life knocks you down just to see how well you do in standing back up and that is what happened to me." That's when I understood what my dreams meant. That shadow was my sister saying goodbye to my mother and I knew that came about because of the unspoken connection between my mother and me. She asked if I understood what she was saying and though I wanted to tell her about my dreams, I didn't, as I pondered that silent bond between us.

I began to wonder if that connection was meant for this moment in time in order for me to understand her sorrow and to provide her comfort. I wasn't sure, because I knew there were always more tests and trials within fairy tales that one had to overcome to survive and make it to the end of the story. But I realized it didn't matter. My mother was being tested now and I needed to be there for her. I was just hoping that this was the last trial she and I encountered but I feared it wasn't. So, I looked at her and asked if my sister had gone to heaven. Clouds formed in her eyes and those raindrops that were in the corners now streamed down her face, yet she still smiled and assured me that Johanna was indeed in heaven because "all the innocents have a special place there."

That was the first time we had ever talked about heaven and I think I asked that question because my mother's blue eyes always reminded me of heaven. Somehow I sensed that she would be comforted by talking about it. As she held me in her arms, I felt and heard her entire body sigh and I hugged her even tighter. And then my mind registered that name. My mother had mentioned a name and I whispered, "Was that my sister's name - Johanna?" She simply nodded and I whispered again, "When you read to me at night, would it be okay if you read to both me and Johanna?"

My mother could do nothing but hold me and cry at that moment, and my father came over and rubbed her back softly. None of us moved for the longest time until my father suggested that it would be a good idea for her to rest. He removed my mother's arms from around me as if she was unable to move them herself and led her upstairs. As I watched them go, I heard my mother's words again echoing within my mind: "All the innocents have a place there." I never forgot those words and whenever I needed to hear them, the words were repeated in my ears and provided me great comfort.

When my father returned, he asked me if I was okay and I just nodded yes. He said mom would be better after she rested and that I had been a very brave little boy. He asked if I wanted to do anything while she slept and I told him I would like to watch some television. Neither "The Andy Griffith Show" nor "The Beverly Hillbillies" were on TV Land, but there was a show on called "Gilligan's Island" so we watched it. I say we watched it, but I think for the most part, we just stared at the television screen. I can't even tell you what the show was about except to say there were some people stranded on an island and a skinny-looking guy named Gilligan did stupid things and a big guy they called Captain helped him fix them. I don't remember laughing at all but I don't suppose there was any laughter in us that could come out that night.

When you are four or five years old, you ask a lot of "why" questions, but I didn't do so at that time. My mother told me what happened but I didn't ask why it happened. Somehow, I knew that neither of my parents had an answer and I was afraid if I asked why I would just cause the pain that I could see surrounding both of them to linger even longer. So, I never asked.

Actually, all I could think of at that time was my father saying that I was brave and I remembered the first time I heard that word. It came from my mother while we were watching an episode of "Andy Griffith." In the show, Opie accidentally killed a mother robin with a slingshot and then raised the little birds that were left motherless in the nest. When they were ready to fly, he opened their cage and let them fly out the window. Mom said Opie was very brave because he didn't want the birds to leave but he knew he had to let them go.

That's when I knew that the unspoken connection between my mother and me was indeed there for a moment like this. My mother didn't want to let the shadow go, but she had to. She was the one being brave and strong. And though my father said I had been brave, I knew I had to be even braver when my mother came back downstairs. She needed me to help her accept that the robins had flown away. And I promised myself I would be just as strong as Opie had been.

My mother came downstairs just before dinner and sat down beside me. I asked her how she was doing and she said she was much better. I asked if I could get her something to eat or drink and she didn't ask me what, she just said that would be nice. So I went into the kitchen with my father and asked him to help me make some hot chocolate with little marshmallows in it. I carried the cup to her and she said she was hoping I would make that.

After she had her hot chocolate, I plugged in the Christmas tree lights and asked if it would be okay if I read "How the Grinch Stole Christmas" to her and she started to laugh. That laugh was one of those special memories that I can hear anytime I want and every time I hear it, I feel strong, perhaps even brave. But most of all, I feel thankful that I had that moment with my mother.

My father helped me read the book and I can remember glancing at my mother's face as we were reading, and each time she was always smiling at us with eyes that glistened. I know now that those were tearful eyes, but at the time, I thought that her eyes just sparkled like the lights on the Christmas tree. Not long after we finished the book, my grandparents came over. I could see they were all sad, but I heard my mother reassure them all that she was okay as they hugged her several times. And then she came over to me and whispered, "The sadness will go away, don't worry, Johnny." And I didn't worry because I knew she could see all the robins that had left Opie's birdcage, too, and had now filled up the tree with song.

A five-year-old doesn't understand the traumatic burden that a miscarriage places upon his parents' shoulders. I believe that is God's plan. He doesn't want children to endure that level of sadness. They cannot comprehend it, nor should they be able to do so at that age. But five-year-olds are also resilient and as such, by January, I had moved on, not realizing that my parents and family had not. I never thought to ask them how they were feeling because they appeared to be fine and for some reason, I didn't sense the sadness in my mother. Maybe it was because she had wanted me to be brave and I had steeled myself to be that for her and in doing so, I had put up an invisible shield around myself. But my mother knew she should eventually talk with me about what happened. And so, she did, just as spring was approaching.

She and dad sat with me at the kitchen table and my mother began by apologizing. I didn't think she should be apologizing for anything but just as I started to say so, I saw her eyes glistening again, and I understood that I should just stay quiet. She was asking me to be brave again without saying so and I knew I should just sit there and let her say whatever she felt needed to be said. So, that's what I did.

She first told me that she and my father should have talked with me and asked me if I wanted a brother or a sister and that in the future, they would do so. She went on to say they should have also asked me if I had any questions about what happened and so they wanted to do that now. The only question that popped immediately into my mind, even though my father had told me she was all right, and she had said she was fine multiple times was, "Are you really okay?" She grabbed my hands and held them in hers and kissed them before she said, "The robins always return in the spring, Johnny," and then smiled.

My eyes widened when I heard those words because it confirmed for me that she had seen what I had seen. The connection, that unspoken connection was there and it felt even stronger. She must have told my father about that particular Andy Griffith episode or else he would have asked all sorts of questions as to why she said that, but he didn't say a word. And I knew. I understood that she was aware I had seen the shadow of my sister saying goodbye and she knew I was going to be okay and she was telling me she was going to be okay too. She said all of that without ever saying anything more than that one sentence.

She then asked if I would want a brother or sister in the future if there was a possibility I could have one and I said, "I think I would make a perfect big brother to a sister or brother or a sister and a brother." They laughed and she said they thought the same thing and hoped one day I would have the chance to be one. And then she surprised me with some of her peanut butter cookies that she always made for me when I was sick. I told her she would have to make a lot more cookies if I had a brother and a sister. She said she was aware of that and would be able to make the necessary changes in her recipe to accommodate everyone. And then she laughed; a laugh that was just like the one I heard when I asked her if I could read her the Grinch book. That laugh had now become a part of me and would always remind me of her.

That spring was a wonderful time. I had an amazing sixth birthday with a hot air balloon ride with my parents and I got lots of cool toys and books. My mother gave me some books that were her favorites when she was growing up. They were called "The Books of Narnia" by C.S. Lewis and they soon became some of my favorites. When she read those to me at night, I never told her that she was reading them to me and Johanna, but I didn't need to. I could see that she knew it by the way her eyes seemed to dance with the smile on her face, as she looked at the pages and then down at me.

Those books generated so many wonderful dreams. After each time she read a chapter, I found myself in Narnia, having all sorts of adventurers with the Pevensie children. I loved Mr. Beaver and Reepicheep, and sailing aboard the Dawn Treader. I had many a battle with Maugrim, the wolf captain of the White Witch's secret police and I always felt comforted by the lion, Aslan. He reminded me of my mother because he was so kind and smart. And though I wished I could have seen Johanna there with me in Narnia she wasn't. But like my mother had told me, it just wasn't time yet, so I didn't worry.

I started school in the fall, and my mother and father suggested to the principal that I skip the first grade. They thought that might be a good idea because I was already very smart and reading books that older kids read. And they were right. I picked up on things quickly and the teacher was always giving me extra assignments because I wanted to learn. But I was also very shy with the other kids. My teacher, Mrs. Reed, told my parents that even though I was extremely bright, she was worried because I didn't interact more with the other children. They told her that they might have misjudged my reaction to my mother's miscarriage. I know because my parents discussed all of this with me.

They told me that Mrs. Reed said I was extremely smart and they were very proud of me. They went on to say that Mrs. Reed thought I seemed shy around the other children and my mother asked if it was because I still felt sad because of Johanna. My mom was very smart and she was doing what very smart people do, which was allowing me to find the answer myself. She knew I felt sad but she didn't tell me I was shy because of it; she asked me if that was the reason.

And I told them the truth. I did think about Johanna when I was around the other kids, especially the girls, wondering if she would have looked like any of them. My mother's eyes became teary for a moment before she said they were so sorry for not understanding all of that earlier. But in my mind, I heard her say the words again, "I love you, little Johnny," and I smiled. She told me not to worry about being shy in class and that everything would eventually work itself out and if I wanted to stay home for a little while and let her teach me that would be okay. I told them I liked school and I wanted to keep going, so that was the end of the conversation. I continued school and though I didn't make lots of close friends, I did enjoy playing with other kids and learning so many different things from Mrs. Reed.

By the time my mother was reading me the seventh and last book of Narnia, called "The Last Battle," it was December and close to Christmas. I was sure my mother would be announcing that I would soon be having a little brother or sister, but I was wrong. My mother didn't get a chance to say much to any of us that Christmas as she was in the hospital or the doctor's offices with Grandmother throughout Christmas and the following year.

Grandmother was diagnosed with breast cancer a week before Christmas. When my father explained to me what breast cancer was, all I could think of was what my mother said last year about this time. When he asked if I understood, I told him I did, and later that evening I went up to my mother and hugged her, and told her I was sorry. I asked if Grandmother would be able to stand back up anytime soon since life had now knocked her down. She took me in her arms and cried and I knew that I would stand there and hug her for as long as she needed me.

Finally, my mother looked down at me as she wiped away her tears and asked how I got to be so smart. I told her I thought it just came naturally, and she smiled and even started laughing and then said, "Johnny, you are truly a blessing to me and I am so lucky to be your mother."

I replied, "Well, I think I'm pretty lucky to be your Johnny," and she hugged me again before she answered my question about Grandmother.

She said Grandmother was very sick, even sicker than she had been herself last year, and that it would take a lot of strong medicine to help her get well. It would not be easy for her and we should pray every night that the medicine would make her better. I promised her I would do that every night before I went to sleep and that I bet Johanna was doing the same thing in heaven even though she and Grandmother had never met.

My mother said Grandmother was lucky that she had two angels looking out for her and as she did, I saw her beautiful blue eyes sparkle again. It was like I was looking at the sparkling blue lights on the Christmas tree again just like last Christmas and I felt that same sense of calm come over me when dad and I were reading the Grinch book to her. I knew right then that Grandmother would eventually "stand up again." And she did. It took a very long time though just like my mother had said, and for almost a year I could only see Grandmother for brief periods and I had to wear a mask when I was around her. It was an entire year and Christmas again, before Grandmother was, as my father said, "cured."

Oddly, time can pass like that without you being aware of it when someone you love is so sick for so long. But that's what happened that year. It was as if time stood still and moved forward at the same time. Things were done because I saw them being done, but it looked like other people were doing them instead of ourselves.

Grandpa Joe made furniture. Papa P made homes. Mammaw made pies. My dad worked. I went to school. We had birthdays and there was spring, summer, and fall, and then it was December again. And though I can't explain it, I do know that when something like that happens, your mind flips some switch, and just like that, you are aware that all that time has passed. But at the same time, you don't dwell on it, because you are happy that a loved one, who has suffered greatly, was now well, and nothing else matters.

I can remember that even though my father said Grandmother was cured, she didn't look well at all. I would even say that she looked pretty scary. She was thin and pale and though she was the same Grandmother in the way she talked, I knew that this cancer had been very hurtful to her body. It was hard for me to understand how something inside of you could change the way you looked so much. I had to ask my father about it and he told me cancer and even some of the medicine that she took to fight the cancer did that to people's bodies. I asked him if it hurt her and he said yes, it hurt her very much, but we should be proud of the way Grandmother came through it all. He told me she was a "fighter" and that we should all be very thankful this Christmas.

I also saw that my grandmother's illness had taken a toll on my mother. She looked like she was sick again and I even asked her if she was okay. She told me she was fine but all the worry that had been inside of her while her mother was sick, had just worn her out. Now that Grandmother was better, she would soon be herself again.

I told her I hadn't expected Grandmother to be so brave and my mother smiled. She said, "At times, it seems like she is more interested in Grandmother than anything else, but that's not true. She has a good heart and she loves us all very much." She then told me to "never judge a book by its cover" and explained to me what that meant - we can never tell what's inside a person by just the way they look on the outside. Another lesson that resonated within me for my entire life.

Though my father had offered to read the final Narnia book to me, I asked him if it would be okay if I waited to finish it with Mom. He didn't even bother to ask why. He knew how special it was to have her read to me and he said that would be perfectly fine. Now that Grandmother was well and we were all able to enjoy the holiday, my mother soon restarted and finished the last book of Narnia. As she read it, I told my mother that the Pevensies coming back to Narnia was like her coming back to us last Christmas and Grandmother coming back to us this Christmas.

She said that was a very smart observation and then said something that surprised me. "I promise you, Johnny, we will take time to enjoy the robins this spring." And when I heard those words, I knew she also understood how time had passed without us being aware that the days had come and gone for each one of us. And that's when I asked her if she could sense someone's feelings without them telling her how they felt. She smiled and said that type of thing "only happens in fairy tales" and then winked at me. I smiled because I knew the magic had indeed returned to the fairy tale.

There was something about knowing how time passed with us just watching it go by, as opposed to being active participants, that made me more aware that both of us were able to sense things in the world around us that no one else did. I couldn't explain how it happened or why it happened, but I knew one doesn't always understand how magic works in fairy tales. All we know is, it is there like the wind, impossible to see without its effect on things we can see and touch and hear. From that year forward, I was always aware of the wind.

I saw my first snow that Christmas, We had so much fun having snowball fights and making snowmen. Mom showed me how to make a snow angel and we made a bunch of them. Though I didn't say anything at the time, when I saw four of those snow angels together I thought about me and Johanna lying there in the snow next to mom and dad. I knew it would make my parents cry if I mentioned that, so I kept it to myself. I just stood there and smiled for a moment as I looked at my sister in the snow before my dad hit me with a snowball and the fight continued.

We had a wonderful Christmas holiday that year, and I could see Grandmother get happier and happier with each present she opened. Papa P always gave her something in a little box. This year there was a key inside and Grandmother looked puzzled. He took her by the hand and we all followed them to the door. When he opened it, there was a brand new black electric Ford Mustang called the Mach-E sitting in the driveway. Grandmother looked at him and then at us and couldn't say a thing. We could tell how happy she was as she hugged Papa P, grabbed her coat, and went as fast as she could toward the car.

Regardless of the snow on the ground, Grandmother made sure she drove that car up and down the road with Papa P and everyone else. My mom told me that car was the best medicine

Grandmother could have gotten and by the way she looked, I understood exactly what she meant.

I also got something pretty cool that year - a Razor MX400 electric motocross bike. Between that car and my motocross bike, Grandmother and I were really happy. I remember Papa P also got a new shotgun that he loved and my mother got some earrings and a necklace from my dad that made her cry, but I wasn't worried as I could tell those were tears of joy. Grandpa Joe got a lot of new saws and tools for his workshop and Mammaw got a mixer she had always wanted and some tickets to a concert to see a group called Journey. She was so excited about going to the concert and talked about it almost every day until well after the first week of January.

Papa P also had told Grandmother that he had tickets for a cruise to Alaska for the summer if she was feeling up to it by then. She said she would make sure and be ready, but she might need to do some clothes shopping first, and everyone laughed, including Grandmother. My mother gave my father season tickets to the Braves baseball games and I can honestly say I don't know who was happier with their gifts that year.

But my mother, always the teacher, took this wonderful time in our lives to remind me that the best gift that any of us got was the fact that Grandmother was no longer sick. She asked me if I understood that and I said I did because if we weren't well, we couldn't enjoy all the gifts we got. She smiled and said, "In a way, Johnny, that's true. But what is more important than any gift that we can hold in our hands, is the ability to hold each other in our hands." That statement is cataloged in my mind, along with many others from my mother, and I can retrieve it whenever necessary. I retrieved that one a lot as I grew up.

Before I knew it, spring had arrived and just as mother promised, she made sure to show me the robins in all the trees around our house. We sat outside on some days and just listened to them and talked about nature. She would ask me what I had learned in school and when the opportunity arose, would show me those things in our yard, whether it had to do with plants or animals. I had a wonderful birthday party at Papa P's house and invited all the kids from my class. The party had a carnival theme with all types of fun games. We even had a magician that did some really neat tricks and made me think about Coriakin, the wizard in Narnia, which provided me with wonderful dreams that evening.

It was my eighth birthday and my mother gave me some more books that she liked reading when she was my age. She said they were a little like the Narnia books, full of magic, and they were called "The Wilderness of Four" by Niel Hancock. Instead of Narnia, the books took place in Alanton Earth and one of the main characters was a bear called Borim Bruinthor, that had been chosen to be the "Guardian of the Light." Just that brief description had me hooked and I couldn't wait to have her read those books to me.

By summer, Grandmother had regained some of her lost weight and was looking forward to their Alaskan trip, but Papa P got some bad news before they left. I didn't know what kind of bad news until they were on their cruise and my mother and father explained everything to me.

Papa P had lung cancer and as soon as I heard the word cancer, I knew it was not good. I asked my mother if it was like Grandmother's cancer and she shook her head no. I then asked if he would get better like Grandmother and she again shook her head no. She told me that he wasn't going to take any medicine to get better. When I asked her why not, tears ran down her cheeks as she looked at me and tried to smile.

"Johnny, I know this is hard to understand but he doesn't see the need to take any medicine. The type of cancer in his lungs has spread throughout his body and he doesn't want to spend any of his time being sick from the medicine."

"But he's already sick with the cancer. I don't understand. Why doesn't he want to get well?"

"Because, Johnny, he won't get well."

I looked over at my father because it was confusing that someone I loved didn't want to get well, so I kept asking more questions.

"But you said when life knocks you down, it's just seeing if you will stand back up, right? That's what you and Grandmother did. Why isn't Papa P standing back up?"

My father came over to me and bent down so he could look straight into my eyes, and told me that Papa P was standing back up, but in a different kind of way. He said that he was standing up by telling the cancer that he would not let it ruin the time he had left with his family. My mother asked if I remembered the last book of Narnia we had just finished this past Christmas and I nodded.

"Well, this is Papa P's last battle and he is being as brave as Reepicheep was when he went into battle. And when the battle is over, he will return to all his friends and family in Heaven. Do you understand that, Johnny?"

I nodded again and started to cry because I now understood what was going to happen. My mother held me close and let me cry until I couldn't cry anymore. She wiped away my tears and told me it was okay to cry, but when Papa P came back from the cruise we needed to be brave for him like he was being brave for all of us.

"You're being tested now, Johnny," she said. "Life is knocking you down real hard and it is seeing how well you will do in standing back up."

I thought about that for a moment and I remembered the robins and how I told myself the very same thing when my mother had lost Johanna. Then I remembered the snow angels and I could sense Johanna with me, telling me to be even braver now for my mother and her parents.

"If you can do it, Mama, and Grandmother can do it, then I can do it too. Plus, I bet Johanna will be waiting to say hello to Papa P when he gets to heaven. That makes me feel a lot better about things."

My mother's face crumpled and I asked her if I said something wrong. She wiped away her tears and said no, I had said something right, but it still made her sad for the moment. She managed to smile as she ran her hands through my hair and asked me how I got to be so smart and I recognized that was my cue. I answered, "I think it just comes naturally," and she smiled again. I could tell from her eyes that the sky had returned and she would soon be okay.

Just before they returned from their trip, my mother reminded me not to mention cancer to my grandparents unless one of them brought it up. Papa P looked very happy when they got home and so did Grandmother. As they were telling us all about their trip over dinner, Papa P said he had a surprise for us. He announced that we were all going to Disneyland and Universal Studios in California just as soon as my mother and father could pack a suitcase!

I looked around the room and no one was saying a word but I could see the biggest smile on Papa P's face and Grandmother was laughing. My parents just looked at one another several times, then looked at me, then over at my grandparents, then back at each other, then at me, before they both looked back at Papa P.

My father said that he wasn't sure if he could get off from work and my grandfather just smiled. "I'll talk to the owner of the company and see what I can do for you!" and he and Grandmother laughed out loud. All the grownups then jumped up and shouted while mom hugged me and cried, "Johnny, we're going to Disneyland!" It took me a minute to understand what everyone was laughing about and then I realized that Papa P was the owner of the company and that he was making a joke when my father said he wasn't sure if he could leave work or not. And then I started laughing as I saw everyone I loved smiling and laughing. Papa P seemed about a foot taller as he embraced my parents and Grandmother.

Papa P told my parents to pack some extra suitcases because after we visited those two places, we were driving up the coastal highway in California all the way up to Washington. "California 1 then on to Highway 101 in Oregon and Washington. Jillian and I have always wanted to do that and we couldn't think of doing it without my favorite daughter, son-in-law, and grandson," he said as he came over and picked me up.

This time I understood his joke right away and I could see what my parents meant about my grandfather being courageous. He showed a little eight-year-old boy that summer that dying didn't mean you stopped living. As Papa P held me in his arms, memories of the times I had spent with him flipped on in my mind as if I was watching some of my favorite television shows.

I could see the first time he took me duck hunting. When he shot the first duck, I told him I didn't like duck hunting so much and he said that was fine. He knew I didn't like seeing the duck killed, so he said we could just sit and watch the ducks and drink hot chocolate and eat some of Mammaw's coconut cream pie and so that's what we did whenever we went "duck hunting." I could see the sunrise reflecting on the pond and us sitting there having hot chocolate and pie for breakfast. After a while, the ducks would fly over and some would land in the pond and swim around in front of us. Those were some of the best breakfasts I've ever had.

I remembered all the times he took me into the factory and to the places where he was building new homes. At those construction sites, he would let me get in the machine that made big holes and he would tell me to put my hand on his. We would dig dirt and pull it up out of the ground and move it onto a big pile next to the hole. I remembered hiking with him at Steele Creek Park and in the Holston mountains and going fishing with him in the South Holston and Watauga Lakes. I caught a rainbow trout once in Watauga Lake. I told Papa P that the fish was "well-named" and he laughed. He had a picture of me holding up that fish in his study and I know he proudly showed it to a lot of people. I dreamed a lot about Papa P that night and I never once was sad, because I knew he had stood up when life knocked him down and he was truly happy.

****

We stayed in the theme parks in California from the time they opened to the time they closed and we saw and did everything in each park. We flew through the air as we rode all sorts of different roller coasters. I had never been on a roller coaster before and I loved them. I couldn't wait to get off the one we were riding and go ride the next one. We saw ghosts and talking animals, and people and bugs and animals that seemed to come out of the movie screen and sit right next to you. I even saw a whole world of wizards in the Wizarding World of Harry Potter and I found out that there were books and movies about that place. Mom said we would read and watch them when I got a little older.

I don't think I ever laughed and screamed so much in my life. I screamed because I was a little bit scared, a little bit amazed, and a little bit thrilled all at the same time. The people who created these parks set up everything so most people felt the same way because I heard many similar screams and then laughter, followed by kids yelling, "Let's do it again!" I thanked Papa P and Grandmother over and over for taking us there and my grandfather said he was having the thrill of a lifetime. He laughed when I said I was having a "thousand thrills of a lifetime." I never understood the irony of those comments until I got older.

When we had done all we possibly could in the theme parks, we started up Highway 1 from Los Angeles, California in a big Lincoln Navigator with a roof that opened up so that everyone in the car could see the sky. It even allowed Papa P to drive without his hands on the wheel on straight parts of the road, though there weren't too many straight parts of the road. I remember him saying when we left Los Angeles, "It will be 1,073 miles to Tumwater, Washington." For some reason the word "Tumwater" made me think about all the poetry he used to read to me.

I couldn't believe I had forgotten how much he seemed to love reading poems to me, and how much I loved hearing them, but that one word triggered that memory. I didn't understand all of the poems, but they always painted pictures in my mind. Papa P could tell when I didn't understand what some of the words meant, and he would take the time to explain the words and what the poet was trying to say. I then remembered one of his favorite poems, so I asked him if we had "miles to go before we slept" which elicited an even bigger smile than I had seen in the amusement parks.

He then recited the entire poem "Stopping by Woods on a Snowy Evening" by Robert Frost. That had always been one of my favorites but became even more special after that. I asked if he knew any more poems (knowing that he did) and he said, "Yes, now that you mention it, I do." He recited another of his favorites. This poem was by Wendell Berry and though it was a short one, it was one he thought was most appropriate and he began:

"And now the remnant groves grow bright with praise,
They light around me like an old man's days."

My mother whispered that was beautiful and her eyes were filled with tears. I didn't have to ask what the poem meant. I could understand it without anyone telling me. It was about him and us and all the wonderful things we were doing at that moment in time. I could feel my mother's happiness because she knew her father was truly happy, surrounded by his family. I remember that moment in time so clearly.

Papa P never complained about being sick during the entire trip and he seemed to enjoy every second of the drive along the coastal highway or the short side trips we took. We drove along the Columbia and Snake Rivers on Highway 101 in Washington and followed the Lewis and Clark trail. I loved hearing Papa P talk about their adventures. At times, it was as if he had been there with Lewis and Clark. He knew so much about everything that occurred and made me feel like I was right there with them too. Before Papa P even mentioned her name, I could see the Indian woman that was with them, and as he started to talk about her, I was saying her name in my mind – Sacagawea. It felt like one of the connections I had with my mother for a moment and I recalled how the passage of time and our feelings had become even more connected.

We stopped to look at some memorials for Lewis and Clark and Sacagawea and I listened to my mother read about them and what they had accomplished and when they had died. But when she said Sacagawea died in 1820 at the age of 24, for some reason, I knew that wasn't true. It was as if someone was whispering to me, telling me that she didn't die then. As my parents and grandparents continued to talk, I saw an old woman in the woods looking at me, and she was pointing her fingers toward the ground.

The woman was dressed in Indian clothes. I knew that from history book pictures I had seen in school. She was wearing a tan leather top and pants. The top was dark green and had long red and tan leather strips hanging down from the sleeves and at her waist. Her hair was grayish-white with long braids that hung over her shoulder in front of her body. At the end of the braids were what looked like small leather badges with eagles on them in the same green and red colors that were on the leather top.

The leaves began to move next to her and I heard whispers again, but this time they were in a language I did not know. Even so, I could repeat them in my head. "Nanga kiidi wi-na-go." The woman pointed down again and I saw a door in the ground that wasn't there just a moment ago. When I looked back up toward the woods the old woman was gone.

I knew instinctively that the old woman was Sacagawea but I didn't know if what I was seeing was real or something that they did at the memorial to make it seem more real. Sort of like what they did at the amusement parks. I wasn't sure what to do so I looked up at my mother and she nodded her head and I knew she had seen the old woman too. She raised her finger to her lips, telling me not to say anything right then. Before getting back in the car, she pulled me aside and said she had seen the old Indian woman and had heard the whispered words but she didn't know what it all meant. She said we should keep this a secret until she could figure it all out and asked if I could do that. We had kept unspoken secrets for a long time now so I knew I could keep spoken secrets to myself just as well.

As we rode toward Tumwater, I wondered if we had seen a ghost. If it was Sacagawea, then it had to be a ghost, but I wasn't sure ghosts were real. Everything I had heard up to this point in my life suggested ghosts were just beings in fairy tales or stories of magic so even if she was a ghost, it didn't bother me at all. After all, I had learned to listen to the wind now.

I would never forget that trip with my parents and grandparents. I could look back on that trip anytime I felt sad or worried and I would be able to make the sadness or worry go away. And if my mother and I had really seen Sacagawea, well that would be something I would tell my grandchildren one day in a way that didn't make me seem crazy. Papa P never even looked like he was sick the whole time and he only talked about how wonderful it was when he got back home. He said it was one of the best times of his life. I believe it was for everyone.

Now older, I realize that in our family's worst moments, we had our best moments. All the problems that we had faced over the past two years only brought us closer together. Regardless of the pain and tragedies that occurred, we always felt like a complete family. And though my father's parents weren't physically there with us on that trip, I felt like they were there with us the entire time. It doesn't seem to make sense, but through sorrow, we found togetherness and came to appreciate the moments we shared even more.

I recounted the whole trip for Grandpa Joe and Mammaw when we got home and they were happy to share in all the excitement that just "jumped" out of my mouth. My mother didn't seem sad at all anymore and that made me even happier. I only had one dream about Sacagawea when I got back home. She was showing me and Lewis and Clark the way to go along the Snake River and the next thing I knew, we were looking at the Pacific Ocean and I woke up. It was a good dream.

****

I loved being in the fourth grade even more than the third because we did a lot more reading and learned more science and history. We studied ecology and biology and got to do some neat experiments and go on some very cool field trips to look at plants and the wildlife that lived where we lived. We also started learning about the beginning of America and the Revolutionary War and before I knew it, it was Thanksgiving.

I wasn't even thinking about the holidays but there we were, all sitting at the large dining room table in Grandpa Joe's home. He had built the table and all the chairs and we were all there getting ready to have Thanksgiving dinner. Mammaw had roasted a gigantic turkey and made many pies and casseroles and homemade bread and even homemade butter. I can remember Grandmother asking Mammaw why she would even think about making butter in this day and time and everyone laughed. Mammaw didn't say anything. She just buttered a piece of bread and handed it to Grandmother. We all watched Grandmother's eyes open wide as she took a bite of the buttered bread. "It tastes like melted honey," she said and Mammaw nodded her head as if to say, "That's why," and again everyone laughed.

Grandpa Joe asked Papa P to say the prayer before dinner and he said he would love to. He began by saying he was thankful for being able to achieve success in his work and provide for his family and the community, for meeting such wonderful friends as Grandpa Joe and Mammaw, and meeting Mammaw's pies on more than one occasion, which made everyone laugh. He then said even though he had a lot of success in his life, his greatest achievement was that he had a loving wife of more than thirty-eight years, a beautiful, kind, and generous daughter, and a brilliant grandson. I thought it was a great blessing but then I realized that no one was eating. I looked around the table and saw my mother staring at Papa P and motioning with her head toward something.

I watched Papa P nod his head and stand back up and tell everyone that he had forgotten something in the blessing. He took his glass of wine in his hand and said, "And I want to thank the good Lord for helping me find the next CEO of Packard Iron Works, Packard Business Solutions, and Packard Construction. Would you please say hello and wish him the best of luck, since he is hearing about it for the first time today? Here's to a brilliant engineer, a wonderful father and husband, and a pretty good ballplayer in his day. Thank you, Charley, for falling in love with my daughter and for being such a good man. I know you will do great things in this new role with the company."

My dad looked like someone had hit him over the head with a baseball bat. He knew he had to say something because everyone was looking at him. He finally stood up and said, "I am at a loss for words, Harold. I feel somewhat overwhelmed." He looked at my mother as if he was asking her what to say and she just smiled at him and I saw her eyes sparkling blue as if the sun was reflected off a summer pool.

Papa P, along with everyone else at the table, said in unison, "Say, yes," and my father looked at my mother and shook his head, and shrugged his shoulders. He took a deep breath and smiled at Papa P and said he would be honored to lead the companies. We all clapped and I could see sparking eyes in everyone, as they all raised their glasses toward my father and took a drink. I raised my glass of water too, a little late, but nonetheless, my father saw it and smiled at me. We had one heck of a Thanksgiving dinner that day.

I didn't think that Papa P had any more surprises in him but I was wrong. Just as we were eating dessert, he told us he wasn't giving anyone gifts for Christmas and he didn't want anyone to give him any. He wanted everyone to spend what they would on gifts for him and Grandmother and give the money to charity and everyone said that was a great idea. In fact, everyone liked the idea so much that they decided to do that for the whole family. Now I was just eight years old, and I loved getting gifts for Christmas, but it had been such a wonderful year that I even thought what Papa P said was a good idea.

Once everyone had agreed, Papa P announced another great idea. When I got out of school for the summer, he wanted everyone to accompany him and Grandmother on a trip to Tahiti. The air seemed to be sucked out of the room as if Grandpa Joe had turned on the large four-foot fan in his workshop that he said "really helped suck the fumes out of the shop" when he was working with stain or paint. No one was saying anything. I stared at my parents to make sure they were breathing and I saw my mother reach over and grab my father's hand and I saw Mammaw do the same thing with Grandpa Joe.

Mammaw's mouth hung open as if she had forgotten how to speak and Papa P winked at me and smiled. He said, "I guess by everyone's expression of enthusiasm that we will all be going and I can't tell you how happy that makes me and Jillian." I was young but I knew what enthusiasm meant and I didn't see anyone expressing anything that closely resembled enthusiasm, so I knew Papa P was making a joke, but this time no one laughed. Papa P looked at me and just shook his head and smiled again and I could see his eyes sparkling, only this time, there were no tears in them. They just sparkled, like he was some sort of magical being that had been described in Narnia or Alanton Earth.

Eventually, my mother was able to say, "Tahiti?" Papa P nodded and said it was always a dream of his to go there and added, "If we don't chase our dreams when we can do so, we will never know if dreams can be reality." My mom smiled and started to cry again as she squeezed my father's hand so hard that he eventually said, "Owww!" before she let go. Everyone else started laughing, so I laughed too. I didn't know what I was laughing about, but I didn't want to be left out of anything.

Grandpa Joe spoke up and said that he and Mammaw would love to go with them to Tahiti and then started asking questions about what we all needed to do before the trip. Papa P said we just had to make sure we were immunized or boosted and he would take care of everything else. He had already talked to a travel agent and we would leave New York on May 30th and return on June 26th. It would be a very long flight and he was going to make sure we had first-class seats so we would be comfortable. He looked at me and said he couldn't think of a better way to celebrate school being out than to fly to Tahiti.

Everyone laughed at that and I knew he didn't really mean we were celebrating school being out. It was a joke that I understood and I looked at Papa P and laughed too. This time when I looked at him, the sparkle was still in his eyes, but I could sense some sadness there clouded by all the joy on his face. Then I understood. This would be his last trip and if I understood that, then my mother was also aware.

Finally, my mother got up and hugged everyone. When she bent down to me I heard her say, "I love you, sweet and brave little Johnny," without saying a word and I smiled. Then she turned around and just like the last time when Papa P said we were going to Disneyland, she screamed. But this time, she screamed, "We're all going to Tahiti!" and everyone talked all at once about what an adventure this would be and thanked Papa P time and time again. Each time I heard them thank him, what I actually heard them saying was that they loved each other and that made me very proud to be a part of this family.

It was hard to concentrate at school between Thanksgiving and Christmas as all I could think about was going to Tahiti, especially after I located it on the world globe in my classroom. I talked to my mother a lot about the trip and said that it felt as if we were going to Narnia. She replied, "Well, maybe not Narnia. Maybe more like Neverland." When I asked her what Neverland was, she took my hand and led me into the living room where our Christmas tree stood and where we had been storing all the charity gifts.

She pulled a small present from beneath the tree and handed it to me. "I know we said we wouldn't give each other gifts this year, my little darling, but this is more than a gift. This is a book that my father gave me when I was a little girl. It's a very special and very old book. I would love to read this to you just as my father read it to me when I was young. Be careful tearing off the wrapping paper. This book means a great deal to me, as I hope it will to you."

As I began to unwrap the present, I could immediately tell the book was old by just its smell. Papa P had lots of books that smelled like that, all along the bookshelf in his study. I never thought it was a bad smell. I always thought that if time had a smell, it would be that type of smell; a smell that triggered immediate memories and one that I always found surprising and enjoyable.

The title of the book was "Peter and Wendy," by J.M. Barrie. Mom pronounced the author's name for me. She told me he was Scottish and that the book was first published in 1911. This was a first edition, which meant it was the first printing of the book, and that made it very valuable. Even though it was worth a lot of money, it was worth more because of what it meant to her. On the inside cover, it was signed "From Dad to Sarah Marie" and then "From Mom to my little Johnny."

She asked if I remembered what we saw and heard when we were in Washington and I nodded yes. She said the words we heard were "nanga kiidi wi-na-go" and they meant "hear cat lily" in Shoshone Indian language. When I asked her what that meant she said that there was an Indian character in this book called Tiger Lily and she was sure that the spirit of Sacagawea wanted us to read this book. She thought it was because the book was over a hundred years old and meant a great deal to her and her father and that's why the spirit of Sacagawea had visited with us. That and because we both could see and hear feelings before feelings.

I asked if we could wait and read the book while we were in Tahiti and maybe ask Papa P to read some of it to both of us. My mother thought that was a beautiful idea. And as if we were reading from scripts, she asked me how I got to be so smart. And this time, along with the appropriate words of response, I shrugged my shoulders as I replied and we hugged.

The day before Christmas, my family delivered clothes, toys, and food to Salvation Army Centers throughout the Tri-Cities areas and to all the food banks. I saw more smiles that day than I have ever seen before, with just as many coming from my family as from the people that received the gifts. I thought about that the whole day and night and when Christmas came around the next morning, I was surprised, but I didn't miss having gifts at all. I remembered what my mother had said about last Christmas when Grandmother was no longer sick. And my mother was right, having each other to hold onto was more important than any gift we could receive.

After Christmas, Mom and I read the final book of "The Wilderness of Four." It was called "The Road to the Middle Islands" and in it, Olthan the Otter and Borim the Bear, along with characters from the earlier books, all come together to destroy the darkness that was threatening to take over Alanton Earth. The title of the last chapter was called "A Final Crossing" and as she read those words, a strange feeling came over me and I saw the connections that were all taking place. I could tell my mother realized the significance of that moment too. My grandfather was fighting "The Last Battle" as described in the books of Narnia and now we were reading about "A Final Crossing" and getting ready to cross over thousands of miles of ocean to a place my mother had referred to as Neverland. Magic now surrounded us.

****

I learned something new and exciting in school every day. Some of my classmates complained about all the different things we were expected to learn, but I never felt that way. My brain felt like an empty library and it cataloged each new entry into my "database." In math, we were doing multiplication and division with fractions and learning about weights, volumes, time, and temperature. We studied geography, especially in our state of Tennessee, and what east, west, north, and south meant and what was in those areas, both close by and far away. We learned a lot about animals, including what cold-blooded and warm-blooded animals were, and what vertebrates and invertebrates meant.

For some reason, I loved hearing those words. I think they reminded me of the words that Sacagawea had said and I couldn't get home soon enough to tell my mom and dad that we were warm-blooded vertebrates (and what that meant), but that the invertebrate animals made up 95% of all animal species and that there were 8.7 million species of animals on earth! I then demonstrated (using what I learned in math) that meant there were 8,265,000 invertebrate animal species, most of them insects, on earth. I'm not sure they were surprised by any of the information but I could tell they were impressed with what I had learned. Looking back, I think it was just one of those moments when the parents get to think to themselves once again how special their child is. I really wasn't doing anything that amazing with my math skills, but they made me feel like I was by the happiness that radiated from their faces.

After dinner, we spent all evening looking up what kind of insects lived in Tahiti. We learned that forty new species of beetles had been discovered there and no poisonous animals lived on the island. I asked my dad if we could go look for some of those beetles when we got there and he said that we certainly could but we had to make sure Mom went with us. I don't know why he said that but when I looked at her she seemed to have a scowl on her face. But then she smiled and said she would love to go on a beetle safari in Tahiti. That night, I dreamed about hunting beetles in Neverland.

Two of my favorite subjects in school were reading and writing. I didn't especially like learning about nouns and verbs and adjectives and adverbs and conjunctions, even though I knew it was necessary to know about those things in order to write and understand what we were reading. We were asked to write a story and I wrote about our trip to California and visiting Disneyland and Universal Studios and going along the coastal highway from California into Washington. I loved writing the part about going along the Lewis and Clark trail since we had recently studied it in class and I described the monuments to them and Sacagawea.

I tried to add as much history into my story as I knew and when I read the story aloud in class, I noticed my teacher smile out of the corner of my eye when I mentioned all of those facts. And then I talked about Sacagawea and how important she was to the expedition. I could see that my teacher liked that too but then she looked a bit confused when I said that the monument suggested she died when she was 20 but I was pretty sure she had lived to be over ninety years old and died of old age.

Later that day after class ended, she asked me why I had said that about Sacagawea. I told her that history wasn't entirely sure when she died and she looked at me oddly and said she didn't think that was true. But when she looked up Sacagawea on the computer, she found that some indigenous people believed that she had come back and married into a Comanche tribe and then returned to her home and the Shoshone tribe where she died when she was 95. "Interesting," she said but then added that all the data and records show she died when she was 20. I just shrugged and said I preferred what some of the Indian storytellers believed. My teacher smiled when she heard me say "storytellers," because she knew I loved reading stories with "magic" in them. She gave me an A on my paper for being so thorough and such a good "storyteller." I smiled on the way home as I thought about the old woman in the trees waving at me and how she helped me get an A on my paper.

My birthday in April came quickly that year and I turned nine years old. My father gave me a wonderful book by John Steinbeck called "The Acts of King Arthur and His Noble Knights" and offered to read it to me before we left for Tahiti. (That's the same book with Latin words that I mentioned earlier which prompted me to tell my mother she was pluperfect). I loved books about knights and I told Dad I looked forward to reading this one and asked him if I could read the book to him instead this time. I had never offered to do that and he said that he would love to hear me read the book. I doubted I could read all the words and he knew that too, but he didn't discourage me.

Papa P gave me the whole set of Harry Potter books and Grandpa Joe made me a bookcase to hold them. He even signed and dated the bottom of the bookcase with his name and the date that he made it. I thanked and hugged them at least a dozen times for those wonderful gifts. Grandmother gave me a bunch of clothes for the trip to Tahiti and Mammaw made a strawberry cake for me. No one in our family had ever had a strawberry cake before because she had never made one. Believe me, after that cake, she realized she would be making many more of them.

We spent my birthday at the lake and went swimming although it was only 65 degrees. Dad and I told mom that the water wasn't that cold, hoping she would jump in - and she did. We both thought we'd hear a loud scream as she came up from under the water but she just swam around us and said we were right, it felt great. My dad and 1 stared at each other until my mom said we were all idiots if we stayed in that water much longer. We were all laughing as we swam back to the boat and dried off.

All in all, it was a great day, and right after I got in bed, Mom came in and said she had not given me my birthday present. I acted like I had no idea she hadn't given me anything by saying, "Oh, I didn't notice," but that bit of acting on my part wasn't that good. She just started tickling me until I said, "Okay, I noticed, I noticed!" She reached behind her back and told me to close my eyes and open my hand. I opened my eyes when I felt her put something in my hands and saw a pocket knife. She told me that this pocket knife was another gift that her father had given her when she was my age. He had told her that every 9-year-old child, boy or girl, should have their own pocket knife.

I asked her what she used it for and she said she used it for all sorts of things: looking up under rocks or moving around big bugs or frogs, carving things out of wood, and, if necessary, using it to protect herself. I asked her what she would need protection from. She replied by saying she never knew what she might need protection from, but the fact that she had something to keep her safe made all the difference in the world.

I thought about what she said for a moment and then asked her if I should be scared. She said that's not what she meant nor what her grandfather had meant when he had given her the knife. She told me about the man that wrote the books of Narnia. He once said, "When I was ten, I read fairy tales in secret and would have been ashamed if I had been found doing so. Now that I am fifty, I read them openly. When I became a man, I put away childish things, including the fear of childishness and the desire to be very grown up."

I looked puzzled and she went on to explain what C. S. Lewis had meant. She told me that I loved reading about all these magical worlds but that when I got older, I may not care to do so anymore. She said the pocket knife can't protect me when I am an adult but it may help me remember how strong it made me feel when I was a child and how much I enjoyed life. She said I should never lose my ability to see the beauty and wonder in the world around me and to always dream like poets and authors. By doing that, she said I would have the best of both worlds when I was all grown up. This pocket knife would protect those dreams for me.

Those memories of my mother and her father were attached to that pocketknife and she always knew she would be loved and protected by him; just as I now knew, I would always be loved and protected by her. I looked at the pocket knife again, and it looked almost brand new. "I'll teach you how to take good care of it," she said, as I examined the knife. She had sensed my question before I even asked it and I could tell that this knife did indeed have special properties.

I asked if any of the characters in the new book had a knife and she said that the main one, called Peter Pan, had a knife and a sword because he needed them to fight off pirates. My eyes widened as I heard the word pirates and she laughed. "Captain Hook was a mean pirate and wanted to kill Peter Pan who had cut off his hand, which was eaten by a crocodile. From that point on, the crocodile chased after Captain Hook to finish his meal." It was as if she was on TV doing a trailer for an upcoming movie and she knew exactly what to say. I couldn't wait to read about Peter Pan fighting off pirates and Captain Hook and the crocodile. And she was right about the pocket knife. Just knowing that I had my mother's knife with me under my pillow, made all the difference in the world as I swam through a sea of crocodiles and fought with pirates in my dreams that night.

From my birthday to the end of the school year, my favorite activity was reading poetry and trying to figure out what the poet was saying in their poems. I loved "Trees" by Joyce Kilmer because it made me think about all the wonderful trees at my grandparents' home. "Paul Revere's Ride" by Henry Wadsworth Longfellow was another favorite because it seemed to tie into all the history I had learned about the Revolutionary War and our Declaration of Independence. "Sick" by Shel Silverstein made me laugh a lot. I read that one to my parents several times and they thought it was funny too. At first, I thought all poems rhymed, but we read a poem by Nikki Giovanni called "Knoxville, Tennessee" and I loved it too. It didn't rhyme but it made me think about summer and running around on my grandfather's land and eating barbecue. The teacher said when a poet makes you think about things after you read their poem, then they were very successful at what they wrote. And then I remembered Papa P telling me the same thing. The teachers and Papa P were both right and all those poets were very successful in my opinion.

School ended and I felt like I had grown so much in just a year, and not just from everything I had learned. I had also grown a couple of inches and was fairly tall for a nine-year-old. And just as Papa P had promised, we flew out of New York on May 30th, all the way to San Francisco before we took another plane to Papeete, in Tahiti. We left New York at eight in the evening and the trip was almost sixteen hours long because we had a three-hour delay in San Francisco. Everyone slept on the plane and when we arrived in Papeete, it was the following day at seven in the morning.

After landing, we had another thirty-five-minute ferry ride to our rental home on the island of Moorea. You would think everyone would have been tired, but no one was. The adults had just as much energy as I did as we saw what I could only describe as Neverland, even though I hadn't even read about it yet. I suddenly knew why Papa P had picked this place.

He had taken my mother to Neverland in her mind when he read to her when she was his little girl. Now he was taking her to Neverland for real and though she may be a mother now, she was still his little girl. She had told me Papa P loved that book and I know he had searched for a place in the world that would allow them to see it in person before he was gone. Thinking back, I know he could not have selected a better place.

We stayed in a place called the Villa Iris on the island of Moorea. Papa P had rented a house with a view of the mountains on one side, and as you walked through the tropical gardens in the back, you soon found yourself on your own private beach. On just the first day, I think I heard the words "beautiful" and "paradise" twenty-seven times, and each time I heard them, I smiled, because the adjectives were so appropriate.

Papa P had arranged for a chef to come and prepare our meals each day. We had grilled tuna for dinner that evening along with lots of fresh fruit, rice, a sweet potato casserole of some kind, and chocolate éclairs for dessert. I asked Papa P if we were going to eat like that for every meal and he laughed and said, "I hope so!" We watched the sun go down on the beach and then went to bed. I don't think I even dreamed that night. I just slept for ten hours and thought this must be what it is like to live in Neverland.

We spent the next week exploring the island. Sometimes we took guided tours into the mountains and the dark green tropical forests that exploded with color from the birds and flowers, or we explored the beach and found more shells than anyone could ever imagine existed. My parents went scuba diving and though I wasn't old enough to do that, they did arrange for me to go snorkeling with them. I saw fish that looked like Dr. Seuss had seen them many years ago before he wrote some of his books. They painted my dreams for several nights after swimming with them.

During the second week, Mom and I went to the beach in the mornings and she would read from "Peter and Wendy" to me. Sometimes Papa P came with us and he read the book to both of us just as we hoped he would. He seemed so happy when he was doing that and when I looked at my mother, her eyes reminded me of the blue waves that flowed onto the ivory-white beaches and I could sense she was full of joy. After reading, we often took a sailboat ride or went fishing or hiking, and when we came back, most everyone took a nap. But when everyone else rested, I continued to read. My mother was right. I loved that book.

I imagined myself as Peter Pan with the ability to fly. It seemed like my vision and hearing became even sharper, just like Peter's. But no matter how hard I tried, I couldn't imagine things into existence as Peter did except in my dreams. My dreams became even more vivid as we got farther into the book. Whenever Papa P was reading to us and Wendy's name was mentioned, I would look over at my mother and tell myself "that's what Wendy would look like if she was all grown up."

Sometimes Mom would find me on the beach pretending to fight Captain Hook with my pocket knife. I would stop when I heard a bird and tell my mother what the bird was saying. She laughed at me and asked, "Should I start calling you Peter instead of Johnny since you seem to be part animal and part fairy now?" Each time, I replied that I was indeed a "betwixt and between" and she would grab me as we laughed and ran in and out of the water along the beach.

One night as Papa P was reading a part about Tiger Lily, I had the strangest feeling again, as if we were being watched. I thought I saw a young Indian girl with long black hair in braids that fell over her the front of her shoulders, standing on the shore. I stood up and started to say something, but then looked down and thought I saw my shadow shake his head no. I looked back at the water and the little Indian girl was gone. I wasn't sure if I had seen another ghost or not but I didn't care. I reminded myself I was in Neverland and that type of thing could be considered normal as I continued to listen to Papa P read.

The next day, Papa P asked me to walk with him into the tropical forest. We stopped at a bench atop a small hill where the woods provided a clearing to see the mountains. He said that I was going to need more books to fill up my new bookshelf that Grandpa Joe had made me. He had heard I enjoyed reading poetry and wanted to give me two of his favorites. He handed me a book titled "Robert Frost Early Poetry Collection," and one called "A Timbered Choir" by Wendell Berry. He said that he had read these poems many, many times in his life and hoped I would too.

I asked him if the "miles to go" poem was in the Robert Frost book and he smiled and said yes. There was another one he thought I would like too and he began to read to me "The Road Not Taken." He asked me if I understood it and I told him I thought I did. I thought it meant that everyone should explore the world. He laughed and said, yes, that was one part of it and the other part was that I should also never be afraid to try new things. I nodded and thought about what my teacher had said about poetry and realized Robert Frost had accomplished his goal. He then read me a poem by Wendell Berry that had no title. He didn't ask me what that poem meant because he didn't feel that it was necessary. He was right.

After reading the poem, he put his arm around my shoulder and we sat and listened to the birds and looked at the mountains. I have read that poem many times since that day and I can see Papa P sitting next to me when I hear the words in my mind:

"Now, surely, I am getting old,
for my memory of myself
as a young man seems now
to be complete, as a story told.
The young man leaps, and lands
on an old man's legs."

On June 23rd we were near the end of "Peter and Wendy" and Papa P asked my mother to finish the last chapters for him. He said his stomach was a little upset and he wanted to rest for a while before dinner. He hugged her and asked me if I had enjoyed the book. I told him that I had never expected to see Narnia in real life or Alanton Earth, but that I had now seen Neverland and it would stay in my heart and mind forever. He said, "Spoken like a true Peter," and kissed me on my forehead. As he walked back inside the house, I looked at my mom and saw that she was crying. I cried too because we could both sense that Papa P's days would soon be over.

My mother asked me to read the final chapter as we sat there together. She cried some more, but also smiled as she listened. When I was finished, I pulled out the pocket knife and said, "He just came back to Neverland. He never lost his ability to see the beauty and wonder in the world around him and he always dreamed like a poet and author," and then I showed her the knife. We hugged and went into Papa P's room where all of us stayed with him that night. He died just after midnight.

Before we left for Tahiti, I believed Papa P would come back with us, but I was wrong. He had left a goodbye note for us all but Grandmother could not read it, so my mother did. Papa P wrote, "Do not mourn for me. I am a lucky man, as in my life I have truly seen paradise on earth and I will soon see paradise in death." He had arranged with the island government to have his body cremated. Just before we left to return home, we sprinkled some of his ashes into the water and watched them disappear into the ocean. Papa P officially died June 24th in Tahiti but he stayed with me forever.

We returned to Bluff City and Grandmother retreated into her home and asked my mother and father to handle the notices required for Papa P's death. I wanted to tell Grandmother that I had always thought Papa P had stood tall when life had knocked him down, but she did not want to be with anyone. My mother said there was "too much sadness on her shoulders for her to carry right now."

She was right. The few times I saw Grandmother during that first week back home, I could tell there was a deep sorrow inside her. I couldn't help but think about Peter and Wendy when I looked at Grandmother because, on some days, it looked like she had lost her shadow and was uncertain as to what to do next. And other times, it appeared as if her shadow had grown so much, that she had disappeared within it.

My parents talked about how to help Grandmother and decided to hold a celebration of life to honor Papa P. My mother was hesitant at first but as she listened to my father talk about the people at work and how they felt about my grandfather, she realized it was something she should do not only for Grandmother but also for those people whom my grandfather had worked with and had called friends.

She talked with those who knew Papa P well and they told her she needed to plan for a large group. My father suggested using a warehouse on the grounds of Packard Iron Works where they stored equipment. They could move the equipment and make the place look nice, and it was large enough to accommodate hundreds, if not a thousand people. My mother thought Papa P would like that, so the event took place in that warehouse on July fifteenth.

Grandmother was reluctant about the service, but Mom convinced her it was the right thing to do. She was overwhelmed by the number of people who came. She shed a tear at first upon seeing the lines of people who wanted to share some words with her and my family, but I could tell the thousands of words she heard from the thousands of people that came made a difference in the way she thought and felt from that point forward.

Life for my mother and Grandmother slowly regained some normality, but life for my father was anything but normal. He spent long hours at work learning how to manage all of Papa P's businesses, but even so, he always had time for me on the weekends to listen to me read him the book about King Arthur and His Noble Knights. I loved the book and had wonderful dreams about being a Knight and helping all those that needed me to save a son or daughter from a dragon or an evil wizard.

****

My fifth-grade year started with a bang and I truly mean that. On the first day of class, my teacher, Mr. Burke, had a scientist from East Tennessee State University come and demonstrate chemistry experiments that made smoke, fire, and loud bangs. He called himself Professor Galaxy and he came back many times to do more experiments. He also show us beautiful pictures taken from the Hubble Telescope and explained things to us about space and the planets.

Every day when I got home from school, I told my parents about what I had learned; whether it was math, including geometry, (which I loved) or about the animal kingdoms and the science of the human body, or ancient civilizations or the Civil War or World War I and II, or how our government is set up to work, or new books we were reading. I loved school and my mother told me she was glad and could tell I was happy but one day she asked me if I would like to invite some friends over to the house to play.

As soon as she asked that question, I knew she was remembering Mrs. Reed telling them I was shy around my classmates a few years ago. I hadn't thought of it again until she said that. I guess I should have told them I no longer wondered if some of the girls looked like Johanna. I also should have told them I was having fun with the kids in my class and I wasn't as shy as I once was. It just never occurred to me that my school friends could become friends away from school. And then I remembered what Papa P had said about not being afraid to try new things.

So, I did what mom suggested and I started asking friends over to our house and eventually became the best of friends with a boy and a girl. Her name was Ann and his was Martin. We all loved the books of Narnia and often pretended we were the Pevensie children having adventures. Ann knew a lot about Harry Potter and she often brought aspects of those books into our journeys of the imagination. They were both very familiar with the story of Peter Pan and so we also played in Neverland too. When I was much older, I came to find out that Ann and Martin were the names of two of the real children on whom C.S.

Lewis based the Pevensie children in the books of Narnia. Once again, a magical connection had occurred and this time I hadn't even noticed the wind.

I don't know how time moved so fast, but it was once again Thanksgiving. My mother warned me that Grandmother might be sad since this would be the first Thanksgiving without Papa P. She was right. Grandmother did seem sad although she didn't cry. When I looked at her at the table, I could see her sitting there, but she didn't really appear to be there at all. It was a strange feeling that only grew stronger when I saw her again as Christmas approached.

Mom was worried about Grandmother and asked my dad if we could do something different for the holidays to cheer her up. He suggested she might need a change of scenery for this first Christmas without Papa P, so we went to Gatlinburg for Christmas. It snowed four inches in Gatlinburg two days before Christmas and seeing the snow seemed to make Grandmother happy. She even laughed when she saw Grandpa Joe and I snow tubing, and though Mammaw tried to get Grandmother to go ice skating with all of us, she said she would just sit back and watch us fall. She was right not to try it because we all fell down a lot. We suffered a lot of bruises and soreness but no one broke anything and the laughter healed everything that hurt.

For Christmas, Grandpa Joe gave everyone boxes he made out of mape, which is a Tahitian chestnut tree. That kind remembrance of our last trip together made Grandmother smile a lot. I asked him if he would show me how to make boxes like that and he said he'd be happy to do that as soon as we got back home. Grandmother gave us all nice clothes and gave my other grandparents an Alaskan cruise. She told them she hoped they would enjoy it. They hugged Grandmother and told her they were sure they would have a grand time.

My father gave my mother a special gold necklace made of three rings of white, yellow, and rose gold. He said the three rings represented the three of us and she cried. My mother gave my father a new leather chair or at least a picture of a leather chair that she bought him for his office. It would massage his back and neck and he said he was sure he would love it. My parents gave Grandmother a pearl necklace that they had bought in Tahiti and had been saving for her for Christmas. Grandmother cried a lot when she got that gift. I didn't need to wonder if she was sad or happy. I knew she was both.

My parents gave me all the Harry Potter movies for Christmas and I was thrilled. All in all, it was a wonderful Christmas. Though I missed Papa P, I remembered that poem as I looked at the mountains outside of our cabin window and thought about the day when we looked at the mountains in paradise.

I was excited to get back to school and tell Ann and Martin that I got all the Harry Potter movies. They said we should have a movie night and watch them together, which we did more than once. Work occupied a lot of my father's time and though I was having lots of fun in school, I could tell my mother was concerned about something. When I asked her what was wrong, she said she was afraid Grandmother was falling into a deep sadness. I asked what we could do to help her and she said the best thing would be to just show her that we loved her. I made sure I stopped by every day to talk to her about school or the latest book I was reading, and even though I knew she appreciated me coming by, I could see a shadow of sadness that draped her shoulders like a shawl that provided her no warmth against the cold and it frightened me. I told my mother what I had seen and she just pulled me into her arms and said she was frightened too but we needed to stand by her as much as she would let us and I told her I understood.

Even with our encouragement, Grandmother seldom left the house anymore. When mom wanted to take her shopping in Knoxville or some other nice places that she liked, she said she didn't want to go. She did go out to eat with us on occasion and appeared to still enjoy going to nice restaurants, but once we got home, she just told us good night and went inside her house. Mom asked her several times to come and spend some time at our house but she never would.

She did come to my tenth birthday party in April and all my friends and I had a great time riding my new go-cart. My dad rented several other go-carts so we could have races. He made sure all my friends' parents came to the party too. He didn't want anyone to get hurt in the go-carts so he always had a parent "riding shotgun" with us. It didn't matter to us. We all had fun riding on the dirt track my father had created on his parents' land.

Grandmother enjoyed the strawberry cake that Mammaw made and I even got her to go on a ride in the go-cart with me, but after the party, she didn't come out of her house again. I can remember seeing her several times in her home and each time I thought back to when she had cancer in her body. She looked just as sick now as she did then, even though she didn't have cancer. But unfortunately, her body could not heal itself this time.

Grandmother died one year to the day after Papa P died, June 24th. My parents held a private graveside ceremony with just family and Grandmother's favorite preacher in attendance. Only my mother and the preacher spoke. Mom talked about how much she would miss her mother but she took comfort in the fact that she was now with her true love in heaven. The preacher read some Bible verses but the one that I still remember to this day was from Psalms: "The Lord is close to the brokenhearted and saves those who are crushed in spirit."

After the funeral, my mother told me that Grandmother died of a broken heart and I think she was right. She didn't like standing up in the world without Papa P next to her and even though she tried, she couldn't do it. I didn't think there was anything wrong with that. She loved my grandfather very much. I had read about broken hearts in many fairy tales and books, so I knew she wasn't the first person who had become sick due to having one, and sometimes, there isn't enough magic in the world to heal them. I would always miss Grandmother and I never faulted her for leaving us. I understood.

****

My parents were concerned about me because I had just lost both my grandparents and that was a lot to handle for a young boy. So, that night they sat with me and asked how I was feeling. I told them I was sad but I knew things would get better. They said that they had never really spoken to me about church or God because they wanted me to find those answers on my own, but asked if I had any questions about life or death or life after death.

I understood no one lives forever but Papa P had said he thought he would see paradise when he died. I asked my mother if that's what the church taught and she nodded her head yes. I told them that the words the preacher had read from the Bible about Grandmother being brokenhearted and that the Lord saves those who have a crushed spirit were very pretty. I said I'd like to hear more of those words from the Bible that made people feel better, so I asked if we could go to church some Sundays and they agreed.

I asked if we could go to a couple of different churches seeing how I thought they all wanted us to get to the same place here and "after here." Mom hugged me and asked how I got to be so smart and I said what was expected as I shrugged my shoulders. They both smiled and my mother said we could certainly go to any church I wanted whenever I wanted to go. So that's what we did. To this day, I'm not sure what religion I am because I never thought that was important. I just wanted to be like my mother and be kind and friendly to all people. And that's what I tried to do. For a while.

We visited a lot of churches after Grandmother died. We went to the one she went to all the time and then to the one that my other grandparents attended and then to others all around the

Tri-City area. I enjoyed them all, even the ones that asked you to get up and down on your knees to listen to a prayer or to pray. And my parents always asked me the same thing after every service. "Did you enjoy it and what did you learn?" And I said the same thing every time. "Love and respect each other." Even if the sermons spoke of Hell or sin or going to Hell, they always ended up the same way by saying that God would want us to "love and respect each other." I liked hearing those words, no matter how long it took to hear them.

At the end of the summer, my mother had a surprise for us. She had read about a production of "Peter Pan" in New York City that she knew I would love to see and thought it would be a great vacation for us before I went back to school. I jumped up and down and asked when we were leaving.

She had already made hotel and plane reservations and we would leave the next Thursday, spend the day Friday seeing a little of New York, go to the play on Saturday, and then come back home on Sunday. I asked her if the play was anything like the book and she said she wasn't sure because she had never seen it. I was surprised that Papa P had not taken her to see the play since they loved the book so much but he never had. They had seen the Disney version of the story but not a real live play and she was looking forward to this just as much as I was.

That made me even more excited and I told her I needed to get busy reading. She didn't ask me what I needed to get busy reading. She knew I would reread "Peter and Wendy" over the next week so I would be ready for the play. She laughed and said to let her and dad know what they should be on the lookout for during the play and I said I would. But as I ran off to my room, I knew she was just making a joke. She knew that book a lot better than me and she was just happy that I was so excited. Mom was smiling as she watched me run off to read and I could see a calmness in her eyes that I hadn't seen since Grandmother had been put to rest. She was happy and that was even better than going to the play, even though I did count the days until we left and I dreamed about Peter and Wendy every night.

We flew first class to New York and while we were on the plane Mom warned me and Dad about not being too surprised when we saw the place we were staying. For some reason, I felt like she was talking to me like she did when I was learning things as a toddler (like telling me that peanut butter was not that easy to paint with) but I wasn't sure why she was talking to dad like that. When we took the large black limousine to the hotel and were escorted to our room, I understood why.

We were staying on the 20th floor of the Plaza Hotel on Fifth Avenue in the Grand Penthouse suite. The first floor of the suite overlooked Central Park and as you took the staircase up to the second floor, there was a large terrace that seemed to look through all of New York. I had never stayed in a hotel room with two floors and I could tell my father had not either. Mom said she had spent a little extra on this trip but that neither of us should get used to staying in places like this all the time.

And then I smiled as I realized that she had never stayed in a hotel room like this either. She was doing this in memory of Grandmother. This type of room was just like Grandmother - expensive and full of class. The room even came with its own butler, which she would have loved. I knew Grandmother was smiling down at my mom for doing something like this and I could tell Mom sensed her presence too.

We went to the Statue of Liberty soon after we got settled into the two-story hotel room. On the way there, I shared what I had learned about it. The statue had been designed by a man named Bartholdi and given to us by France to celebrate our first 100 years as a nation. The seven rays on the top of Lady Liberty represent the seven continents of the world and I thought that was very fitting since people from all seven continents made America their home. "My son, the walking encyclopedia," my father said.

When we got there, mom asked if we were both ready to walk. My father asked where we were walking and she said to the top of the statue. "It's only 393 steps to the crown. Surely a baseball player could do that many steps." And though she didn't use the words, "I double dare you," I heard it as if she did. So, we walked. It took us about thirty minutes to make it to the top and as we started up the spiral staircase toward the crown, I looked back at my mom and dad and they were holding hands and smiling. It was the best walk up a flight of stairs that I had ever been on in my life. It's unfortunate, but I don't think I ever heard any other person there say they were excited about going up that flight of stairs. I think that's because they just weren't doing it with the right people at the right time in their life.

On the way back to the hotel, Mom told us that there were 25,082 restaurants in Manhattan, where the hotel was located. If we ate three meals a day, it would take us 22.9 years to eat in each restaurant. I knew she had gathered those statistics just for me and she asked what I thought of them. I said we needed to get busy. She said she already had dinner planned for the evening and she had the Uber driver let us out five blocks away from the hotel.

As we walked along the street, we ran into a vendor that sold hot dogs and Mom said, "Dinner is served!" We each got a hot dog, with ketchup and mustard, and a bottle of water. I have to admit, it was a really good hot dog but I was still hungry. We walked another block and we bought the largest pretzel I had ever seen from another vendor and it was even better than the hot dog. And for dessert, we stopped at an ice cream shop that made its own ice cream. I had my first banana split at that shop with chocolate, strawberry, vanilla ice cream, marshmallows and extra whipped cream, and three cherries on top.

My mother had a chocolate sundae and my dad had some pistachio ice cream. I think they both said their ice cream was good, but I wasn't sure because eating that whole banana split made me somewhat deaf. That had never happened before, but then, I had never had a banana split before. I'm not sure if that happens every time you eat one, because I have never had another one since that day.

The next morning, we went to the 9/11 memorial, and just like the day before, I was amazed at what I was seeing. This was a different kind of amazement, though, that came from deep inside me and made me feel very sad. 2,982 names were engraved on the bronze memorial where they found the victims. My mother said the two waterfalls were the largest man-made waterfalls in the world, but all I could think of was that they needed to be even bigger because they reflected a lot of tears. We spent over two hours there just looking and not saying much to each other, but it was one of those times when you didn't need to talk because the voices that were present said more than enough.

I felt like I was back in Washington again when I saw Sacagawea in the woods, but this time, I didn't see only her. Many others were walking around but none of them were sad. I wanted to ask my mother if she saw them too, but I didn't. I heard the people tell me it wasn't necessary and that everything would be okay. I nodded my head in agreement because if anyone could know that, it would have been them.

Mom said we had one more thing to do that afternoon before we ate at a very nice restaurant and then went to the play, and that was to go for a carriage ride in Central Park. The man who drove the carriage was named Henry and he was very knowledgeable. I think Mom had prompted him to recite some statistics about the park and I loved hearing about the 170 different species of trees in the park and that the Sugar Maple, Ash, and Black Tubelo were the most stunning trees in autumn. He took us by the Pool, Tavern Green, the North Meadow, and Strawberry Fields. Just as we were approaching what he called the Ramble, where Belvedere Castle was located, a loud explosion went off in front of the horse and spooked it, throwing Henry off onto the ground.

As the horse galloped past the castle, my father climbed to the front seat of the carriage and got hold of the reins of the horse and somehow slowed him down. All I could think of as I watched him do that, was "The Noble Acts of King Arthur and His Knights." I could imagine everyone cheering his name, "Sir Charles of Fulwider," even though only a few people saw it happen. They did clap, but they didn't yell out that name.

When he got the horse stopped, he turned the carriage around and went back to where we had been, and we found Henry sitting there on the ground. Some teenagers had thrown some firecrackers in front of the horse, thinking it would be funny, but it wasn't funny at all. Henry said he just had some bumps and bruises but he would be fine. He apologized for the incident and told us our ride would be free.

My mother said we had an even more exciting ride than expected and not only paid Henry for the ride but tipped him a couple of hundred dollars, telling him that she hoped he would be okay and thanked him for showing her that she had married a heroic knight. My mother saw the same thing as I did in my father but for some reason, I think she saw something else too. I don't know why I had that feeling. I just did and it made me feel a little strange, but I didn't worry. I was too excited about where we would soon be going.

My mother had one last surprise for me back at the hotel. I followed her upstairs to the terrace where I saw two plastic swords. One looked like a cutlass that Captain Hook carried and the other like a rapier that Peter Pan used. I didn't ask how or what, I just ran over and grabbed the rapier, and cried, "Defend yourself, you scurvy pirate!" My mother laughed as she picked up the cutlass and we began sword fighting.

I jumped on and off the chairs, trading blows with my mother as we thrust and parried around the porch. I wasn't even aware I was so close to the edge of the terrace when I jumped onto a large table and lost my balance. Just as I was falling, I felt my mother grab me and then she fell over the rail. I watched her fall toward the ground but all I could see was Wendy flying away from Peter. I heard my father yelling as he came running and though I could see his arms around me, I could not feel them.

****

I don't remember much of what happened after that. The next thing I remember is waking up in my room several days later and finding Grandpa Joe sitting beside me. When he saw I was awake, he hugged me and said he was so very sorry. I knew why he said he was sorry, but I didn't feel sad. I just was. It was as if all the magic in the world had disappeared and not one fairy tale had ever been written. Time had stopped again. The hands on the face of the clock may have moved but my body remained motionless.

It took all the energy in my body to speak and I asked where my father was. Grandpa Joe told me he was downstairs with Mammaw and I said I wanted to go see him. He helped me up out of the bed and took my hand as we walked down the stairs. When my father saw me, he rushed over and hugged me, and said he was sorry. I looked up at him and I said, "She saved me, Daddy. Momma knew I couldn't fly, so she did."

Mammaw started crying and my father held me even tighter and said everything would be all right. He repeated that so many times that I couldn't hear it anymore and I soon found myself on a ship. I could hear the tick-tock of a clock and I knew it was the crocodile looking for Captain Hook and I needed to be very alert. I knew Captain Hook was around somewhere because the crocodile was close by and then I sensed something behind me and ducked just in time to miss the captain's cutlass as it swiped over my head.

"You won't escape me this time, Peter," Captain Hook yelled and as he lunged toward me, I stumbled backward and fell over the side of the ship. The jaws of the crocodile were waiting for me but I pushed away and felt myself flying upward. I could fly!

I flew around Captain Hook and it felt like my shadow was helping me thrust and parry with my sword. I finally got Captain Hook off balance and kicked him over the side of the ship into the jaws of the crocodile and then everything went black.

When I opened my eyes, I was back in my own bed and my father was holding my hand. He smiled and asked how I was feeling. I told him I was hungry. He wasn't surprised because I hadn't eaten in almost two days. He said we could go to Grandpa Joe's to grill some hamburgers and that Mammaw had made me a strawberry cake. I thought that sounded good. He asked if I felt strong enough to take a shower and I told him I could. I knew he waited outside the bathroom door, but I understood why.

The food tasted really good but it seemed like everyone was afraid to say very much to me. Grandpa Joe talked about the weather and his new saw that he had just gotten and asked if I wanted to see it after dinner and I nodded yes. He told me it was an old antique tabletop circular saw and that you had to be real careful when you cut wood on it, making sure you didn't cut against the grain. He had told me before that "cutting against the grain of the wood can be dangerous" so I knew what he meant and I just nodded again.

Mammaw asked me if I had enough to eat and I told her that everything tasted great and smiled. She smiled back at me but I could tell she was doing everything she could to make sure that smile didn't disappear under a stream of tears. My father didn't say anything at all but I could see he was happy that I was eating and I suppose that was good enough for him. After I finished my strawberry cake I asked if I could go out and sit on the porch and my father said that would be fine.

That's when I heard the whispers similar to the time when I saw Sacagawea. At first, I thought it was my grandparents and my dad talking about me but when I looked back at them, they were just sitting there at the table staring at me. Their mouths weren't moving and the more I looked at them, the more they didn't look real; more like mannequins that had been positioned to sit at a table in a storefront window, pretending they were eating.

As I looked into the woods, I saw her for the first time since she flew away from me. I heard her whisper my name and smile as those kind blues eyes reappeared. I asked her if she was okay and she said she was fine but was worried about me. She apologized for leaving me and I told her that she shouldn't keep apologizing for things that weren't her fault. She said it wasn't my fault either; it was just an accident. I cried when I heard her say that. I don't know how long I cried before I felt my father take me in his arms and tell me again that everything would be all right.

I didn't see Grandpa Joe's antique circular saw that evening. I told my dad I just wanted to go home and go to bed. After he asked me if I wanted the door left open and a light on in the hallway, I told my father that I was sorry. He sat down on the bed and hugged me and said it was just an accident. I told him mother had just said the same thing.

I wasn't sure how he would react when I told him I had spoken to my dead mother, but he made me feel like that was perfectly normal. And though I was pretty sure he didn't believe I had talked to her, he said that sounded like something she would say. I could tell he didn't care if I had truly heard her voice or not. It didn't matter to him. What mattered is that's what I said I heard and that was all he needed to know. My father was like that. He was always there to support and help me whenever I needed him. I then remembered Mom looking at my father in the carriage that day. She saw the knight that he needed to be now and like one, he was there with me every day and night.

I had dreams about Captain Hook again, except this time bright red blood dripped from the hook and his other hand. I had never seen blood in my dreams. Ever. I couldn't remember reading about blood in the book either, and it scared me. I woke up with my father sitting next to me on the bed. I told him that Captain Hook was trying to kill me and I had seen a lot of blood.

That's when I saw the tears falling down his cheek that he couldn't wipe away.

I said I would be fine but I needed the pocket knife that mother gave me. He got up and retrieved it from the dresser drawer and handed it to me. I smiled and tucked it under my pillow. I soon went back to sleep, feeling much better knowing that I could protect myself with the pocket knife, and with my mother and my father watching over me.

I didn't go to school all that week and my father stayed home with me. I began re-reading Harry Potter's first book about the Sorcerer's Stone. Dad sat with me as I read, working on his computer. We didn't talk about Mom at all. We just talked about the book and he would explain to me what he was working on. Then we would eat and I would continue to read and he would continue to work. We did that until it was time to go to sleep and then every night it would happen again.

I would be flying through the air in my dreams as if I was Peter and I would see familiar places in Neverland, like the Mermaids Lagoon, where the Lost Boys and I saved Tiger Lily. I always saw the familiar faces of John and Michael Darling and no matter where I went or what I did, I always saw Wendy. I could tell Tinkerbell was jealous of Wendy but she also knew Wendy meant a great deal to me, so she never acted in a jealous nature. And each night I could hear the tick-tock, tick-tock of the clock and when I did, I would see Captain Hook coming toward me. And each time I saw him, he looked even bloodier.

At first, Captain Hook had bright red blood only on his hook and his other hand but as the dreams progressed, the blood became noticeable elsewhere. It was on Hook's face, then his entire body, and even his clothes eventually appeared drenched in blood. And each night when I woke up, my father was there holding me and I was holding onto my pocket knife.

After a week of the same thing happening over and over, my father said I needed to go and speak with someone who could help me with my nightmares. That was the first time I had even considered my dreams were nightmares so I asked him why he called them nightmares and not dreams. He told me that dreams didn't cause little boys to wake up screaming, "Get bloody Captain Hook away from me!" I had no idea I was screaming. I never heard myself screaming in my dreams. So, I went with my father to talk to a doctor about my nightmares.

The doctor asked me to tell him about the dreams. He asked me questions about my mother, Papa P, and Grandmother. He just nodded and scribbled something on a notepad after each reply. He asked if I was sad that I had lost my grandparents and my mother and I said, "Yes." The doctor stared at me for a few moments and I could tell he expected me to say more than just "yes" but I didn't. I wasn't sure what else needed to be said.

He then asked me a question that I wasn't expecting. He asked if I felt guilty for my mother's death. I shook my head no and said that I knew it was an accident and my mother had told me the same thing. I saw him glance at my father and his eyebrows moved downward as if they were bushy caterpillars adjusting their position on his forehead. He thanked me for talking with him and then asked if he could talk to my father alone for a moment. I said that would be fine and went outside and sat in the lobby. The secretary and I talked and she was very nice. She reminded me of Susan Pevensie. She had a gentle tone in her voice and a kind look on her face.

My father soon came out and took me home and that night just before I went to bed, he asked me if I thought it was helpful to talk with the doctor. I told him that I preferred talking to him and my father chuckled. And true to his character, he told me the truth about what the doctor thought was the cause of my nightmares. He said that I had endured more trauma in five years than any ten-year-old should, and that horrible vision of my mother falling was making me connect the play and book that we loved, with the image of her death. That's when I told my father that I never saw any blood on my mother and never even saw her on the ground. He said that didn't matter; the trauma I experienced was creating those images in my mind and the blood represented guilt.

I asked him why he thought I felt guilty, and he told me that deep down I might be feeling responsible for my mother's death, but he reassured me once again that it was not my fault. I wasn't sure how to respond so I didn't say anything except that I wanted to go to sleep. He understood and we lay down in bed, with my pocket knife under the pillow and my father beside me. I was soon in Neverland again and I heard Wendy saying goodbye to the Lost Boys. I told her that I was sorry she was leaving but she told me that she needed to go home and get back to her family.

I took her hand and we flew into the sky but a cannon went off and knocked her down through a bunch of trees, landing on an island. I swooped down to help her and as I knelt by her, I could hear the tick-tock, tick-tock all around me. This time, instead of running away, I went toward the sound. I followed it through the forest and I soon found Captain Hook. He was in a dark red building and was, as usual, covered in blood. He turned around as if he knew I would be there and said, "See what you made me do!" And then I saw what I didn't want to see.

There were strips of what I thought were skin next to his black boots. Something was hanging from a hook that once had a human form, but was now just bones and ribbons of skin. I kept screaming, "No! Take it off the hook!" and when I opened my eyes, my father was holding me and telling me that it would be okay. We went back to see the doctor again the next day. This time before we talked about my dreams, he asked me more questions about Papa P and Grandmother.

He wanted to know what we did to have fun together and I told him about the wonderful trip to California, Oregon, and Washington, and of the Tahiti trip we all took together. I then spoke about Papa P and said that I loved seeing all the places that he had built and I loved it when he read poetry to me. I told him about the books he gave me and when he read the poem to me while we were looking at the mountains on the day before he died. I recited the Wendell Berry poem for him, just as Papa P had done for me.

This time the furry caterpillars arched their back as if he was surprised a ten-year-old boy could recite a poem like that, but if I wanted to remember something, I could. I never wondered why, I just always could. He then asked me about Grandmother and I said that I knew she loved me and she liked to do a lot of shopping. I told him I didn't particularly like doing that, but I went with her because I knew it made her happy. I told him that she died of a broken heart and I was sorry there wasn't enough magic in the world to fix it because she had lost Papa P. He asked me why I started going to church after she died and I told him that my parents asked me if I wanted to and I said I did, so we started going.

I was puzzled for a moment when he asked me what I hoped to find in church. I told him that I didn't expect to find anything in particular; I just liked hearing the words of kindness that the preachers spoke about. I told him my mother was the kindest woman I have ever known and that I thought after her mother died, she would like hearing those words too and though she never said that to me, she smiled a lot after we had been to church.

He then asked me about Johanna. I told him that losing Johanna had made my mother very sad. I was sad too because I never got to meet her but I always sensed she was around us. He looked at me and asked me what I meant by "around us." I explained that I saw her in some snow angels we had made in Gatlinburg once, and I had told my mother that Johanna was praying with us all when Grandmother was sick and that I thought Johanna would be waiting to see Papa P in paradise when he got there.

He asked if I knew what the tick-tock in the crocodile meant and I told him that it meant that the crocodile was nearby and he scribbled something on his paper. He asked if I had ever thought the ticking of the clock was a symbol of time, and that since we only have a limited amount of time here on earth, sometimes that makes our minds feel anxious.

I told him I didn't feel anxious about time or seeing paradise. I had seen it here and I was certain I would see it when I died, remembering what Papa P had said in his note. And then I said something that just popped out of my mouth without me even meaning to say it. I told him I would see Johanna someday too. The doctor thanked me for talking with him and said he wanted to talk with my father for a moment. I went outside and waited with the nice secretary again while they talked.

On the way home, my father said the doctor thought guilt was still very present in my mind and that the images in my "night terrors" were a combination of everything in real life and fictional life coming together in my dreams. He explained to me that night terrors were nightmares that seem so real that they woke you up, scared and screaming like what had been happening to me. He said the doctor thought I suffered from something called disassociation which meant that I could not come to terms with my mother's death and also from the death of my sister. He said I had become "disassociated from reality" and that was causing me to suffer in my dreams as I learned to live with everything that had happened.

I told my dad that I didn't want to go back to the doctor. He said he understood, but thought it was important that I continue to go and talk things out. He said it would be good for me and since I knew he only wanted the best for me, I agreed to continue. But I did ask him if he would make sure the doctor spoke to only both of us from this point forward and he said he would make sure that happened.

My dream that night started the same. Wendy was leaving Neverland and as I was flying her home, she was shot out of the air with a cannon and injured. I then heard something besides the tick-tock sound; it sounded like a saw. As I neared the red building, I saw Captain Hook and the monstrous image of a body hanging from a hook, but with more blood covering the floor and the sides of the building. And this time, besides strips of skin that lay on the ground, there was a hand with a green ring on one finger and a blue ring on the finger next to it. I woke up screaming.

When we went to the doctor the next day, my father told him that we would all talk together from now on and the doctor agreed. He asked about the dream from last night and I told him everything I had seen. He asked my father if Mom had a blue or green ring. My father replied that she always wore an emerald ring that her father had given her for graduation, and had a turquoise ring she wore on occasion.

The doctor looked at both of us and then asked me if I had ever heard the term, "let someone off the hook" and I told him no. He explained that it meant someone was being freed from their obligations or, in my case, it was me asking myself to be free of guilt. He said I felt guilty for living when my sister had died, and now, in addition to that, my mother's death had led to even more guilt. He said that I may not feel that way when I was awake but my subconscious mind was coming forward and telling me all of that.

He looked at my father and said the tick-tock and the saw were combinations of the sounds that I heard in my grandfathers' workshops and places of business and that time was chasing after me, as it had caught up with my grandparents and my mother. My father looked disturbed and asked the doctor if he thought my mother was fated to die. The doctor told him no, he didn't, but that he thought I did. Dad asked him why I would think such a thing and the doctor said it was because I wanted to remain a child in Neverland and not have to deal with any of the deaths that had occurred.

My father stood up and announced we were leaving. As we were walking out the door, he told the doctor he appreciated his theories on the nightmares that I was having but, in his opinion, they were "bullshit." I had never heard my father use that word before. In fact, I had never heard anyone but Grandpa Joe use that word and each time he did, Mammaw would scold him for "swaring." I smiled.

On the way home, my father apologized for putting me through all that and I told him he didn't need to apologize for anything. I told him that it would be okay and he looked at me and nodded and said, "Yes, it will."

Unfortunately, the dream was even worse that night. When I woke up, I told my dad about all the blood and the hand and rings and then I told him that the horses outside the red building were throwing up. I asked if he thought the horses were throwing up because of all those horrible things in the barn. He told me horses can't throw up and I looked surprised. He said that was the first time I had mentioned a barn in my dreams. I explained to him that in the dream last night, right before I went to the barn Wendy also said something she had never said before. She said that Jan Burris was gone. I asked if he knew who that was since she wasn't in the book. He didn't know but said he was going to make a few phone calls while I had some breakfast.

Later that afternoon, some men came to our house and asked me about my dream again. And when I told them, they showed me a black-and-white photo of a teenage girl and asked me if I recognized her. I said I didn't know that face and they thanked me for talking with them and I heard them whisper to my father before they left. Dad told me those men were detectives and that my nightmares had made them curious. I didn't think any more of it, but that night I heard Wendy say that not only Jan was gone, but another girl by the name of Jill was also missing and that Captain Hook had burned her blue horse.

The next morning, after I told my father about my dream, those same men came back to visit me. They showed me another picture of a young woman, but I didn't recognize her either. They asked me if I saw horses in the barn and I said no. They then asked me if I could see anything else and as I closed my eyes, I told them yes, I did see something else. I told them I saw a lot of green grass in a valley, but that was all.

While they talked to my dad, I went out on the porch and I saw my mother again standing out in the woods. I could hear her whispering to me and I ran back inside and told them that I remembered something else from my dreams. I know it wasn't really in my dreams, but I didn't want to tell them that my mother had just told me to tell them something fearing that I would be taken back to see the doctor. I told them I saw the words "caballo de batalla" and they looked at me and said that was a big help.

I had no idea what that phrase meant until Dad looked it up on the internet. It was Spanish for "hobby horse," but that meant nothing to either of us. That night, everything was the same in my dream except this time Captain Hook wasn't in the barn. I could walk right up to the bloody body that hung from a hook and when I did, I threw up. It looked like a monster and it opened its eyes and yelled, "Run!" But before I could run, Captain Hook grabbed me. I managed to twist out of my pajama shirt and get away but Captain Hook was yelling at me saying that he would find me and kill me and that's when I heard the tick-tocking all around me. I couldn't see the crocodile but the ticking sound was so loud, all I could think of was what the doctor had said about time, and when I did, I saw a building that was filled with clocks. It was surrounded by a grassy valley, just like the red barn had been.

Those same men came back again the next day and asked if we could go with them to Greenville, Tennessee, and look at a place to see if I recognized anything. My father agreed, but only after they assured him that I would be safe. They said I would never even have to get out of the car. So we drove to Greenville that day. They took me to the farm and the red building on it looked just like the one I saw in my dreams.

It was an abandoned farm with a big green pasture and the red barn was off on a hill by itself in the woods. I didn't get out but I told the detectives what I had seen in my dreams. When they examined the area, they found an old blue hobby horse up in the barn loft and some other "items of interest," as they described them. They called in some other police officers to continue the search while they took us into Greenville to get something to eat because I said I was hungry.

We went to a place called the Tannery and while we ate, I noticed an antique store on the other side of the street that looked interesting. That was one of the kinds of stores that I didn't mind going to with Grandmother and my mother and I asked if we could go in there after lunch. The detectives said they didn't mind. So after lunch, we walked over there and peered in the window. There was a whole wall full of clocks and I heard the tick-tocking all around me again. I froze at the sight of them, and my father asked what was wrong. I told him I was afraid to go in the store. One of the detectives took me and Dad away while the other one went inside to check things out.

On the way home, the detectives told us they had found some things that they had been searching for at the barn and also at the antique store. Since some of those things seemed to be represented in my dreams, they were going to have a policeman stay at our house for a while until they could figure things out. That night the dream started the same way as it did every night, but this time I could actually feel and smell everything around me. And just like the last time, when I saw the body hanging from the hook, it opened its eyes and told me to run, but this time, I looked around and realized that I was in Grandpa Joe's workshop and there was a tall shadow staring at me.

The shadow rushed toward me and I ran over and turned on my grandfather's large fan. I could see Tinkerbell flying around the shadow sprinkling pixie dust in its dark eyes. The shadow was swiping back and forth at me with a large knife but I knew he couldn't see where I was. I can't say whether I imagined kicking him off the deck of the ship into the crocodile or not, but I did hear my grandfather's saw come on and I saw the shadow fall forward.

I yelled for my father as I woke up and ran out of the shop. My dad stayed with me while the policeman rushed into the workshop. He found a man sitting inside with both of his hands cut off, dying as the blood flowed onto the floor as if two water spigots had been turned on. Next to him was a Kukri machete, which I heard the policeman say was an Indian blade, three feet long.

The man they found that night owned the antique store in Greenville with all the clocks and had killed those two women I had seen in my dreams. That night, the dreams of Captain Hook were gone but my dreams were far from settled. Tiger Lily was crying and when I asked her why she said because the girl was about to die. I asked her where she was and she pointed to a sign that said "McMahan."

I told my father about the dream and he immediately called the detectives. They found a place called the McMahan Indian Mound in Sevierville, Tennessee. The murderer owned a second antique store close by there, and the detectives discovered another young girl in the cellar of that store. She was barely alive, but alive, and would eventually recover after spending a week in the hospital.

The police referred to the killer as "Captain Hook." I understand now that was their way to humanize a monster and minimize the horror that his actions prompted in their minds. But when I met with them again, I could tell it didn't work. I knew that each of them saw the picture that the killer had made every night and it would haunt some of them and I tried to help those that I could.

I would ask them if they had children and if they said yes, then I would tell them, you took away a nightmare for them. That made a lot of them smile. I also told them that the community, not just local, but the entire world, appreciated what they did. I could sense some of them felt better by what I said, but others would never be able to make the bad memories go away and would be haunted for a very long time, if not forever.

****

No one understands why I was the only one who saw the face of Captain Hook and lived. I am certain Wendy had a lot to do with it. The real one and the fictional one because they were both looking out for the Lost Boys in their lives. There will be those who read this and say what happened was pure coincidence. I am not going to try and convince those readers it wasn't. As my mother would have said, those that understand, will; and those that don't, won't, and it's not cause for me to worry with either way.

I wish I could have told my mom that the first non-professional actor to win an Oscar was Harold Russell. He was a World War II veteran that lost both his hands in the war and had hooks on his hands. The name of the movie was "The Best Years of Our Lives." Mom would have appreciated the fact that he was a war veteran and she would have been kind and welcoming to him should she ever have met him. And she wouldn't have said a word about the hooks on his hands. "'The Best Years of Our Lives.' What a wonderful title for a movie, Johnny. Yes, that seems appropriate. So very appropriate," she would say and together we would have probably seen that connection in our life was no coincidence.

I have learned that the best years of our lives are not in the past, but are being made with the days of the future that add magic to our life. Even if those days bring you sorrow, you learn from them. It's not always easy to see that reason but over time, hopefully, you understand. Your memories are a constant retelling of your life and that is never a bad thing, even if bad things happened. One would not know what good meant if one didn't understand what bad meant. I do understand the meaning of both words very well.

I believe that this life on earth can be anything you want it to be. Heaven or Hell and perhaps at one time or another, it may be a little of both. I never cried so much in my life as when my mother died but I haven't experienced all of life's woes either.

Granted I have had my fair share, as they would say, but I suspect that there will come a time when I may cry even more. I hope that's not the case but I wouldn't be surprised if it happened, because nothing concerning life can be anything but surprising. I don't have all the answers and you don't have all the answers. One day, if we are lucky, we will. But on that day, I know we will not be of this earth.

The name of the girl who was saved from that cellar was Johanna Clark and she said a woman with black hair and sky-blue eyes told her I would come to save her and that she made her feel safe when she was in there by herself. She said the woman's name was Wendy and I'm sure that's who it was, but I doubt it was the fictional Wendy. I have no doubt it was the Wendy that I called my mother.

Johanna happens to be a descendant of William Clark; you know, the one that went with Meriwether Lewis to map the land west of the Mississippi and meet Sacagawea. And if you recall, when I saw Sacagawea in Washington, she was pointing to a door in the ground as if perhaps there was something important in a cellar. Sacagawea also allowed William Clark to adopt her two children, Lisette and Jean Baptiste, to save them from her first husband. William Clark called Jean Baptiste "Little Pomp" in an affectionate manner much the same way my mother called me "little Johnny." Interesting coincidences, don't you think?

Some may ask why my mother had to die to save Johanna Clark, and my reply to that question would be that she didn't die to save her. She just died. Sort of. She's never been dead to me. Whenever I hold the pocket knife she gave me, I can see her, sitting next to me on the porch, or at the supper table, or by my bed. She's never far away and when I want to talk to her, I do. Sometimes I hear her say something wise or kind but then I wonder if it's just me remembering something she told me that was wise or kind. When I do wonder, I'm inclined to believe that I am hearing my mother talk. That comforts me as I am not afraid to see or hear what others cannot.

I am never haunted by all that happened because I have such wonderful memories that fill me with joy. I can always hear my mother's laugh and sometimes I think it is a part of the air I breathe. I remember the trips to California and the real Neverland, "funny sayings," coconut cream pie and strawberry cake, chicken noodle soup and peanut butter cookies with M&M's, my grandfather reciting that poem to me in Tahiti, and my other grandfather showing me how to work with wood. I can recall my grandmother being courageous when it mattered, my father reading "Fox in Sox" and forever being there for me and my mother, and my mind is never without wisdom from all of the spoken and unspoken lessons my mother taught me.

Funny how life makes those strange connections that, at the time, we don't recognize as such. But later in life, if we allow our vision to take us back there, we recognize just how linked one aspect of our life is to others. My mother and I were fortunate in that way.

Johanna Clark had red hair, just like William Clark. She also had the same sky-blue eyes as my mother. If you know anything about statistics, you can understand how rare a red-haired blue-eyed girl is. It only happens .17% of the time. She and I have become the best of friends, almost as if we were brother and sister. I have never forgotten the fairy tale life I lived, and as an adult, I believe in fairy tales much more now than I ever did as a child.

Let someone off the hook

John Doriot has wanted to be a writer since he was in the second grade and is fulfilling a dream every day when he sits down to write. He has published 11 books to date. Two of his books, Litter and Grimmer Folk Stories, were recipients of the Georgia Independent Author of the Year Awards in 2022, for best Horror/Thriller and collection of short stories.

John was born in Roanoke, Virginia, and grew up in Bristol, Tennessee. A graduate of The University of Tennessee, he has lived in Augusta, Georgia for 31 years, where he retired after a long career in healthcare. He has been married for 42 years and has one son, one granddaughter, and a dog, Oreo. When he is not writing, he loves working in the garden or traveling with his wife and dog, especially to visit their new granddaughter. If he is not doing any of the above activities, you will find him reading or searching for the next great book to read!

www.ingramcontent.com/pod-product-compliance
Lightning Source LLC
Chambersburg PA
CBHW072119300726
48975CB00003B/860